THE GARDEN HOUSE

www.**penguin**.co.uk

Also by Marcia Willett

For more information on Marcia Willett and her books,
see her website at www.marciawillett.co.uk

THE GARDEN HOUSE

MARCIA WILLETT

BANTAM PRESS

TRANSWORLD PUBLISHERS
61–63 Uxbridge Road, London W5 5SA
www.penguin.co.uk

Transworld is part of the Penguin Random House group of companies
whose addresses can be found at global.penguinrandomhouse.com

First published in Great Britain in 2020 by Bantam Press
an imprint of Transworld Publishers

A CIP catalogue record for this book
is available from the British Library.

ISBN 9781787632264

Typeset in 13.25 pt/15.5pt Fournier MT
by Integra Software Services Pvt. Ltd, Pondicherry

Printed and bound in Great Britain by Clays Ltd, Elcograf S.p.A.

Penguin Random House is committed to a sustainable
future for our business, our readers and our planet. This book
is made from Forest Stewardship Council® certified paper.

1 3 5 7 9 10 8 6 4 2

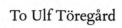

To Ulf Töregård

THE GARDEN HOUSE

PROLOGUE

The church is full. The service has ended and the organist plays quietly as friends and family file out of their pews to follow the coffin into the churchyard. The nave is flooded with bright slanting sunshine sliced by sharp black shadows, and long-stemmed flowers, purple and blue, cast splashes of colour across cold grey stone.

Half hidden behind a pillar at the back of the church, struggling to control her tears, not wishing to be seen, Julia watches them. One or two she recognizes from photographs; most are strangers to her. As she stands up, preparatory to slipping away, she sees the tall young man that she noticed outside before the service. Her sudden movement catches his attention as he makes his slow progression down the aisle, and their eyes meet, hold for a moment, before he is drawn into a group of friends just inside the porch.

Julia quickly makes her way out of the church, skirting the groups of people in the churchyard, hurrying away into the little lane that leads into Duke Street, heading back to the car park. Climbing into the car, casting her bag on to the passenger seat, she takes a huge breath, slumping for a moment, giving herself time to regroup. Martin is dead. Martin, who was so full of life, is dead because he stabbed his finger on some black-thorn and died of sepsis within forty-eight hours. Julia still doesn't know how to process this: the shock, disbelief, and the devastating loss.

Sitting quite still, staring unseeingly ahead, she recalls moments of their love. She remembers their first meeting at The Garden House, his first text to her:

`Crosby, Stills, Nash & Young. Woodstock.`

Suddenly she knows where she must go, as if he is showing her the way. The words sing in her head: 'We are stardust, we are golden . . . And we've got to get ourselves back to the garden.'

She switches on the engine, pulls out of the car park, and drives away into the warm, late summer sunshine.

CHAPTER ONE

On this journey to claim her inheritance, El is filled with nervous anticipation. As she drives past familiar signposts and landmarks, she is wondering how it will feel to turn the key in the lock and walk in, knowing that this time it's not just for a holiday or a visit; knowing that the Pig Pen belongs to her. El remembers how Pa phoned her during her first term at Durham.

'I've found the perfect place to live, El,' he said. 'But you won't believe what it's called.'

Even as she remembers, she is seized with this new sense of grief that overwhelms her at unexpected moments. Pa is dead. How can that be true? She wasn't with him. She was celebrating with her university friends in Durham, having got a First in English. Thank God he'd known that; that she'd dashed down to see him as soon as she knew her results and that they'd celebrated in the Royal Oak at Meavy.

'I'm so proud of you, darling,' he said, raising his glass to her. 'So very, very proud.'

'You'll come to my graduation, won't you?' she asked anxiously.

Her father hesitated, cutting up some food, pretending to think about it. Even now, five years after the divorce, events that might involve both her parents are fraught with difficulty. Her mother has never forgiven him for being unfaithful; never shifted from her position as the betrayed wife. Nor has she forgiven El for continuing to love him.

'I shall be furious with you if you don't come,' she told him fiercely.

Now, as she drives through the early autumn landscape, she wishes she hadn't said that. The graduation was hedged about with grief and shock. Her mother was there with Roger, El's stepfather, but the event was coloured with a terrible sadness that couldn't be dispelled. Roger was gentle and kind because it is his nature to be so, but her mother, even on such an occasion, was incapable of hiding her bitterness. El could see her consciously making the effort to hold back some blighting remark. She almost expected her to say, 'Serves him right.'

How awful, thinks El, pulling in to the Exeter motorway services for a pit stop – that's what Pa always called them: 'Time for a pit stop' – how very sad, to be able to bear a grudge, to keep hatred and jealousy so vividly alive, for so long. She parks the car and reaches for her bag, checking her phone. There's a text from Angus. Angus has guided her through the mysteries of probate, kept her focused despite her grief, and now, as Pa's senior partner and closest friend, is welcoming her home.

Home. She needs some coffee and to concentrate on what lies ahead, to stay strong, but it's been difficult to remain positive in the face of her mother's opposition.

'You can't seriously be considering living there?' she asked incredulously. 'In a cottage with a ridiculous name in a small village in the middle of Dartmoor? What on earth will you do?'

Her mother has never seen the Pig Pen. After the separation, and as soon as the family home near Plymouth was sold, she moved back to Dorchester to be with her own father, taking sixteen-year-old El and her older brother Freddie with her. Freddie is a peacemaker. He tries to be all things to all men; he arbitrates between their mother and El with inarticulate affection. She understands that her obstinate love for her father is seen as disloyalty by her mother, but how can you help loving? How can you simply switch off such an instinctive emotion? It doesn't help that deep down she can sympathize with the reasons why Pa might have been tempted by the offer of unconditional love, of warmth. Her mother is critical, touchy, driven.

'She just wants us to do well,' Freddie would say consolingly when there were tears over homework, or, 'She likes us to feel proud of ourselves,' when there were criticisms after the end-of-term concert. When Freddie went to Manchester to study medicine their mother was delighted. Freddie is her darling, her golden boy, and his loyalty to her is unquestioning. El loves him very much but, even at sixteen, she could see that it is sometimes necessary to take a stand, to choose a side, even if you might be on the losing team.

'I can't stop loving Pa,' she shouted crossly during those awful early days of separation, 'just because he's done something wrong. Everybody does a wrong thing sometimes but it doesn't mean you can just switch off everything you feel for them.'

Her mother tried to explain the values of faithfulness, of loyalty, the difference between right and wrong, whilst Freddie watched anxiously, willing them both to arrive at a manageable, peaceful conclusion.

Remembering, El smiles wryly. Even now, six years on from the initial parting, this is still a consummation devoutly to be wished. Barely two years later her mother married a boyfriend from her youth, Roger Bennett: a widower with a son, Will, six years older than Eleanor. Pa became a senior partner in the law firm in Plymouth where he'd worked all his life and then bought the Pig Pen from a farmer out on the moor not far from Tavistock. It was one of two conversions from old agricultural buildings: square stone buildings, slate roofed, separated from each other by an orchard and set about with dry-stone walls.

'He says he doesn't hold with all these fancy names for conversions like the Linhay or the Old Dairy,' Pa told her, laughing. 'He's called the other one the Hen House. Don't you just love it? I can't wait for you to see it. It's small but perfect for everything I need. Hope you approve.'

Now, El replies to Angus's text, shoulders her bag and locks the car. She loved the Pig Pen from the very first moment she saw it, and now it belongs to her. Despite her fears, her anxieties that she should follow her mother's advice to sell the Pig Pen and look for a job in London, El feels driven to take this opportunity: to try to make a life for herself where she has been so happy with Pa. Swallowing down tears, straightening her shoulders, she goes to find some coffee.

Over the moor in Tavistock, Angus emerges from the Pannier Market, pauses to buy a loaf of bread from the stall just outside, and heads across the square to the Bedford Hotel's car park. As he loads his shopping into the car his phone pings: it's a text from Eleanor. He reads it and then goes into the hotel and up the stairs. In the bar he glances round, and then smiles at the sight of two women sitting at the table by the window, laughing together over the coffee cups. Cass and Kate have been meeting here for more than forty years to discuss husbands, lovers and, latterly, their grandchildren. Cass's daughter Gemma is married to Kate's son Guy, and their twins, just off to university, are the joint delight and concern of the two older women, as is their extended family who own and run a sailing school down on the Tamar. Angus orders his coffee from Lynn at the bar, catches Kate's eye and is warmed by the way both women wave, indicating that he must join them. Their friendship is all the more precious to him since his beloved Marina died nearly three years ago. She was very fond of Cass and Kate.

'They're such fun,' she'd say, after a coffee session in the Bedford. 'And yet they're so different. Cass is a hedonist and Kate is an idealist. It must be wonderful to have a shared past that goes back to your schooldays, and then all those years as naval wives, supporting each other.'

Angus agrees with that. Very old friends still see in each other their former selves. In this way, they never truly grow old.

'El's moving in today,' he tells them, as they transfer coats and bags to a spare chair to make space for him. 'She's stopped off for coffee at Exeter. Now tell me, would it be a good move to go over to the cottage to be waiting for her so as to welcome her, or is this something she should do alone?'

The two women look at each other. Cass, her fair hair silvery now, long and twisted into the back of her neck, is elegant, whilst Kate, dressed in jeans and a guernsey, still has an oddly youthful look.

'Alone,' suggests Kate. 'I think she needs to have time to take it all in. I know she's been there once or twice since Martin died but it's different this time, isn't it?'

Cass nods her agreement. 'Yes. If you're there she'll think she needs to concentrate on you rather than just being able to enter into the whole thing naturally.' She pushes aside her cafetiere to make space for Angus's coffee. 'But you could let her know that you're around?'

They glance at him, concerned, slightly wary, and he suspects that they're wondering if this is reminding him of Marina. He is touched but has no intention of allowing the conversation to become maudlin.

'Good,' he says cheerfully, pouring his coffee. 'That confirms my gut reaction. So what's the latest news? You were looking rather conspiratorial when I came in. How's Tom?'

Cass rolls her eyes. 'He's got his nephew staying with us. Dear fellow but he can't eat this and he can't tolerate that and he's given up booze. Utterly dire, darling.'

Kate grins and Angus bursts out laughing.

'Sounds like a fun visit,' he observes. 'How's old Tom dealing with that?'

'Not very well,' admits Cass. 'After all those years in submarines he doesn't have much patience with fads. It's lucky we've got Kate staying, too, so she and I can sneak off when the going gets tough.'

'He is rather too precious to live,' admits Kate. 'He asked us why our sixties generation was so degenerate. You know, drugs, sex and rock'n'roll? And Cass said, "FOMO, darling," and he just stared at her blankly.'

'No sense of humour,' says Cass bleakly.

'Hang on,' says Angus. 'What's FOMO?'

They look at him disbelievingly, then at each other and shrug at such ignorance.

Cass sighs. 'Fear of missing out,' she says slowly and patiently. 'Got it now? Do keep up, Angus.'

Angus laughs. 'I'll try. So, in that case, why don't I invite you both to lunch?'

He drinks his coffee, watching them as they look at one another, deciding, and he hopes that they will accept his offer. He's beginning to understand the ruthlessness of the really lonely but he fights against it, and so he waits, determined to say nothing else that might persuade them.

'I don't see why we shouldn't,' says Cass at last. 'Tom can manage lunch for them both but I'll have to phone him.'

Angus glances at his watch. 'Nearly midday. Why don't I finish my coffee and then get us a drink while we have a look at the menu?'

Cass beams at him. 'Sounds good to me,' she says. 'There's not a good enough signal to phone from here so I'll have to dash outside.'

She gets up and goes out. Kate smiles at Angus.

'This is very kind of you. I must admit that life at the Old Rectory is a bit stressed at the moment. Tom's irascibility hasn't improved with age. So do you think El's right to be moving in?'

He's slightly surprised by the change of direction and sips his coffee to give himself time to think.

'I don't know,' he says at last. 'I hope so. I know she loves the place, but it's going to be very different without Martin and I'm not sure what she's considering career-wise. She says that her mother isn't very happy about it.'

'Well, I can understand that,' says Kate. 'It's been a very unhappy situation anyway, hasn't it? But this is a big step for a young girl. Quite a distance from her uni friends and her family. No job. I can imagine that Felicity would be anxious about her.'

'El's got friends here, too,' says Angus. 'I think she needs time to come to terms with things. After all, lots of young people take a year out after university, don't they? They don't all immediately start on a career. She needs a bit of space.' He shakes his head. 'I still can hardly take it in. It was so quick. Poor old Martin. He was so proud of her.'

Before Kate can answer, Cass is back.

'Tom's not pleased but he sends his regards, Angus, and says have a wet for him.'

Angus grins at the naval expression. 'I certainly will. We all will.'

He feels cheerful at the immediate prospect and meanwhile he'll wait to see if El needs any kind of support. As her lawyer, and as Martin's closest, oldest friend he feels a strong sense of responsibility for her.

'Let's have that drink,' he says.

As he moves to stand up his foot encounters something soft and there's a small yelp. He bends down to see a flat-coated retriever coming out from beneath the table, tail wagging, her whole bearing apologetic.

'I'm sorry, Floss,' exclaims Angus, bending to stroke her. 'I had no idea you were there.'

'It's OK,' says Kate, holding the lead. 'You know how much she loves coming into the Bedford so I didn't have the heart to leave her in the car. We've already taken her for a walk up around Burrator so she'd crashed out by the time you arrived. She'll be fine.'

She strokes Floss, settling her again.

'How long are you up from Cornwall for?'

'I'm decorating my cottage in Chapel Street in preparation for new tenants,' answers Kate. 'So I'm here for as long as it takes, unless Tom chucks me out. If he does, then I'll have to come and stay with you.'

Angus grins at her; he enjoys these little flirtatious moments with Kate.

'Open house,' he says. 'You know that.'

'I'll come and help you carry,' offers Cass, and they go to the bar together. Angus is still thinking about El and Martin, and Cass takes his arm for a moment as if to comfort him.

'Don't worry too much about El. She'll be OK,' she tells him. 'El's tough. We're not far away and Martin had a good network of friends. We'll be looking out for her.'

'I know,' he answers gratefully. 'It's only because she has such little family support. Now, what are you and Kate drinking? Let's get some menus and then you can tell me all the news.'

CHAPTER TWO

As El drives towards Postbridge she notices the change in the seasons. When she drove down to bring the glad tidings of her exam results it was very hot. The countryside was languorous, dozing in the heat; tall foxgloves glowing against granite walls, creamy cow parsley nearly head high, sheep seeking shade under a thorn tree; the white vapour of a plane smudged across the blue board of the sky. Today the landscape looks as if it has been chalked in with a casual hand – dusty golds, faded pinks, bronze – and tattered clouds race before the strong south-westerly winds.

She drives through the village, passing the old clapper bridge, remembering journeys with her father, walks, picnics. In earlier days these had included her mother and Freddie, and it was odd and rather nice, after the divorce, to find that Pa was such a good companion, such fun to be with. Without her mother's controlling influence, her irritation at any kind of foolishness, he was relaxed, funny, always ready for an unexpected jaunt.

Cloud shadows race across the tors and a flurry of crows disappear into Bellever Woods. El drives warily, always aware of the grazing sheep, the ponies cantering amongst the boulders at the road's edge. She leaves Princetown away to the left and heads towards Tavistock. Soon she will turn off into smaller lanes and then she will be home. Her hands grip the wheel a little tighter. Angus's text is comforting – Here if you need me – but she has to do this on her own. She doesn't want to put on a brave face for Angus's benefit; she needs to be able to react naturally.

She leaves the high moorland road behind her, passing between dry-stone walls and banks of furze, and now she is here, turning into the gateway that serves both properties, and then into the yard beside the Pig Pen. She parks in the small open-fronted barn, switches off the engine, opens the door and climbs out. It's only a few weeks since Pa's funeral but already everything seems different. There's nothing now to distract her from the fact that she is here alone, the Pig Pen is hers, and she will never see Pa again.

She turns the key in the back door and lets herself into the utility room. It leads into a hall that divides the two bedrooms, each with its loo and shower. The Pig Pen and the Hen House were built as holiday lets and are practical and convenient. El drops her case just inside her bedroom, picks up some letters from the mat inside the front door, and climbs the wooden staircase that rises up to the big room, which is kitchen, dining-room and sitting-room. Its high roof, criss-crossed with heavy beams, has Velux windows, which fill the big space with light, and at the end is a sliding glass door that opens out on to a large paved area. At this end the ground floor of the house is built against the bank and there are steps leading down from the terrace into the small garden. Everything is paved to make upkeep simple, but the dry-stone walls support foxgloves, stonecrop, ivy-leaved toadflax and ferns, and the orchard with its old apple trees is a delight.

El stands beside the long wooden table separating the kitchen from the sitting-room, looking around her. Nothing has been changed since Pa died. Her own things, belongings that she's left during the few years he has lived here, are here too. Her books are amongst his on the shelves, some pottery she bought at the Pannier Market in Tavistock is on the table, her shawl thrown across one of the two sofas. Oddly, her first reaction is a sudden weariness. It occurs to her that she has been fighting for years: fighting for her right to see Pa; fighting the pressure to accept her mother's viewpoint; fighting the insidious feeling that she is disloyal. And all the while she's had Pa at her back to lean against. Now she has the odd sensation that she is falling. Desolation seizes her and she feels afraid. What made her think she could do this? Is it simply stubbornness that led her to announce she intended to live in the Pig Pen; to try to make a life for herself here?

El looks up at the massive beams supporting the roof and then out on to the terrace where Pa has filled big terracotta pots with shrubs and bulbs. She glances down at the letters she is still holding in her hand: the usual circulars and advertising leaflets, Pa's *Dartmoor News* magazine. One, however, is hand-written and addressed to her, so she drops the others on to the table and tears open the envelope. The address at the top of the single sheet of paper is 'The Old Rectory' and underneath is a telephone number. She reads the words.

'Don't be lonely, El. We would love to see you. We miss him, too, so stay in touch. Very much love, Tom and Cass xx'

El gives a little gasp – something between tears, laughter and relief. These are her father's old friends, people that he loved and who loved him. She looks at her phone and rereads the text from Angus. Suddenly she is filled with courage. Presently she will make a plan: go shopping for supplies, let people know she is here. She turns and fills the kettle and switches it on. She is home.

The lunch party at the Bedford has reached the possibility of a pudding stage.

'You haven't told us how Plum is,' Cass says. 'Has Ian seen the Appointer yet?'

Angus lays down the menu. He's delighted with the news that his son-in-law is to be posted back to the West Country, to Devonport, but ever since Plum told him the news he's been turning an idea over in his mind. He wonders whether to share it with these two friends; to ask their advice.

'He has. They're coming back,' he tells them. 'Plum is so pleased. She's coming down tomorrow. They wondered whether to let the London flat but I think now that they've decided to keep it for long leaves and for when the girls are home, and to look for somewhere small to rent down here. I had this idea that they could stay with me. After all, the house is plenty big enough so it's silly for them to be renting. Ian will be at sea a great deal so it seems the obvious thing. What d'you think?'

'I think it's great that they're coming back,' answers Cass at once, 'even if it's just for a couple of years. That's really good news. Why don't you suggest that they stay with you until they find a place of their own and then let it gradually dawn on them that it's not worth moving out? Especially if they've still got the flat in London to dash away to when he's on leave, or for the theatre or to meet up with the girls.'

'That's a good idea,' agrees Kate. 'They won't feel pressured and then they'll begin to see that they have the best of both worlds. It's like me. Living down on my rock in Cornwall and then coming back to stay with Cass and Tom when I need to party and see the family.'

'How devious you are,' observes Angus admiringly. 'I would have just come straight out with it and put them on the spot.'

'Will they be home in time for Christmas?' asks Cass.

He nods happily. 'It's going to be a good one. They were still out in Washington last Christmas so we've got to make up for lost time.'

'Excellent,' says Kate. 'It's the sensible thing for them to come to you for Christmas and then you just let things take their course. There's always my cottage, remember, if they decide to rent. I haven't got new tenants yet.'

'We must have a party,' says Cass. 'All of you and all of us . . .'

'Not forgetting El,' adds Kate, 'though she might go back to her own family, I suppose.'

'We must still make sure she knows she's invited,' says Cass firmly.

'I think we need several parties,' suggests Angus, entering into the spirit of this idea. 'Plum is first class at parties.'

He thinks how wonderful it would be to have her back, filling his big, quiet house with her life-affirming presence, with her friends and their children. Plum is so positive, so all-embracing.

'I think it's the perfect answer all round,' says Cass. 'Ian will be off to sea and Plum will be missing both her girls now that Lauren's gone off to uni, and didn't you tell us that Alice is flat-sharing with a friend? Plum will be suffering from empty-nest syndrome. Anyway we need something to keep Tom cheerful. He's doing his GOM thing about downsizing and it's driving me mad.'

'GOM?' Angus is puzzled.

'This man is hopeless,' says Cass to Kate. 'First FOMO. Now GOM. We need to take him in hand.' She turns back to Angus. 'Grumpy old man, darling. I can't believe you didn't know that.'

'That's the trouble with living with sailors,' says Kate, smiling at Angus's expression. 'Have you never heard the definition of a conversation in the Mess? Insult, followed by personal abuse, followed by physical violence, but don't take my word for it. Ask Plum or Ian. Now then. Who's having a pudding?'

CHAPTER THREE

El moves about the cottage, switching on the heating and the fridge, unpacking her things, trying to accustom herself to her father's absence, wondering what she might want to change. Nothing immediately springs to mind. The cottage has always seemed like a shared space. When he first moved in, she came to stay and they chose furniture, paintings, kitchenware together. Her mother had taken most of the family belongings with her, and Pa had decided that the Pig Pen was to be a fresh start. They had a great deal of fun choosing what might work in this big open area. Occasionally El wondered if they might be enjoying themselves too much: this, after all, was the result of a divorce, of his unfaithfulness. Sometimes she wondered if it were a kind of relief for both of them to be free of her mother's controlling personality. This made her feel guilty, but didn't prevent her from enjoying the experience.

Freddie came to visit. El knew that she and Pa felt very slightly like naughty children who have behaved badly but aren't really sorry.

'I hope he likes it,' Pa said just before Freddie's first arrival, looking around anxiously lest there should be something his son might find tasteless. El knew that he felt badly that there were only two bedrooms and so it was difficult to accommodate Freddie. One of the sofas could be converted into a comfortable bed made up with duvets and pillows, which is where Pa put his friends when they came to stay, but Eleanor knew that Freddie would be relieved. He would feel less compromised, less disloyal, if he could say to his mother that he wasn't actually staying at the Pig Pen. He booked in at the Bedford Hotel and El guessed that he would be more comfortable knowing he could make his escape; that he need not be drawn into those long intimate after-supper conversations, which might demand too much of him or compromise him. He is non-confrontational; he likes everybody to be happy. He can't see that his expectation is a triumph of hope over experience. It was a good visit, though. He and Pa did their one-arm, man-type hug when Freddie left, promising to return soon.

'I think he was OK with it,' Pa said, as they waved him off up the track.

He stood for a moment, listening to the sound of the car engine fading, and then turned back, stooping to twitch the dead head from a flower in a tub, tweaking out a weed. She hadn't known what to say. Pa never spoke of the divorce or the reason for it. Sometimes she wondered if he might still be seeing the woman with whom he had the affair but he never mentioned her, nor was there ever any sign of another female presence at the Pig Pen.

El wishes that she had the approval of her family for this big adventure in her life but, although it has been agreed that Freddie should inherit everything their mother took with her in the divorce settlement and that El should have the Pig Pen, there is no sense of encouragement. Nobody could have expected that Pa should die when he was barely sixty, so none of them had thought much about the future, but she would have appreciated a friendly voice from the people closest to her.

She goes out from the sitting-room on to the little terrace and looks at her phone. Freddie messaged her yesterday, sending his love, Angus has offered company or help, or anything she might need to settle in, but there are three new messages. Two are from her uni friends, sending love, asking when they can come to stay. The third one is from Will.

Hope you're OK. Have you moved in yet?

She stares at the message, surprised, and pleased, too. Will: she hadn't expected anything from him. Her relationship with Will is an ambivalent one. When her mother and his father became an item, Will was as unenthusiastic about it as El and Freddie were. He and Freddie were nearly twenty-three, Eleanor seventeen.

'But how are we all supposed to live together?' she demanded of her mother. 'I mean, we don't know these people. We can't just suddenly become a family.'

She was indignant, Freddie was troubled, Will was cool and unapproachable. It was fortunate that Freddie was already in his fifth year of his medical course and Will had joined an airline as a junior first officer. He often spent holidays abroad with friends. After the wedding, El hated moving into Roger's house; being allotted a small bedroom, bumping into Will on the landing on those rare occasions when he came home, adjusting to Roger's presence. It wasn't that she disliked Roger – he was an inoffensive, kindly man – it was all just so weird. Her mother managed to imply that it was her father's fault, that if he hadn't behaved so badly they wouldn't be in this position now, but El was very relieved when Pa bought the Pig Pen and

she could escape for the major part of each holiday and alter-
nate Christmases, despite her mother's wrath and Freddie's
pleadings. Will kept clear, too. El went to university and their
relationship, such that it was, continued at a distance.

Yet she understands Will. She knows that he was resentful
that his father should marry this strong-willed woman, who
moved in and clearly intended to take over all their lives. Will
made no scenes, caused no arguments, he simply disappeared
away into his own life. Several times he brought home his flat-
mate, a gay man called Christian. El liked him, and liked the
way he and Will bantered together, but her mother was convinced that Will was gay after he brought him to the first
New Year's party Roger gave soon after the move back to
Dorchester from Devon.

Now, as she stares at his text, El remembers how touched
she was when Will asked if he could attend Pa's funeral; pleased
when he hugged her afterwards and told her how well she'd
organized it.

She suddenly remembers that very first Christmas after the
wedding, with them all together in the new house, at the Boxing
Day party that her mother insisted should be given so that their
mutual friends should see how happy they all were. El was
embarrassed and not at all happy. Towards the end of the party
she took rather a large swig from Freddie's wine glass and, in a
silly fit of devil-may-care misery, she seized a piece of mistletoe, held it over Will's head and kissed him. It was not
intended to be a sisterly action – quite the contrary, as if she
were trying to show their parents that she refused to accept the
relationship. Taken off guard, he responded, pulling her close
to him, before suddenly pushing her away. Both of them were
shocked, and El, feeling confused by her reaction to his kiss

and humiliated by her foolishness, dropped the mistletoe and fled to her room, hoping that in the crush nobody would notice. She stayed in bed until late the next morning and by the time she made a reluctant appearance it was to find that Will had already left to visit friends for the rest of the holidays. By the time she saw him again she was able to pretend that it was all part of the Christmas madness; almost that it had never happened. Certainly Will never mentioned it.

Now, four years on, she looks at his message, remembers his kindness at the funeral, and wonders if some kind of friendship might be salvaged. She types a reply – Not really. Missing Pa. Got to sort his clothes – and sends it before she can change her mind. She looks again at her messages and she goes back into the cottage. It's time to do the thing she's been dreading for the last few weeks, which is to clear out Pa's bedroom. Soon she will have visitors to stay and she has to make his room a guest-room.

Slowly, reluctantly, she goes downstairs and opens his bedroom door. Standing just inside, she looks around. She's done this several times since he died: looking for echoes of him, reminders of his presence. When Freddie stayed for the funeral she changed the sheets, tidied the bathroom, but she left the essentials of him so that Freddie should remember the father they'd shared.

'You don't mind?' she asked tentatively, the night before the funeral. 'Me having the Pig Pen, I mean? You'll get all of Mum's estate, of course, and Pa's life insurance will be split between us, but it seems a bit weird somehow, me having this now . . .'

'It's fine,' he answered quickly. 'Honestly, El, it's not a problem. I wouldn't want it anyway. It's not my scene.'

'No, I get that, but it would be more fair to sell it and split it between us.'

He shook his head. 'It's all been dealt with. Let's not talk about it now.'

Once he'd gone she'd stripped the bed, flung a throw across it and closed the door, but now she looks at those built-in cupboards and drawers full of Pa's clothes and knows that she must sort them out, take them to a charity shop. When she asked Freddie if there was anything he'd like to keep he selected two pairs of cuff links, several books and a small watercolour of a moorland scene, asking first if she minded.

'Of course not,' she said, pleased that he wanted these special things. 'And I shan't be getting rid of any of the books or paintings or things like that. Only his clothes and shoes. So if you think of anything else, let me know.'

He hesitated and she wondered if he might be going to ask if he should take anything for their mother. Pa's death had been so sudden, so unexpected, that she decided it would be unfair to Roger to cancel the expensive holiday they had booked and they hadn't appeared at the funeral. Freddie did his best to explain this tactfully, reasonably, but El knew how humiliated her mother would feel to face all the friends who knew what Pa had done and was glad to have an excuse to stay away.

But all Freddie said now was: 'Do you need any help with anything?'

'There's really only his clothes. Angus is going to check through all his papers, all the official stuff. But thanks for offering. I'll let you know if I have problems. And I hope everything goes really well with you and Sarah.'

He was telling her at supper after the funeral about his new girlfriend, a radiologist at his hospital, and how they might be getting a flat together. El was pleased for him, told him that she must bring Sarah down for a visit. She found him a bag in which to put his keepsakes, gave him a hug.

Now, as she opens the cupboard doors and stares inside, she realizes that she will need bags into which she must pack the clothes. Resisting the urge to close the doors again, to postpone the moment, she begins to bring out the trousers, shirts and jackets and pile them on to the bed. She glances at Pa's radio and CD player standing on top of the chest and switches it on. The CD starts turning and begins to play. Earth, Wind & Fire: 'Star bright, star light . . .', one of Pa's favourites. Eleanor hesitates, her arms full of clothes. Tears rush to her eyes and she bows her head, burying her face in his soft cotton shirts. After a moment she straightens up, piles them on to the bed and begins to fold them. A text pings in and she takes out her phone to look at it. It's from Will.

Would you like some help with that? I could come down on Wednesday morning for twenty-four hours.

It's odd how unexpected kindness is the undoing of her. She sits down on the edge of the bed beside the pile of shirts, takes a deep breath. Why not accept his offer, accept help? She's sometimes wondered how it must have been for Will when his mother died, how he felt about his father remarrying, and how much he must have resented her mother. She texts:

Thanks. That would be great. I'll send directions.

Once she's sent it she is washed through with relief. This dreaded moment can be postponed. It will be easier to deal with it once Will, calm, pragmatic, is with her. She switches off the music, goes out and closes the door behind her.

*

Kate is walking Floss in the woods above Burrator Reservoir. How strange but how familiar it is to be here: a glint of water between bare, black branches, the high outcrop of rock that is Sheepstor, the croak of a raven circling above her. As she wanders slowly, crunching through rusty dead bracken, watching Floss skittering ahead, Kate tries to analyse the sensations of happiness, contentment – and an odd feeling of loss. From the very beginning when she moved here as a young naval wife with her twin baby sons, Dartmoor – bleak, mysterious – has been her spiritual home. The colonial bungalow in Dousland, the cottage near Horrabridge, the Victorian semi in Whitchurch: these places were home and the moor was her refuge. It consoled her when her first marriage failed, when her love affair with Alex broke apart, and then again when her second husband, David, died.

As she picks her way amongst the mossy boulders, checking on Floss, watching a buzzard surfing the thermals, she wonders why it should have been then, when she felt most alone – David gone, both her boys married – that she left Tavistock, selling the house, which was much too big for her, and renting a cottage from one of David's friends in St Meriadoc on the north Cornish coast. David was an artist, an RA; Bruno Trevannion is a writer. He owns the small estate at St Meriadoc but prefers to live in a stone folly on the cliff rather than in the pretty house, Paradise, set amongst sheltered gardens, or in one of the three terraced cottages set round the long-disused harbour. It was in one of these cottages that Kate lived, though, and taking advice she'd bought a cottage in Chapel Street in Tavistock, which she rented out as a naval hiring. Her son Guy with his wife, Gemma, and their two boys have been living in it since they came home from Canada. Now they've moved down to be closer to the little family group that run the sailing school and Kate must find another tenant. Staying with Cass whilst some redecorating is done at the cottage, she's falling back into old familiar ways: walking on the moor, going to see old friends, coffee with Cass in the Bedford.

'Why don't you move back?' asks Cass. 'This is home really, you know that. I know you're very fond of dear old Bruno, and it's beautiful down there on the coast, but this is where you belong.'

Kate thinks about this as she walks. In a way, Cass is right. She ran away when David died. At that moment it seemed this place she loved so much represented failure: the collapse of her marriage with Mark, the heartbreak of a failed love affair, David's death. She was looking for a new beginning, something completely different. The move to St Meriadoc gave her a whole new perspective and she is happy in the little cottage, with Bruno out on his rock, writing his novels, and his kindly relatives around her. She remembers another occasion like this when she felt torn between her two loves, and Bruno saying, 'Home is where the heart is,' but she is still not sure where that is. She misses Bruno when she is away from him. In some ways he's like David. They're both creative artists and so are slightly detached, but they both know how to share, how to love.

She looks around for Floss, calling her name. She can see her now, following a scent amongst the trees on the slopes below, and Kate calls again until Floss comes dashing back to her.

'Good girl,' says Kate, fastening Floss's lead. 'It's time for tea.'

They walk back to the car, Floss tugging at the end of the lead and Kate suddenly wishing that they were going to her cottage in Tavistock rather than back to the Old Rectory. Just at the moment there's a great deal of stress between Cass and Tom. Tom feels very strongly that the time has come to sell the Rectory and move into a smaller house in Tavistock.

'Things have changed,' he says. 'The village shop and post office have closed down. There's no bus. I'm seventy-five this year and we need to make the move while we still can. We don't want to leave it too late and be pushed into it.'

Whenever he says this kind of thing, Kate can see Cass shrink a little; her eyes flick around her home as if to reassure herself of all that is dear and familiar to her. Kate feels huge sympathy for both of them. Tom is right: the Rectory is very big and very remote. It's beginning to look shabby and the garden is becoming a wilderness. Tom has had a knee replacement and can't do as much as he once could, and they are starting to lose their grip on it all. At the same time, Cass has lived there for forty years and there are too many memories, too much of her life there, to be cast aside easily. Each of them appeals to Kate for support and she's finding it a very difficult situation. Although she's never lived for any length of time in Chapel Street, she wonders what it might be like to be going there now: going home. She thinks of El. How she is feeling now that the Pig Pen is truly her home; not simply a place she goes to for holidays or weekends to stay with her father, but the place where she lives?

As she helps Floss to scramble into the back of the car and settles her on her rug, Kate thinks about Martin, and imagines how proud he would be of El. She remembers the woman she saw with him in the Walled Garden at The Garden House, and again one winter's morning on a beach in Cornwall, arm in arm, heads bent close together against the wind. On both occasions instinct warned Kate to stay clear. As she gets into the car and drives away, she thinks about how she saw the woman again at Martin's funeral, slipping out from her seat at the back into the shadows and disappearing on to Church Lane, unwilling to be noticed. It was then that Kate recognized her: the pretty, dark-haired woman was Julia Braithwaite. She'd presented a programme recently on local television called *Cakes and Ale*, celebrating the pubs and tearooms around the coast of the south-west peninsula, but Kate made no attempt to approach her, nor did she mention Julia to any of her friends. Clearly Martin wanted to keep their affair a private thing, a secret, and Kate has no intention of betraying it.

CHAPTER FOUR

All is dark on the flight deck. Will leans forward, gazing out at the stars, his preparations complete, absorbing these last few moments of serenity before descent. The moon casts its glittering light across the cloud sheet below him, obscuring the fainter constellations. He cannot see the swan clearly tonight but he knows where it flies. Deneb and Vega, two of the summer triangle stars, glitter to the right of the aircraft nose, marking the position of Cygnus in the night sky. This is what he has worked for, these moments of privilege and peace, and it is with reluctance that he returns to the management of the flight. He reaches down for the microphone on the throttle quadrant.

'Good morning, ladies and gentlemen. This is the captain.'

For a moment Will pauses: he knows he will never get tired of that phrase. He begins to brief his passengers, explaining that it is a clear and cold morning in Bristol but that the wind might make for a bumpy approach to the airport. He thanks them for flying with the company and wishes them safe onward journeys before he reaches up and turns on the seat-belt signs. In the dark of the flight deck his first officer grins at him. 'Making excuses for your landing?'

Christian is a good flight deck companion. When he was posted to Bristol, Will's home base, it seemed logical for him to move into Will's house in Backwell. For Will this was a steep learning curve, never knowing quite whom he would meet at the breakfast table. But taking Chris home to meet his critical stepmother was a joy that Will cherished for months. Chris is the eccentric counterpart to Will's conventional nature, hedonist to Will's ascetic, and gay to Will's straight. They have been friends since they met in flight training nine years ago. From their earliest days at flight school to the point where they set off separately to build hours, they've got on well together despite their obvious differences. In a strange sense they complement each other. Without Will, Christian would not have had the focus to make it through training. Without Christian, Will, scared by the loss of his mother, might have been swallowed up by introspection, melancholy and obsession. Will acknowledges that he has had the luck and, critically, the money, where Chris has not. It was Will who got his airline transport pilot licence first, Will who reached an airline first, and Will who helped Chris join that same company after he qualified as an airline pilot. No one in the business was surprised when, at the age of twenty-seven, Will was the youngest first officer at his base to be offered a command course. With his customary diligence he passed with ease.

And here they are, Will in the left seat and Christian in the right: a disciplined and effective team.

'Descent, please, Chris.'

Chris activates his microphone and obtains clearance. 'London Silver Star Two Fifty, request descent.'

'Silver Star Two Fifty descend flight level two four zero, further shortly.'

As Chris reads back the clearance, Will reaches up to the altitude dial on the flight control unit, turns it till the numbers read two four zero and pulls. On the screen in front of him the selected altitude changes to read FL two four zero and turns blue.

'Two four zero blue,' he reports.

'Check,' comes the response.

Gently the nose of the aircraft dips below the horizon and the altimeter begins to wind down, marking their descent.

Not far below them is a faintly visible layer of cloud, like a rumpled bed sheet, glowing faintly in the starlight. It does not take long for the aircraft to descend the few thousand feet needed to meet the cloud layer, and Will experiences the familiar rush, the sudden and rare awareness of the speed at which he is travelling. Cloud streamers race pass the flight deck windows as they drop into the mist.

In his left ear he can hear the incessant measured communication between the controller in London and the many aircraft he is managing tonight. On the central navigation screen in front of him he can see the symbols that mark the aircraft in his vicinity. Yet it is rare actually to see those aircraft: they are invisible performers in a stately dance in the skies.

Will adjusts the scale on the moving map and makes a quick mental calculation, miles to go versus altitude passing. If anyone had told him at school to learn the three times table up to 150 he would have laughed. The pilot's mantra, one mile three hundred feet, ten miles three thousand feet, one hundred miles thirty thousand feet, plays in his mind. The aircraft is on profile.

Momentarily, Will catches a glow below him to his left, then another: a hazy view of light across the nose as the aircraft descends out of the cloud layer. And then . . . London.

Red stars upon gold, silver and diamond. A confused cascade of sparkling light strewn upon a black field that is, at first, merely glimpsed through the haze as the airliner breaks out of the high cloud. For a moment the lights blur again, a deep glow penetrating the cloud cover and illuminating the dark flight deck, and then, quite suddenly, sharp focus again. In the darkness below there are no discernible features, just lights revealing patterns of black. There, the dark ribbon of the Thames; there, the absence of light in Regent's Park; there, the encompassing ribbon of light that circles the whole, the M25. Here is Heathrow, a patchwork buried in the expanded metropolis. To his left a cluster of lights out in the country shows the presence of Gatwick. In front of the aircraft's nose he can see the M4 stretched out to the west. In places near London it is illuminated by the diamond white of the new motorway lights. Further west it is a thin ribbon of white headlights and red taillights, the motorway traffic sparse at this time of the morning. Far out to his left he can see the south coast, Portsmouth and Southampton. Far to his right, through Chris's windows, he can see to the north the faint light of Birmingham and Coventry, whilst in front, Bristol – home – and beyond that the south coast of Wales. He allows his eyes to be drawn south, looking for the as-yet-invisible ribbon of the M5. On the far horizon he can see the faint lights of Exeter, and the dense darkness that is Dartmoor. It is a singularly privileged view which, of the 229 people on this Airbus A321, only he and Christian can share.

As they are approaching their designated level the London controller calls them again.

'Silver Star Two Fifty. What's your heading, please?'

'Two seven five degrees, Silver Star Two Fifty.'

'Roger. Maintain two seven five degrees, descend flight level one eight zero. Call London one three two decimal four. Good night.'

Releasing the microphone switch, Chris leans forward to dial up the new frequency and checks in, whilst Will sets the new flight level and pulls the heading control knob to disable the navigation following mode. When Chris has checked in with the new controller, Will reads out the new settings.

'Flight level one eight zero, heading two seven five, blue.'

'Checked.'

For the next twenty minutes the pilots are kept busy as they are routed around traffic inbound to London from the west. Will can see other aircraft of interest as they appear on the navigation screen in front of him, but he knows these are only a fraction of the traffic that is in the sky over the south of Britain this morning. This is the start of the rush hour, as aircraft inbound from the Americas are making their approaches to London or routeing far overhead to a myriad of European destinations.

Once he and Chris are handed over to Bristol Approach the radio traffic becomes much quieter. They cross the M5, heading out into the Bristol Channel before they are turned inbound to Runway 09 at Bristol.

As Will reduces their speed for the approach he begins to reconfigure the aircraft for landing, concentrating hard. Bristol has an unusual runway that slopes downhill from the west to the east. Landing on Runway 09 requires the pilots to fly manually as the approach is too tricky for autoland systems. Will knows he needs to land accurately in the touchdown zone so that he isn't left in the air, floating down the hill. But this is his home base and this is his moment; this is what he lives for. As they pass through three hundred feet the wind catches them, throwing the aircraft off balance, but Will is ready for the disturbance and corrects the flight path almost before it is deflected.

'Decide.' The order is from Chris.

'Land,' responds Will.

He has timed it perfectly. The main wheels touch the runway firmly, preventing any side-slip. He feels the ground spoilers deploy as he holds the right wing down with the stick, lowering the nose to the runway as the automatic braking system kicks in. At the same time he selects full reverse thrust. It may be early in the morning for loud noise but Will is making sure the aircraft will stop on the runway as it rolls downhill. As soon as he is confident of his landing he moves the thrust levers back to idle and the engine noise dies away from a roar to a murmur. His heart is beating fast, he exhales fully and feels the familiar exhilaration of a job well done.

Chris says, 'Nice one, Will.'

Will doesn't respond, he doesn't need to.

Bristol is a small airport and it is not long before Will is braking the aircraft to a halt and they are shutting down the engines and turning off the anti-collision lights. As the passengers disembark, Will and Chris work fast to secure the aircraft, complete the electronic paperwork and flight reports and brief the ground engineers on the minor faults that this flight has revealed. Then they are out of their seats, packing their flight bags and putting on caps and jackets before they leave the flight deck to join the cabin crew, who are waiting on the crew bus.

They dump their bags on the floor and sprawl on to the seats. Soon they will be on their way home.

El sleeps fitfully. It's not the first time she's been alone at night in the cottage since Pa died, but it's the first night of this whole new life ahead of her. Restlessly she turns on to her back, trying to keep sadness under control; trying to recreate the sense of adventure that she experienced as she drove down, planning what she might do and how she might live. Now, her hopefulness is diminished and she fears that her mother might be right: that it's a crazy plan. She's never told her mother about her secret dream that she might start to write, to attempt a novel. For some time now she's been wondering what form it might take, how she would begin, and she makes notes continually about her feelings, things she sees, how people behave. Pa encouraged her simply by allowing her to escape into other worlds, to read voraciously. It worries her that, even in her grief and loneliness, a part of her stands detached observing these emotions, wondering how they might be described, used. It makes her feel callous, but at the same time she thinks that it might be necessary if she is to write with any depth about people and how they think and feel and have their being.

'Cardboard cutouts,' Pa would sometimes say, tossing a novel aside. 'Two-dimensional characters.'

She is determined that she will never be snared in this trap and as she lies there in the darkness, in the deep rural silence, El wonders how she would describe her mother if she were to write about her; how she would try to show the need to dominate, to control, so as to maintain her grasp on events and the people around her. She needed order, rules, familiarity, to hold at bay her own insecurity. El could see now how much Pa's faithlessness had undermined all these things, stripping away her mother's fragile structure and support, leaving her exposed. Explanations and forgiveness were not an option. She took everything and left, expecting those closest to her to be absolutely on her side. Her motto was, 'Those who are not for me are against me.'

Just occasionally in this last year Pa came close to talking about his private life; the separation before the divorce.

'Why?' El asked him once, tentative and nervous, after a companionable supper.

She couldn't quite say the words outright. He stared into his wine glass, turning the stem in his fingers so as to catch the gleams of ruby light, not pretending to misunderstand her.

'Just for one moment, I was allowed to be me,' he answered at last.

His downturned face was serious, almost stern, and she was silent. He glanced up at her and smiled apologetically.

'You might say that it was a very costly moment.'

She could see that to continue the conversation would be complicated. She guessed that he enjoyed his freedom but at what expense? He lost companionship, family life, Freddie's respect. Yet there was a contentment, a self-sufficiency, about her father. She longed to ask who the woman was but knew she never would. He made no excuses or apologies: his pleasure in his daughter's company and ongoing love was evident. It pleased her that their friends were clearly in his corner, he wasn't condemned or cast out, and she wondered whether her mother – critical, pessimistic – had ever been popular with them. Even Marina, Angus's wife, was unmoved by the gossip surrounding the divorce. Marina was a generous, warm-hearted woman but her sympathy for the wronged wife seemed well under control.

El rolls on to her side, hugging her pillow, remembering those morning coffee sessions in the Bedford with Marina and Angus, Cass and Tom, Kate if she happened to be staying with Cass. They had such fun together: shrieks of laughter, gossip, shared anecdotes of family. They welcomed El into these, praising her cleverness, her prettiness, her youth in general, and she felt herself expanding into the warmth and friendship of these much older people. She simply couldn't imagine her mother as a part of this group.

'Much too busy,' she would have said, with that familiar look that was part irritation, part contempt, 'to sit about drinking coffee and gossiping.'

How sad they all were when Marina died. The little group still met, encouraging Angus, sharing in his grief, but still with that underlying, life-giving humour that raised the spirits. His daughter and her husband were posted to Washington and, though Plum made short visits to see her father, they were too far away to bring any real comfort.

'It's such a pity,' El heard Cass say to Kate whilst the men were at the bar. 'Plum would be so good for him. She's so strong and positive. I've only ever seen Plum desolate once, and that's when she had the stillborn child. How terrible that was.'

And then the men came back to the table, carrying drinks, and Kate raised her glass encouragingly to Angus.

'People don't know what to say to me,' Angus told them. 'Some people are embarrassed, some try to avoid me. Some keep telling me that it doesn't change but that I'll learn to handle it. Others tell me that they know how I feel.'

El wanted to give him a hug but she felt too young and inexperienced to know what to say. Cass leaned forward.

'But the worst are those who tell you how sorry they are for your loss,' she said. 'As if you'd left Marina at the railway station like poor old Paddington Bear.'

There was a tiny silence, then Angus burst out laughing. 'You are so right,' he exclaimed. 'Where has that awful expression come from?'

The mood lightened, and when the party broke up Cass smiled at El.

'The crucial thing,' she said, 'is never to lose one's sense of humour or we're all done for.'

Now, lying in the dark, El remembers this and instinctively thinks of reasons to be cheerful. She is here at the Pig Pen, she has good friends, she can make a start on her novel, and Will is coming down on Wednesday. A combination of relief, expectation and anxiety tenses her. How will that be? She hardly knows him, and yet here he is offering sympathy, understanding, prepared to drive down to support her, just as he'd driven down for the funeral. She remembers his instinctive reaction to that kiss all those years ago and wonders if her mother could be right: that Will is gay. El is well aware that Will enjoys winding her mother up. She remembers a New Year's party when Christian and Will wore matching pink shirts, and her mother's reaction, yet she can't forget how kind Will was at Pa's funeral.

'You did well,' he told her after the service at St Eustachius.

'I didn't want to read,' she told him, 'but Father Steven thought that Pa might like it. That passage from Paul's letter to the Romans, "Who shall separate us from the love of Christ?" was one of his favourites. I was so nervous.'

'You didn't look it,' he assured her. 'Father Steven was right. Is he the rector?'

'No, he's the curate,' she said. 'He's been so kind. Come and meet him.'

How odd it was, thinks El now, introducing Will to Pa's friends and not knowing how to describe him. Somehow she couldn't quite bring herself to call him her stepbrother though she didn't know why, which confused her further. To her relief Freddie behaved as if Will were an old friend so there was no awkwardness.

She groans aloud as memories jostle in her head, longing for sleep, wondering what the time is, and suddenly remembers a comment from Tom to Angus on that same morning in the Bedford.

'When you wake in the night watches never ever look at the clock. It's so disheartening to know that it's only three o'clock.'

'So what do you do?' Angus asked.

'I recite the shipping forecast,' answered Tom. 'Never get past Malin.'

Smiling to herself, El makes herself comfortable and silently begins to recite Carol Ann Duffy's poem 'Prayer'.

By the time she reaches 'Malin' she is asleep.

CHAPTER FIVE

Plum is glad to be home again: in England, in the flat in London, and here in the big Victorian house in Whitchurch on the edge of Tavistock. Washington was amazing, a wonderful experience, but it's good to be able to see the girls, her friends and her father without the travelling.

She stands in her childhood bedroom, which she prefers when she visits on her own, dumping things out of her suitcase on to the bed, fishing out the chocolates she's brought for her father. It was good of him to let them use his big double garage to store their car whilst they were in Washington; keeping it checked over, letting the girls drive it when they came down from uni to stay with him.

And it's clear, thinks Plum, that he is very happy to have her and Ian home. He was so pleased to see her as she got off the train at Plymouth, hugging her, kissing the top of her head, which always makes her feel like a child again and helps to ease the sadness now that her mother is no longer standing there on the platform beside him, waving, hurrying to greet her.

This is the first time she's seen him since they arrived back in London, so there's a lot of catching up to do. She's relieved to see him looking fit and in such good spirits and she's enjoying the prospect of spending a few days with him before taking the car back to London.

'No need to be in a rush,' Ian told her. 'It's been a long time and he'll be so pleased to see you. My debrief will take days, so enjoy yourselves.'

She can hear her father calling up the stairs and she leaves her unpacking and goes down to find him in the kitchen, a big room with a high ceiling and tall sash windows with painted wooden shutters. Her father's two golden Labradors, Blossom and Dearie, come to greet her, tails wagging, and she bends to smooth their heads, talking to them. She looks around, smiling at the old familiar things: the cream Aga, the built-in dresser crammed with a muddle of plates, photographs, small objects; her mother's cookery books on a shelf above a shabby old sofa.

She sinks on to the sofa, a dog at each knee, and smiles at her father.

'This is so good,' she says. 'So. Where shall we start?'

Angus has no idea where to start. It's been such a long and lonely three years without Marina, and with Plum and Ian so far away, that he still can hardly believe she's here in the kitchen sitting on the dogs' sofa, beaming at him. In her jeans and a shirt, her long fair hair looped back casually over her ears, she seems unchanged.

'You'll get dog hairs all over you if you sit there,' he says automatically, and Plum laughs, hugging the dogs, who are ecstatic to see her.

'No change there, then,' she says. 'So I told you all our news in the car, there must be something new happening in Tavistock.'

'First of all let's decide on what you want to do this after-noon. Anything special?'

'Yes,' she answers promptly. 'I want to take the dogs up on the moor for a walk. I've been dreaming about that for weeks. And it's such a heavenly day. Are you OK with that?'

'Very OK,' Angus replies. 'It's what I would have been doing. So lunch and then a walk. How about some soup?'

'Great. Something quick and easy. But I'm still waiting to hear the gossip.'

As he begins to prepare lunch, heating the soup, she stands up to help him, laying the table, peering into the fridge, and he feels an uprush of pleasure, of gratefulness for her company. He casts about for something to tell her and suddenly thinks of El. Plum knows that Martin has died, though she and Ian were still in Washington, but she doesn't know El's plans.

'Well, you know about poor old Martin,' he begins.

'Yes,' she says opening a drawer, her back to him, taking out spoons and knives. 'That was . . . just awful.'

He glances at her. He knows how fond she was of Martin, how distressed by his separation and then divorce, which hap-pened a few months after she'd given birth to her stillborn baby. It's a very sensitive subject and coupled with Martin's death Angus knows he must tread carefully.

'Well, El has decided to keep the Pig Pen. She wants to live there.'

Plum turns to stare at him. 'In the Pig Pen? Alone?'

'Yes. In fact she moved in yesterday.' Plum looks so shocked that he is surprised, but he smiles at her encourag-ingly. 'I think it's very brave of her. Of course, Felicity is out of her mind.'

'Felicity?'

Angus shrugs. 'Well, she would be, wouldn't she? She's never approved of El sticking by Martin and she thinks this is a crazy idea.'

Plum puts plates on the table. 'How old is El now?'

'Nearly twenty-two. She's just graduated with a First in English from Durham. She doesn't quite know what she wants to do career-wise yet, but she wants to keep the Pig Pen.'

Angus pours soup into two bowls and puts them on the table with baguettes and some cheese. He is puzzled by Plum's reaction. There's a kind of grim introspection, a distant look on her face that worries him. It's still a shock to think about Martin, of course, and the suddenness of his death, and he wishes that Marina were here to guide the conversation back into more light-hearted channels.

'Anyway,' he says, as they sit down, 'that's the latest news. Tom and Cass are looking forward to seeing you. Kate's staying, so we thought we'd all have a get-together. Have you got any plans?'

She glances at him and almost visibly pulls herself together.

'Not really. I've texted a couple of friends to say that we're back so I'll probably see them while I'm here. Just for coffee, nothing special.'

'So it's just me and the dogs?' he asks, and is relieved to see her smile return.

'Just you and the dogs,' she agrees.

He pushes the bread board towards her and she takes a baguette and breaks it, cuts some cheese.

'So where would you like to walk?' He wants to steer the conversation away from Eleanor and Martin. 'Pew Tor? Whitchurch Common?'

'The Common,' she says at once. 'Willy's ice-cream van might be there. The weather's still warm enough.'

He laughs, relieved by her response, feeling that the awkward turn in their conversation has been safely negotiated. He begins to talk about his granddaughters – Lauren just settling in at Warwick University, Alice working at a literary agency in London – and soon he feels that Plum is relaxed again and all is well.

Whilst Angus prepares himself for the walk, Plum wanders out through the utility room into the garden. Her mother kept it as a moorland garden. Mossy boulders edge a thin trickle of a stream, and in the spring ferns and primroses grow amongst the roots of the silver birches, and there are lakes and pools of daffodils and bluebells.

Now, on this warm October day, there are cyclamen on the grassy banks and along the border; under the high sheltering stone wall are golden rudbeckia and tall purple salvia. Plum stands beneath the beech tree, gazing out across the Down, thinking about her mother – always so present here in her beloved garden – of Martin, and of her baby.

'His name is James,' she told the naval chaplain firmly, as he sat by her bed in the hospital. Ian was at sea, not able to be present at the small private ceremony in the hospital's chapel. The chaplain kept her strong. As she stands in her mother's garden, Plum remembers the words prayed at her funeral.

'The souls of the righteous are in the hands of God and no torment shall touch them . . . In the eyes of the foolish they seem to have died . . .'

The moor flows away, hazy and mysterious to the horizon. A tiny movement of warm air stirs in the branches above her and suddenly she is surrounded by gently twirling flakes of gold that land lightly in her hair and in the crook of her folded arms. To catch a falling leaf means a year's good luck and she takes one and smooths it in her fingers. Suddenly the silence is disturbed by the thud of feet and here are the dogs, nuzzling her legs, tails wagging. Blossom and Dearie. Her mother brought them home as puppies just after James was born. Perhaps she hoped that these wriggling, engaging little creatures would go a little way to heal the pain.

'Blossom, Dearie,' she said, hoping to make Plum smile. 'They're litter sisters. Adorable, aren't they?'

And they were. Kneeling to gather their warm little bodies into her arms, Plum felt comforted. Now she bends to pat them, to lead them towards the car where her father is waiting. Plum knows that he is worried about her, confused by the pain she was unable to hide at lunch, and she is determined to put it aside, but almost on cue a text pings in. She takes her phone from her pocket and reads the text.

Good to hear you're back. Looking forward to a catch up.

The text is from one of her oldest friends, Isla: Issy. They were at primary school together, then at Plymouth College. Issy has a research post at the university. She is quick, clever, spiky – and suddenly, just at this moment, Plum wishes that she hadn't been so quick to tell her oldest friend that she was home. She remembers a conversation with Issy, quite a few years back, when she'd been a little too confiding. Issy was being so sweet about James, so understanding, the wine was flowing and the combination of these things made Plum more talkative than usual. Somehow, whilst Ian was at MOD and they were living in London, and then in Washington, this moment of indiscretion hadn't caused more than a pinprick of regret. Now, as they are about to move back into closer contact again after nearly five years, Plum feels uneasy. Her instinct is to delay answering Issy's text; to wait until she is back in London. Her father is coming out, calling to the dogs, and she goes to meet him, pushing her phone back into her pocket.

'Come on,' she says, helping the dogs into the back of the car. 'Last one in's a cissy.'

She climbs into the passenger seat and smiles at her father. He looks happy, ready for the walk, and she leans over briefly to kiss his cheek.

'It's great to be home, Dad,' she says.

As they drive up on to the moor, bumping over the cattle grid, turning right into the car park, Plum feels all her tension and sadness slipping away from her. She climbs out of the car and looks around her at the familiar landmarks: the bony outline of Cox Tor, that distant glimpse of shining water that is the River Tamar and, to the far west, half hidden in mist, the Cornish hills vanishing into eternity. Two crows are in contention over a discarded piece of ice-cream cone but they fly upwards, squawking angrily as the dogs are released from the car.

'Willy's here,' she says, nodding towards the ice-cream van, and her father smiles.

'Walk first. Ice creams after.'

Blossom and Dearie hurry out on to the sheep-grazed turf, following a scent, tails waving. He locks the car, their leads in his hand, and they all set off together towards Vixen Tor.

El crosses Duke Street into Church Lane, hesitates for a moment beside the path that leads through the churchyard and then turns into the café opposite. She orders a pot of tea and goes out into the courtyard. It's still quite warm enough to have her tea outside and she sits at a small table, looking across the wall at the church. Even the memories of Pa's funeral there a few weeks ago can't diminish this new excitement she's feeling. He would be proud that she's taken her courage in both hands, gone into Book Stop and talked to the owners, Simon and Natasha, about the possibility of working there. Of course, they knew Pa very well – he was a regular customer – and they've been very kind to her. Nevertheless she felt rather shy just coming out with it.

To her relief neither of them was particularly surprised at her question and she could hardly believe it when Natasha said that they were thinking of taking someone on in a part-time capacity before Christmas. Of course, she added, they would need to see El's CV and any job references.

Sitting in the afternoon sunshine, sipping her tea, El can hardly believe her luck. Of course, nothing is settled yet, but it isn't a refusal. Mentally she reviews her CV and plans to get in touch with the owner of the small second-hand bookshop she worked in during her last holidays from uni. Perhaps she should have gone straight home and got it sorted, but she felt a need to celebrate this wonderful opportunity rather than to go back to the Pig Pen where there is nobody with whom she can share the news. She longs to tell somebody, to have some encourage- ment, but both her closest friends are out of the country – one working with a charity in Ghana and the other on a family holiday – and she knows that Freddie's enthusiasm would be muted because he hopes that she will regret her decision to move to the Pig Pen. Despite these high spirits she is still very nervous about her decision to start a new life here – sometimes her courage evaporates and she is filled with panic – and she can't allow herself to be unnerved.

For a brief moment she wonders whether to share the moment with Will, to text him, but she rejects it almost immediately: she doesn't feel she knows him well enough. When he comes down will be soon enough. The prospect of Will arriving tomorrow distracts her from thoughts of the bookshop. It seems slightly surreal that he will be there with her at the Pig Pen.

'So what's Will like?' Pa asked her once, not long after the marriage. 'What sort of fellow is he?'

She shrugged.

'I don't know. I've only seen him a couple of times. I don't think he likes the situation any more than we do. Freddie and he are polite and he hardly notices me. He's just finished training as a pilot.'

'Standoffish, then?'

She thought about it. 'No, he's always polite. It's more like he's totally detached from it all.'

'Perhaps he needs time to adjust,' Pa said.

But Will hadn't adjusted — if anything he became more detached — and now El wonders how she will deal with this stranger who is so cool and remote. Yet she remembers his kindness at Pa's funeral when she glimpsed another side to him. She thinks about his text, and she feels glad that he's offered to help her. As she finishes her tea, El wonders if she'll introduce him to Angus, to Cass and Tom; draw Will into her small circle of friends. It's a new beginning and it's up to her to make it work.

CHAPTER SIX

'Are you still going on this madcap trip to Devon then?' For a moment Will pauses. It has been another long night and the lure of heading home with Chris and getting some sleep is strong. But then, he has made a promise, told El he would be driving down to Devon.

'Yes, I suppose so,' he answers. 'I should be there in two and a bit hours if I don't get lost.'

Chris snorts. 'Well, I hope you've got the sat nav set up. I'm not sure I'd trust your navigation at this time of the morning.'

Will nods. 'Programmed it on my phone this morning. I should arrive about seven if I'm lucky.'

It doesn't take long to check in at the crew room, talk to Ops and file the flight reports. Will and Chris say their farewells to the cabin crew and walk together out to the staff car park. Normally they share a lift from their house if they are flying together, but this time they have come in separately.

They reach Chris's battered Mini first and as he fishes his keys out of his nav bag he says: 'Well, take care, Will. Stay awake. I'll see you tomorrow.'

Will grins. 'See you then,' he answers, as he walks on towards the corner of the car park.

The black car gleams under the overhead lights and, as he presses the button on his keys and the indicators flick, he takes a moment to appreciate its lines. To the untrained eye it is like any other large saloon, but to the enthusiast it is an understated achievement, quiet power and quality. The Phaeton is his pride, joy . . . and money sink. Bought to celebrate his command – and to irritate his stepmother – it is the perfect vehicle for a new captain.

Walking up to the car he activates the electric boot and hoists his flight bag into the cavernous interior next to his overnight bag. Then he presses the button to close the lid while he pulls off his jacket and tie and opens the driver's door. He hears the unmistakable sound of Chris's Mini misfiring as it pulls out of its parking slot with a cheery toot of the horn. Will raises his arm in salute and then climbs into the driver's seat and shuts the door.

Within the car there is the silence of quality. It is like a flight deck in here, silent and expectant, like an airliner waiting. He reaches down to the gear lever control panel and presses the start button. The car comes alive, a symphony of reds and blues and silvers. As the engine starts there is a faint rumble and then almost inaudible quiet, unnatural calmness in a car capable of such power. He enjoys the moment, allowing the engine to warm a little before he takes the solid automatic lever in his left hand and shifts the car into drive.

He eases out of the parking slot and down towards the exit. Even at 4 a.m. the roads are busy with traffic leaving and arriving at the airport. He turns right around the roundabout on to the A38 southbound and drives past the threshold of Runway 27. Soon he is leaving the bustle of the car parks on the south side of the airfield behind him. The unfamiliar sign ahead says 'M5 South 15 miles' and for the first time he permits himself to wonder why he is heading for Devon, for the Pig Pen and for El. Then with an impatient flick of the wrist he turns on the audio system and calls up the first loaded CD. He hits play and allows the opening riff of 'Layla' to propel him south into the darkness.

An hour later, Will glares balefully at the analogue clock in the centre of the cherry wood dashboard. It is not yet six o'clock, and it has just occurred to him that, at his current rate of progress, he will be arriving at the Pig Pen well before sunrise. Again he wonders at the impulse that is driving him south towards Devon. It is not as if he and El are close. He can't remember the last time that they communicated, apart from her father's funeral. But he knows about loss, about grief – Martin's funeral has reminded him of the bleak loneliness after his own mother died, has reawakened his battened-down misery – and he could not help but respond to the honesty in El's text. Nevertheless he can't imagine her being pleased to find her stepbrother – how he hates that word – banging on her door before seven in the morning.

So now what? He could stay here in these sterile services, drinking coffee for an hour, but at the thought of it Will snorts out loud. 'Not bloody likely.'

He looks again at the map display on his phone. The blue line that takes him to the farm shows that he will arrive in fifty-one minutes, but there are two other options available to him: the A38 to Plymouth and a route over Dartmoor.

A snippet of conversation slips into conscious thought: 'Pa and I loved the moor. I suppose that's why he moved there . . .'

The moor. Around him he can see that, at last, it is beginning to get light. The few stars that, up to now, have been challenging the bright white lights of the service area have begun to dim and wink out. He looks at the clock again. Sunrise will be at about seven thirty at this time of year.

He decides. OK, then it's up on to the moor, find somewhere to watch the sunrise and then down to El's for breakfast . . . if she eats breakfast. On this gloomy thought he taps the screen to activate the route through Two Bridges and then presses the start button. With the engine running he snaps the buckle home on his seat belt and, reaching to the console, he chucks Christian's Kylie CD in the glove compartment and sets a new CD on the auto changer before he eases the big car out of the parking bay.

Passing the lights of the petrol station and the green traffic light at the exit to the services, he rolls down the hill towards the motorway junction. A few seconds later he is powering up the slip road, back on to the M5.

It is not far to the A30 junction, and sweeping round the sharp right-hand bend on to the dual carriageway he gives the car its head and surges on towards the west. The car is in its natural element now, treating both hills and descents with elegant equanimity. Will is enjoying the drive, dawn is beginning to reveal the hills rising ahead and to the left of the road, and soon he is approaching the Whiddon Down junction and taking the road towards Moretonhampstead. He needs the powerful full beam on the headlights now as he follows the winding road.

As he approaches a sharp left junction the sat nav instructs him to enter a narrow lane ahead. Almost immediately he regrets the instinct to follow blindly instructions from a computer. The lane is extremely narrow for such a large car. Gingerly he presses on, half considering finding a place to turn round and go back, but fortunately, at this hour, he is not meeting any other traffic. The lane begins a long, steady and confusing descent. Surely he should be climbing up to the moor, not rolling down into a valley? And then his route becomes positively alarming. Ahead of him there is a narrow stone chicane. As he eases up to it he realizes that he will have inches to spare either side of his vehicle. He retracts the wing mirrors and passes the obstruction gingerly. Immediately, the reason for the chicane is obvious: it protects an ancient, very narrow stone bridge with high stone walls that crosses the river in the bottom of the valley.

'Well I got through the entrance, I ought to be able to get through this,' he mutters.

Holding his breath, as if by doing so he will make the car narrower, he eases over the bridge, keeping as close as he can to the right-hand wall, half expecting to hear the scrape of metal on stone. It is not easy in the semi-darkness. Beyond, there is an exit chicane that has to be navigated before the road begins to climb again. His heart is racing, his palms clammy. This is not the place to bring a luxury saloon.

The narrow lane continues interminably and he has to nego-tiate several turns and junctions, trusting and cursing the sat nav at the same time. Eventually he gives up, stops and has a closer look at the route he is following. He can see that there are still a couple of miles until he reaches the main B road across the moor. Cursing himself for a fool again, he stows his phone in its cradle and eases on up the narrow lane.

At last he is leaving the network of small stone-walled fields he has been traversing and is climbing up into the light and on to the moor. Yet more problems: every fifty feet or so there are sheep on the road. They seem oblivious to the approaching black predator until he makes the car growl by selecting neutral and revving the engine. Startled, they move off into the scrubland, but progress is slow until he reaches the junction and turns with relief out of the lane and on to a proper road. He laughs aloud at his foolish little adventure as he allows the car to accelerate at last.

It is getting light. The whole landscape is being revealed to him. Behind, the countryside stretches back towards Exeter and the dawn, whilst ahead the moor obscures the view. He presses on, looking for that point on the road when he will reach the summit and begin his descent towards the west.

And here it is. Two '40' signs, designating the speed limit, are painted on the road. As he crests the rise the landscape opens up before him, stretching away into darker lands ahead. The road is straight, descending. He slows a little, looking for a place to stop. Ahead in the dawn light he can see a line of stones that lead to a small car park on his left. As he approaches, his eye is drawn momentarily to a stone pillar beyond the markers, but then he has to swing wide to turn left into the tarmac entrance. He pulls up on the gravel and sits a moment before turning off the engine.

All is silent. He opens the driver's door and climbs out, stretching in the cold breeze. He reaches into the car and grabs his jacket, shuts the door and drapes the jacket about his shoulders. With the practised instinct of the city dweller he locks the doors and then steps up on to the low turf bank in front of the car.

From his vantage point he is looking at a gentle hill capped at its highest point with an outcrop of rock. To his right a long low valley stretches out to the south-west, towards his destination. In the far distance he can just see the beginnings of farmlands and dark woods. To his left, towards the light, is the road descending from its summit, and there, close to him, is the stone pillar. He walks towards it, through a marked exit from the car park and down a narrow path etched into the ground by footfall. He crosses a gully on a white stone slab, and walks on, towards the grey pillar across the grass growing between tufts of windswept scrub.

As he approaches, he can see that the stone is not a natural addition to this landscape, nor is it a pillar. It is a cross, hewn from a single piece of granite. It is beaten and weathered by the elements. The arms, very short, are invisible from the wrong angle, disproportionate with the main trunk. It is primitive, elemental, simple. The dawn's light shows a covering of yellow lichen that seems to invite the sun to rise, to shine upon it.

Will stands staring at the cross, ignoring the chill morning air. The light grows, the sun will rise soon. From where he stands it seems that the trunk of the cross is bent, curving a little to the left then a little to the right, so that it appears con-torted, agonized, as if the stone mason has carved suffering into the granite. Unbidden memories of his mother are sum-moned from the locked spaces in his mind: her stoicism in the face of the cancer that destroyed her; the tremor, the weakness in her voice the last time she spoke to him.

'No tears, Billy. Promise me, no tears.'

At twelve years old he wasn't ready to make that promise, to accept that burden. He wanted to scream out his fear, but he obeyed, complied, tried to control his anguish.

After her death no one ever called him Billy again. He wouldn't permit it, couldn't stand the intimacy, the reminder. He never cried in public, not even in front of his father, who tried to help him but was having difficulty in managing his own suffering.

Will moves closer to the stone. Putting his hand on the rough granite he acknowledges the pain and loss that dwell deep within him. Slowly the light grows stronger, he feels a faint warmth caressing his back and, momentarily, it seems as if he is being held and protected.

He turns, leaning back against the cross, facing the rising sun as it lifts above the hill. Before him the moor seems to be quaking, dissolving in the brightness of golden light. He shuts his eyes against the dazzle. Bathed in the gentle warmth, encompassed by the glow, he laughs softly, dispelling the gloom.

'Hello, Mum,' he says.

Half an hour later Will drives through the open gate into the small courtyard of the Pig Pen. He shuts off the engine and sits looking at the little house still decorated by the last of the year's climbing roses. He ought to be nervous, to be unsure, but somehow those feelings have been left on the moor, by the cross. He climbs out of the car, pulls off his jacket and, slinging it over his shoulder, strolls up to the door, and knocks.

El is waiting for him. She was up early, feeling apprehensive about this meeting with someone who isn't a brother, a friend or a colleague. To have invited him here for twenty-four hours now seems a crazy thing to have done and she is nervous. As she showered and dressed – deciding to be casual, leggings and a loose shirt – she wished, not for the first time, that she was thin and elegant and had silky smooth hair, rather than being rather solid and round-faced with very thick brown curly hair. Staring at herself in the glass as she wound her hair into a rope and pinned it up, El made a face at her reflection and turned away. If Will is gay, it couldn't matter less.

No platitude had been spared throughout her teenage years as her mother underlined El's own dissatisfaction by assuring her, in various terms, that beauty was only skin deep.

Now, hearing Will's knock, she comes to the head of the stairs and shouts to him: 'Come in, Will.'

She goes down a few steps to meet him as he stands in the hall, gazing round before he looks up at her.

'It's an upside-down house,' she explains. 'Come on up.'

She backs up before him as he climbs the stairs, smiling at him, wondering how she should greet him. His surprise at the huge space, however, drives away any embarrassment.

'Wow!' he exclaims. 'I wasn't expecting this.'

She laughs. 'What were you expecting. Troughs and sties?'

He laughs, too. 'Not exactly. But this is really good.'

El is relieved by this quick easing into familiarity. She watches him as he looks around and up at the huge beams and suddenly her anxiety dissipates and she feels calm.

'Have you had breakfast?' she asks. 'I haven't had mine yet.'

'Only coffee,' he answers. 'Thanks. Yes, please. Whatever's going.'

As she makes toast and scrambles eggs, he wanders round, sliding open the door on to the terrace and going outside, peering from the window over the kitchen sink, commenting on the wood-burning stove.

'The floor was strengthened to bear its weight,' El tells him as she sets things out on the central oak table. 'It's a bit of a fag bringing logs up, but worth it.'

He picks up a long wooden pole and examines it.

'It's to let down the blinds.' She indicates the big Velux windows. 'It can be a bit bleak when it's dark and raining so Pa had blinds fitted.'

Will sets the pole back in the corner and comes to the table with a more serious expression. Somehow, by mentioning Pa, it's as if she's reminded him why he's here and a slight constraint creeps into the former cheerfulness. El sits opposite him and pushes the coffee pot towards him.

'Did you have a good journey down?' she asks randomly. 'Which way did you come?'

Will pours himself some coffee. 'I came over the moor. It was . . . quite an experience.'

There's a note in his voice that makes El glance at him. He sounds as if he's been affected by his journey but she doesn't feel able to ask him directly what it might be.

'It's an amazing place,' she says lightly. 'Especially at sunrise. Or at sunset.'

'I believe you,' he answers. 'I'd love to see some more of it.'

'Well, that's easily achieved. I shall take you on a guided tour.'

'I'd like that,' he says, eating his breakfast with evident relish. 'If there's time.'

Once again she's reminded of the real object of his visit, but the prospect of showing him some of her favourite places, perhaps taking him for a pub lunch, is surprisingly attractive.

'I think there will be,' she answers. 'It's going to be another fine day so we could go for an explore, perhaps have lunch somewhere, then we'll have the rest of the day to sort out Pa's things.'

He looks at her directly then, as if assessing her mental state, and she smiles at him as if to reassure him that she's fine with it. He nods.

'I'll get my bag in from the car then,' he says, 'if you'd like to show me where I'm sleeping.'

She follows him downstairs and when he comes in with his bag she's already waiting in Pa's bedroom.

'There are only the two bedrooms,' she tells him, suddenly feeling rather shy. 'I hope you'll be comfortable in here.'

'Are you OK with that?' Will glances round the room and then at her. 'I mean, I could doss down on one of the sofas upstairs.'

She smiles her gratitude at this sensitivity but shakes her head.

'This will have to be my spare room,' she tells him. 'I hope people will come and stay so I've got to get over it. Freddie slept in here for the funeral. I'll let you get sorted and then we'll decide what we're going to do.'

She leaves him, going back upstairs, clearing the table and filling the dishwasher. It's a little while before she begins to wonder why there's no sight or sound of him. She stands at the top of the stairs and calls tentatively and then goes down into the hall. The bedroom door is still open so she taps lightly and when there is no reply she looks into the room. Will is sprawled across the bed, his head buried in his forearm, heavily asleep.

El remembers that he's driven straight down to Devon after his flight and smiles sympathetically. She studies the long bony length of him, the floppy fair hair and the half-hidden face, and thinks that it's rather a pity that he's gay. On the other hand it makes everything simple and easy between them. She backs out of the bedroom and goes quietly upstairs.

Will wakes out of dreamlessness, rolls on to his back and stares at the unfamiliar ceiling. He groans and sits up. It's a fairly normal procedure to crash out after a night flight but not here: not on his first visit to the Pig Pen. He glances at his watch and groans again. He's been out for at least half an hour. Pushing himself off the bed he wonders if he should shave, shower and get dressed as if nothing has happened but instead he goes out and up the stairs.

El is sitting at the table, her laptop open, and she glances up as he appears. He decides to behave as if she's guessed what's happened and he simply opens out his hands and shrugs.

'Sorry,' he says. 'I sat down on the bed to check my phone and the next minute I was gone.'

He can tell by her amused expression that she knows, that she probably came down and saw him, and he feels a prat.

'I'm not surprised,' she says. 'I didn't ask you about your flight but you said you'd be driving straight down. I should have asked when you arrived if you just needed to sleep. Sorry. Would you like some more coffee?'

'I'd love some,' he answers, grateful for her calm response. 'Give me ten to shave and shower?'

'There's no rush,' she tells him. 'You made such good time that the day is still all before us. Let me know if there's anything you need.'

Back in the bedroom, he unpacks his bag, takes out jeans and a shirt and jersey. As he does this he's puzzled by an unfamiliar lightness of heart, an odd peacefulness, and then he remembers that moment up on the moor, the old stone cross, that intense moment of mourning for his mother; his tears for her and all that he's lost. He stands, holding his clothes, remembering the feeling of release, of being held and comforted: the weight on his heart beginning to lift with the sun as it rose above the hills.

Looking around the room he thinks about El, wonders how she feels about her father, and he feels apprehensive at what lies ahead. He respects her for what she's doing, for how she stuck to her guns and stood by her father despite Felicity's anger. Nevertheless, it must be tough to take this decision without any family support. He knows what it's like to feel alone and he feels even more determined to help her through this. It's as if his little vigil at the stone cross has strengthened him just when he needs it.

Shaking his head at this rather fanciful thought, Will picks up his shaving gear and goes into the bathroom.

CHAPTER SEVEN

Plum comes out of Crebers, turns left and then dives into the little passage that leads into the Pannier Market. She glances at the tables outside Dukes, wondering if anyone she knows is having coffee outside in the sunshine on this warm October morning, and then pushes open the door and goes into the market. The bustle, the colour, the wonderful variety of stalls is familiar yet always interesting. The possibility of buying for someone a present that is quirky, unique, is always here. She wanders in the aisles, smiling at the stall-holders, stopping to chat, and once again the sense of being at home clutches at her heart.

'Hi,' says a voice behind her.

She turns quickly and here is Issy, friend of her youth, smiling at her. Plum has no time to analyse her mix of reactions – surprise, affection, anxiety – before the exchange of hugs, expressions of delight, amazement that they should meet by accident.

'I was going to text to arrange to meet once we've moved down,' Plum says, before Issy can imply any kind of neglect, 'but this is just a quick dash to pick up the car. Look, this is great! Have you got time for coffee?'

She's aware that she's gushing, overdoing it, and that Issy is giving that little secret smile to show that she knows it, too.

'I certainly have,' she answers. 'No tutorials, no papers to be marked. But I'm having lunch with my mum so I can't be long.'

Plum can barely suppress her relief. 'Let's go to Dukes. It looked so nice as I came through with everyone sitting in the sun.'

She's leading the way, trying not to babble about the weather, wondering why she was so weak and foolish to admit her biggest regret to this friend who is now sitting down opposite, watching her. She remembers the occasion of her indiscretion – Ian was at sea, the children at boarding school – and Issy had come to supper at their naval hiring in Horrabridge. She was still off balance after James, still mourning him, but there was something else that was weighing on her conscience, and after several glasses of wine the temptation to talk, to tell all, was too great. How kind Issy was: how sympathetic and understanding.

Even now Plum bitterly regrets the disclosure. Not long afterwards Ian was posted to Portsmouth, then to the MOD and then to Washington. It has never been spoken of again between them, but instinct warns Plum that Issy is waiting her moment, and as they order coffee and exchange news Plum is alert, watchful.

'I can't think why you are so fond of her,' her mother used to say. 'She's such an odd child.'

Plum could never analyse her feelings. Issy was an enigma: witty, edgy, but surprisingly empathetic. It wasn't until she was much older that Plum realized that she always told Issy much more than Issy ever told her. She is the middle child with two clever, successful siblings, and as Plum enquires after her sisters and their partners and their children she remembers how Issy spoke once, very briefly, about her own love affair. She let the name George slip out but she quickly glossed over it and then changed the subject, and Plum suspects that he is a married man, though she's never asked. There's something so private about Issy that even now Plum doesn't question her about her love affairs in that jokey way that she might with her other girlfriends. Instead, she talks about where they might live now that Ian has been posted back to Devonport and the girls have left home, how they intend to keep the London flat and how good it is to be back in Tavistock.

Isla watches her. Plum still looks so young, so pretty. It was always easy to attract school friends like Plum – easy-going, open, confiding – easy to make them laugh at her spiky wit, thrill at her daring, and respond to her ability to empathize; to lay herself alongside their fears and doubts and tragedies without ever displaying her own weaknesses. But Plum was always special. Isla wanted Plum for herself, her own special friend; to detach her from her loving family. She wondered if Plum – adored only child – could possibly imagine what it must be like to have two clever, good-looking sisters, one older, one younger, their mother's darlings, their father's pride and joy. She was always pushed to the background despite her own achievements; never taken seriously.

'It's great to see you, Issy,' Plum is saying.

She hates being called Issy, dislikes nicknames, thinks it's silly and affected that Plum is so called because her name is Victoria, but she smiles back at her old friend. She asks after Plum's girls and carefully bats away any questions about her own situation. She remembers mentioning George and knows that Plum remembers, too, and is dying to ask but is too tactful to broach the question. The relationship with George

– Georgina – didn't last very long. She said that Isla was too possessive, too demanding, but Isla can't help her overwhelming need to bind those whom she loves closely to her. She wonders whether Plum regrets her own indiscretion – that fateful need to confide – when she admitted to a lapse that surprised and shocked Isla, though she didn't show it. It's quite a few years ago but old sins have long shadows and now, watching Plum across the table, still so attractive, so warm-hearted, Isla longs to mention it; to draw Plum closer again. But this is not the right time or the right place. The moment will come and she knows how to wait.

When Issy says that she must go, Plum conceals her relief. As they hug, agree that they must meet again soon, she's glad that Issy holds a post at Plymouth University, where she lives in a flat on the campus, so that the possibility of bumping into her in Tavistock is unlikely. This morning was just a coincidence. She was on her way to her mother at Lydford but stopped to buy her a birthday present in the Pannier Market. Surely that wouldn't be likely to happen very often. Nevertheless Plum feels unsettled, guilt and remorse knocking at her heart, knowing she will never forgive herself for that one foolish act that had such far-reaching consequences.

As she crosses the square, glancing at her watch – it's well after midday – she realizes she's rather later than she meant to be to meet up with her father, but she knows where she'll find him. She hurries up the steps and into the Bedford. Her father and Tom Wivenhoe are having a pint at a table near the bar. Tom stands up as she approaches them and this small act of gallantry warms her heart and so does the hug he gives her. It reminds her of other returns – from school, from university, from other naval ports – and she responds, smiling at him.

'What will you have?' he asks her. 'Coffee? Or do you fancy a wet?'

She's about to refuse and then changes her mind. She doesn't want any more coffee but a glass of wine might just steady her.

'A small one,' she says. 'Pinot Grigio? That would be great. Thanks, Tom.'

Her father smiles at her as she sits down beside him. Presently Cass arrives and, to Plum, just for a moment it's as if nothing has changed, as if time has stood still, held like a fly in amber. She sips her wine, listens to the flow of conversation, and wonders what they would say if she suddenly spoke out. Plum shivers, imagining their shocked expressions, the disbelief and – worse – the disappointment.

Cass turns to her, asking her how the girls are doing, whether they'll be home for Christmas. She's drawn into a conversation about parties, celebrations, and suddenly Cass asks: 'How's El, Angus? Tom and I thought we'd invite her to Sunday lunch. Will you still be here, Plum?'

'No,' says Plum quickly, rather too quickly. She sees her father's brief glance and adds, 'I have to be back in London by the weekend. Lauren's home. I hardly see her now she's at uni so I like to make the most of her visits.'

It's true, but somehow she feels that it doesn't sound it.

'Never mind,' says Cass. 'Lots of time ahead. So how's El doing, Angus? Have you seen her?'

'No, but I've had a text,' he answers. 'She's very excited because Natasha and Simon at Book Stop are thinking about offering her a part-time job. She was getting her CV sorted out. And then Will is coming down to help her sort out Martin's things.'

'Will?' questions Cass. 'Didn't we meet him at the funeral?'

'Can't Freddie help her?' asks Tom. 'Surely he should be the one supporting her at a time like this.'

'Well,' Cass shrugs, 'I think it was all a bit tricky after the divorce, wasn't it? Freddie feeling that he needed to be on Felicity's side and El sticking by Martin. I think she's so brave to move in and try to make a life here. Would she mind, d'you think, if you were to give me her mobile number, Angus?'

He hesitates, always cautious. 'I'll ask her. I'm sure it's OK but I think that might be best.'

'Once a lawyer, always a lawyer,' says Cass, resigned. 'Poor girl. How awful it is. I still half expect Martin to come walking in.'

Plum puts down her glass, swings her bag on to her shoulder and gets to her feet. 'Just going to the loo,' she says as they glance up at her. 'Shan't be long.'

She walks out of the bar, through the lounge and along the passage. The cloakroom is empty and she stands for a moment both hands resting on the washbasin, head bent. She wants to scream, to cry. One small foolish act, just one, has caused such chaos. And now Martin is dead. Plum raises her head and stares at her face in the mirror. Her reflection gazes bleakly back at her. She hears voices outside, the door handle rattles as someone opens it, and Plum hurries into the nearest cubicle and locks the door behind her.

Hidden by the Endsleigh Gardens Nursery lorry in the square, Isla watches her old friend hurry across the road and up the steps into the hotel. Isla remembers how Plum's parents used to meet friends there, taking up several tables, enjoying themselves. Several times, way back, Plum invited her to join them and Isla was amused and fascinated by these people – confident, so at ease with each other – and how they welcomed her as Plum's friend.

It would be interesting, thinks Isla, to walk in there now. To take Plum by surprise, pretending that she's forgotten something she wanted to ask her, and to watch her reaction. Plum was ill at ease, however hard she tried to cover it, and Isla knows why. Secrets are so dangerous. How ironic that they both have something to hide. As she makes her way back to her car, Isla decides that she might make another visit to Tavistock and have coffee in the Bedford.

The prospect pleases her and she smiles as she gets into her car, heads out of the town and drives towards Lydford.

CHAPTER EIGHT

El stands with Will in her father's bedroom, steeling herself for the task ahead. She's aware that Will is waiting for her to take the lead, not wanting to rush in. She's really enjoyed their day, driving him around, showing him the beauties and the mysteries of the moor: steep-sided river valleys, high stony tors with unexpected glimpses of the distant sea, a dry-stone wall that looked like granite lace against the blue sky. The day was warm and sunny, and she was delighted by his reaction to this place she loves so much. He didn't exclaim or enthuse but paid it the true compliment of silent contemplation.

They had lunch at the Warren Inn, drove back with a diversion around Burrator Reservoir, and then home. At first she dithered, emptying the dishwasher, checking what they might have for supper, until Will simply said: 'Shall we just get on with it? Then we'll be able to relax.'

She nodded. He was right. Gathering up some black plastic bags they went downstairs and into Pa's bedroom.

Now, Will is still waiting and, making up her mind, El steps forward and swings open the cupboard doors.

'I made a start,' she said, 'but I lost my nerve, and when you said you'd come down I put everything back so as to get the room ready for you.'

Will nods. He stands looking into the wardrobe and then down at her.

'How do you want to play it?' he asks. 'Shall I bring everything out and lay it on the bed and then you make decisions?'

She nods, trying to imagine what Pa would say if he knew that Will was here, handling his clothes, but she's too near to tears to put it off any longer. Will begins to slide the clothes out, laying them gently across the bed, working quickly along the rail whilst she smooths and folds the shirts and trousers, making a neat pile.

'There's no point,' she says, trying to sound calm, sensible, 'in keeping anything. Pa wasn't very tall, not as tall as Freddie. I asked him, of course. Freddie, I mean. But he didn't want any of these things. He's taken what he wants. Books. A painting . . .'

She rambles on whilst Will works silently beside her, folding, filling the bags. Soon the wardrobe is empty and El opens the top drawers. Inside, Pa's socks are rolled into neat balls, brown, navy, dark green. She stares at them, picks one up, thinks about him putting it there, not dreaming what lay ahead, and wants to burst into tears. Gently, Will moves her to one side.

'Shall I do this?' he asks.

She nods, and with the same deft movements he empties the drawer, then opens the next and the next, and works quickly through them. El stands beside the bed, fingering this garment and that, before putting them into the bags. Soon the small drawers are empty and Will starts on a chest, which is full of jerseys.

'I've kept a couple of his jerseys for myself,' El tells Will, determined to sound calm. 'He didn't care much about clothes. Books were his thing. So I'm keeping all those.'

Will works quickly and efficiently but he is respectful with Pa's things, always ready to pause if El needs time to consider. Gradually the drawers and cupboards are cleared and the room is stacked with black plastic bags. El stares at them despondently.

'I'll take them to Tavistock in the morning,' she says reluctantly but gratefully. 'To one of the charity shops.'

'I was just wondering,' Will says quickly, 'how you'd feel if I took them.'

El stares at him in astonishment. 'You? Why would you do that?'

'I know a very good hospice shop. Our local hospice was just great to my mum at the end and I'd really like to do that, unless you feel the same about a charity here, of course.'

She remembers that his mother died of cancer when he was still a boy of twelve and this time she can't prevent the tears. He puts an arm around her, holds her tightly for a moment then lets her go.

'Life's shit,' he says. 'Look, I'll get all this stuff into my car and then we'll have a drink. I think we deserve one, don't you?'

She nods and they take the bags out of the bedroom, into the hall, and she stacks them beside the back door whilst Will unlocks his car, opens the boot, and makes space. The bags soon fill it up and the rest he piles on to the back seat.

El goes into the bedroom and looks around her. Only Will's things remain, apart from the books in the bookcase. She comes out again and then sees Pa's coats hanging on the hooks in the utility room. His Wellington boots stand underneath, beside his walking shoes, and she hesitates. Instinctively she decides against giving the coats to Will. These she will keep a little longer. She touches Pa's navy-blue fleece gilet and then takes it down and tries it on, hugging it around her, feeling its softness. She closes her eyes, squeezing back tears as she remembers him wearing it, knowing that she can't bear to part with it. It's only a little too big for her and she puts her hands in its pockets, thinking that it would fit quite well over a big jersey on a cold day. Her right hand encounters something smooth, oblong, hard, and she brings the object out. It's Pa's mobile phone. She stares at it, remembering how she looked for it just after he died and then forgot about it. Will is coming back. Quickly she shrugs herself out of the gilet, hangs it back on the peg and hurries into her bedroom. She puts the phone in a drawer and then goes out to meet him.

'All done?' she asks. 'That's amazing. Shall we have that drink, then? What would you like?'

She leads the way upstairs, realizing that she knows so little about him, and yet he's just helped her through one of the most important and difficult things in her life so far. As she pours him a gin and tonic El decides to tell him about the job at Book Stop; how she's hoping they will take her on part time. Will is impressed that she's got off to such a promising start and asks questions about the shop, what hours she'd be working. Warmed by his interest and enthusiasm, she expands, showing him her CV, telling him about her previous work experience while he lights the wood burner. She finds it hard to believe how easy it is to be in his company, remembering all those years of coolness and avoidance. She also remembers her mother's insistence – after she met Christian – that Will is gay, and El wonders if this is why there is no constraint affecting them. Anyway, it's not important. Just at the moment she's grateful for his kindness, his company and his empathy. He knows what it's like: the shock, the loneliness, the grief.

'Who's your neighbour?' he asks as they sit down to supper. 'I see there's another cottage the other side of that little orchard. Who lives there?'

'The farmer's son, Andy.' she tells him. 'He works on the farm and his wife's just had a baby. They're great. Very down to earth and fun. They've been really sweet since Pa died, and I have to admit that knowing they're there was quite a big part of giving me the confidence to move down. Secretly, it's all a bit scary.'

Will raises his glass to her. 'It's a big step but it's definitely worth giving it a go.'

She smiles back at him, thinking how nice he is and rather regretting all these years of animosity.

'I know you said you could manage twenty-four hours,' she says. 'Does that mean an early start tomorrow?'

He nods. 'Straight after breakfast, if that's OK, but maybe . . .' He hesitates, embarrassed, and she steps quickly into the silence.

'But you'll come again, won't you?' she asks, casually. 'I'd like to show you Tavistock. You must see the Pannier Market. And you haven't begun to get to know the moor yet.'

'Can't resist an offer like that,' he says.

As they finish supper she wonders whether to mention Christian but decides against it. Remembering how Will fell asleep this morning after his night flight and then his drive down, she wonders if he's tired and decides to aim for a fairly early night. Will makes no protest and she watches him go downstairs, then begins to tidy up. Suddenly she feels exhausted. It's been such a huge thing, clearing Pa's clothes, and she guesses that tomorrow, once Will has gone, the reality will hit her. El sighs, follows Will downstairs, goes into her bedroom and closes the door.

As Will drives away the next morning he wonders if El really believed his little fiction about the charity shop or if she was simply relieved to have the problem totally removed from her. After all, she knows he now lives in a village west of Bristol, near the airport, whilst his mother died upcountry. Probably she wasn't thinking straight, and he's glad he was able to take from her the task of delivering the bags to a charity shop in Tavistock.

He turns up on to the moor, getting his bearings, looking out for landmarks that they'd driven past yesterday. It's another golden day and he drives carefully, watching out for sheep and ponies, whilst trying to take in the immensity of the landscape. He passes the Two Bridges Hotel and turns left on the road towards Moretonhampstead, determined to take a more direct route than the sat nav showed him on the way down. And all the while, he's remembering the old stone cross, trying to place its whereabouts in his mind and looking out for it. He'd half wondered about mentioning it to El, but couldn't quite bring himself to talk about it. His experience there was still just a little too raw.

He's hoping to find it, to walk out to it again, yet a part of his mind warns him against disappointment. He's had his moment, his feeling of release; it's not the kind of thing that happens twice. He can see now how foolish he was to hold El and Freddie at such a distance for so long, but it was so hard for Will not to see his father's remarriage as a betrayal of his mother.

His father took a long while to let go of his memories of her, and no attempt was made to clear away some of her belongings for several years. This gave Will the feeling that there was plenty of time to find special keepsakes, photos, and then he'd come home from flying school for the Easter holidays to find almost every trace of his mother erased, and suddenly Felicity was in their lives.

He's driving slowly now, remembering and watching for the cross. It occurs to him that El is not much changed from the girl that came into his life five years ago. He remembers that Felicity used to nag at her to lose weight, embarrassing her at those family gatherings he made such efforts to avoid. Will always admired El's dogged refusal to be separated from her father and he's impressed with her determination to make a success of her new life. She's such a pretty girl, so interesting and amusing, and he's glad that at last they can be friends.

Will wonders what Freddie might think of this new friendship and whether he minds that he, Will, has been clearing out his father's things. No doubt if Freddie had wanted to do it there would have been no question of El needing Will's help. There has never been any antagonism from Freddie; he is too placatory, too peace-loving to make trouble. Both he and Will simply avoided any confrontation. They had no desire to be brothers.

Suddenly, from nowhere, comes a memory. Eleanor marching up to him at a Christmas party, holding up some mistletoe and kissing him firmly on the lips. Will can remember how instinctively he jerked away from the contact. Somehow, weirdly, they were supposed to be stepbrother and -sister, and he was horrified at how her mother might react. Luckily nobody noticed and El, overcome with embarrassment, fled away to her room. Remembering, Will laughs aloud. Perhaps it was her way of completely repudiating the relationship in the only way she knew how, and now he rather wishes that he hadn't reacted so brutally.

As he passes the Warren Inn, where he and El had lunch yesterday, and drives across the moor he sees the cross standing just off the road on his right. Its blunt twisted shape is diminished in the vast bleak landscape and, slowing as he approaches, Will is almost relieved to see that the small parking space has three cars in it. Their owners are not there – probably out on the moor walking – but he decides not to stop. It won't be the same on this bright sunny morning. The atmosphere will be different. Glancing in his driving mirror, he pulls into the side and brakes, reaches for his phone and takes a photograph of the cross.

A car is approaching. Will lets it pass, lays his phone on the passenger seat and then accelerates away.

'I'll be back,' he says.

It's a promise.

CHAPTER NINE

After Will has gone, El stands at the door for a moment listening to the sound of the engine fading. In the orchard a blackbird is foraging amongst the long grass, feasting on the remains of the windfalls. She hears voices, a door slams, and then there's the sound of the quad bike starting up and she knows that Andy is off to work on the farm with his sheepdog, Boy, perched up on the bike beside him. She likes Andy and his wife, Trish. They're good neighbours, and the baby is sweet. She's careful not to impose on Andy when he offers to bring in logs, clear the orchard. At this moment she's tempted to cross to the Hen House, to bang on the door, and shout, 'Hi, it's me, Trish. Want to come over for coffee?'

But still she stands, oddly unwilling to go back inside. She's trying to decide whether looking at Pa's phone is a dishonourable thing to do, like reading someone's private correspondence. Yet she wonders, too, if there might be something she ought to see, some message that might be important, someone she ought to contact. Pa had a very comprehensive database of names and addresses, which she and Angus used to contact people after he died, since she hadn't found his phone.

Now she guessed that Pa was wearing his fleece gilet in the garden as he worked, just before he stabbed his finger, and he'd gone back into the cottage, hung up his gilet and hurried to wash his hands, to try to stop the bleeding. The gilet, with the phone in its pocket, has hung there ever since. Somehow the little scene is horribly vivid in her mind. She can imagine the water running whilst he tries to wash away the mud and the blood and how he would be cursing as he tried to get out bandages and plasters and fix them to the wound with his left hand . . .

She can hear the postman's van rattling down the track and she turns quickly and hurries inside, unwilling to be caught in an emotional state. She takes the phone from the drawer and goes upstairs. She knows the battery will be flat and she takes it over to the little table by the bookcase where Pa always kept its charger. She plugs it in, switches it on. There's a battery symbol, a red line and a cable, and then the screen goes black again. After a few minutes the white apple appears and then the phone comes alive. She knows the password because she set it all up for him, and now there are the little red circles which show that there are unread messages and missed calls.

El stares at the screen. Now she must decide. Another memory slides into her mind. He'd phoned her later that evening from his landline and left a message.

'Hi there, El. It's Pa. I managed to stab my finger on a thorn in the garden earlier, clumsy idiot that I am. It's my right hand and the bandage is a bit bulky so I won't be texting any time soon. I hope you're out celebrating. Love you, darling.'

By the time she answered there was no reply. She didn't know it but he was already in hospital and she didn't have the chance to speak to him again. Impulsively she taps the messages and here they are. There are the texts she sent when she got no reply from the landline, one from Angus suggesting meeting for a pint, a couple from Pa's walking group confirming the next hike, and one from someone simply headed J.

`Where are you? x`

El stares at the message and then scrolls up. Pa's message reads:

`Sounds like a plan. See you there.`

Quickly she slides up through the messages in reverse.

`Yes please. Nancy Fortescue. 10.45?`

`Coffee tomorrow?`

El tries to remember anyone she knows called Nancy Fortescue but can think of nobody, although the name has an odd familiarity. Looking at the date, thinking back, she can see that the meeting was planned for the day after Pa died. She flicks back to the home screen to look at the missed calls and then notices the red dot on the voicemail. Hesitantly she touches the icon, then presses the key to listen to the message.

'So where were you?' asks a warm, flexible female voice. The voice sounds amused. 'Hope you haven't had a drama. Let me know.'

Resisting with great difficulty the operator's invitation to return the call. El stands in complete confusion, her mind in a tumult of conjecture, disbelief and surprise. Even as she stands, trying to puzzle it out, her own phone buzzes. She stares at the text. Simon and Natasha are very pleased with her CV and would love to have a chat. They'll be in the shop all morning if she's around, otherwise let them know when she can meet up with them again.

Still in a state of bewilderment, El sends them a message saying that she's on her way. Leaving Pa's phone on charge, she hurries downstairs, grabs her bag and goes out to the car.

*

All the while she is with Natasha and Simon she is still thinking about the messages. It is difficult to concentrate while they talk about what her duties will involve when she's longing to say to them: 'Do you know anyone called Nancy Fortescue?' They knew Pa very well and might recognize the name. With an effort she pulls herself together and as she talks with Natasha about checking books in, scanning them into the computer, dealing with wholesalers, El is glad that she's had holiday jobs in bookshops. It all sounds reassuringly familiar. She loves Book Stop, with its two floors of books and, up on the third floor, the Music Room. Pa once found a remastered CD of Miles Davis's *Kind of Blue* up there. El remembers how delighted he was and thinks again about the messages.

There are several customers needing attention now and the phone is ringing, so El agrees that she will start on Friday morning at nine o'clock and goes out into the street. She can't focus her thoughts: partly excited at the prospect of starting work in Book Stop, partly still struggling with the idea of Pa having a relationship with someone she doesn't know, or at least with a voice she doesn't recognize. As she pauses on the corner, trying to pull herself together, she sees a woman at the end of Church Lane waving to her. It's Kate. El waves back, waits for a van to pass between them and then hurries across the road. Kate gives her a hug.

'Are you OK?' she asks. 'You looked a bit lost, standing there, as if you weren't sure where you ought to be going.'

El nods rather ruefully. 'I do feel a bit like that,' she admits. 'I've got a job in Book Stop and I was just wondering how to celebrate. It seems a bit flat just to go home.'

'That's easy,' Kate says at once. 'Come back to the cottage with me and have some coffee. The decorating is nearly done and it's looking so nice that I can hardly bear the thought of letting anybody else live in it.'

El laughs as they walk along Duke Street. 'Then why don't you stay? Everyone wants you to.'

As they turn into Chapel Street and she follows Kate into the cottage, El wonders what Kate would say if she were to ask her about Nancy Fortescue. Kate leads her into a living-room, two walls lined with bookshelves, a big table in the centre, and indicates one of the armchairs.

'Would you like to sit down while I make some coffee? The kitchen is very small so this is where I tend to live when I'm here. Gemma and Guy haven't been gone long so it still feels homely. I think I'll let it furnished, but I shall take advice.'

'So you won't move back?' El leans against the kitchen door, watching as Kate fills the kettle, spoons coffee into a cafetiere and sets the mugs on a tray. She doesn't answer for a moment.

'When I'm here,' she says at last, 'with everyone around, I feel really tempted. But then again, I love being at St Meriadoc, too. I wish I could be more single-minded.'

'But why?' asks El. 'Surely you have the best of both worlds?'

'Not really,' answers Kate. 'I can't afford to leave the cottage empty and come back to it whenever I feel like it. It's great staying with Tom and Cass, but I sometimes wonder what it would be like actually to live here. Really make it my home.'

'At least it's here for you, though, if you should really need it,' says El. 'You've got it waiting for you and meanwhile you can enjoy your other life as well.'

Kate smiles at her. 'You're like your old pa,' she says. 'You're a comforter. You take the positive line. I like that. We all miss him terribly.'

El is silent for a moment. She is pleased that Kate has spoken so directly and with such affection but tears fill her eyes and she wipes them away quickly.

'I'm thinking of writing a novel,' she says, almost randomly, to distract herself from this sudden stab of grief. 'I've always wanted to. I've got a few ideas and I'm making lots of notes.'

'Now that really is amazing,' Kate says warmly. 'Martin would certainly be thrilled with the idea.'

El stands aside so that Kate can carry the tray into the living-room. She sets it on the table and El pulls up a chair. Kate sits opposite.

'So you think he'd approve of what I'm doing?' El asks.

Kate glances across at her, considering the question. 'I think he'd be very proud of you for giving it a go; for wanting to make it work. And he'd be delighted about your job at Book Stop. He practically lived there.'

El smiles. 'It's only part time, three days a week and flexible, but it's a really good start for me. I feel fantastically lucky.'

'It's such a friendly place,' agrees Kate, 'and you'll probably know lots of the customers by sight, if not by name.'

It's as if Kate has offered her an opportunity and El seizes it.

'Talking of names,' she says, casually, 'do you know anyone called Nancy Fortescue?'

Kate frowns, sipping her coffee thoughtfully. 'The name certainly rings a bell but I can't place it. Why?'

El's ready for this one. 'I've been clearing up a bit and there are things scribbled down on bits of paper. Phone numbers, names. I'm just making sure I've contacted everyone who should know.'

'That's horrid for you to have to do on your own,' says Kate sympathetically. 'Isn't there anyone to help? What about

Freddie? Angus was saying that his friend has been helping you sort out the clothes.'

El is thankful that none of Pa's friends here in Tavistock knows about her mother's new family. He never discussed it with them but El wonders if, now she is living here among them, it will be much more difficult to maintain that silence, especially if Will comes to see her again. She wonders why it is so difficult to describe Will as her stepbrother, how they would react to him, and why it matters. Perhaps, because Pa was so reluctant to talk about it all, she's simply followed his lead. She wonders whether to tell Kate the truth and then decides that she will talk to Will about it first. She remembers how vague he was at the funeral, happy to be introduced as one of Freddie's friends.

Kate is talking about Sunday lunch. Cass is inviting everyone, will El be able to come? They discuss it, and then Kate says she must be getting back to the Rectory, that she's left Floss with Cass while she came in to do some shopping. They finish their coffee, El offers to help clear up, and then she's out in Chapel Street, heading back to the car park and still wondering about Nancy Fortescue.

CHAPTER TEN

Hidden away in the lanes above Buckfastleigh, in the pretty little Georgian house at the end of the mossy drive, Davy Callaghan strides up and down the old-fashioned square kitchen, pausing at intervals to grip the back of the Windsor chair at the head of the old farmhouse table so as to emphasize a point.

'It's just silly of you to go on being so stubborn,' he cries. 'The job might be made for you, Jules. At least let me put your name forward. You were brilliant at presenting *Cakes and Ale*. What's the matter with you?'

He stares crossly at Julia as she continues to roll out pastry, chop ingredients, pauses to brush back a strand of hair with a floury wrist.

'I've told you,' she says patiently. 'I've done it. Been there. Got the T-shirt. I'm tired of sitting in meetings with mere children who say, "It's so last year to have a brain, darling. Just look everything up on Google."'

'I don't believe you,' he answers flatly. 'You love it. It's something else. These last few months you've been in the dumps. You can't just sit around out here in the middle of nowhere staring at the wall.'

'I don't intend to. I've always been freelance and I shan't change now. I intend to write some articles on famous local people for *Devon Life*.'

'It's been done,' he says flatly.

'OK.' She laughs at him. 'Then I'll think of something else.'

'And meantime you'll just live here on your own?'

'I've got the boys,' she counters.

He snorts. 'Only in the holidays. Remember, they're both away now, not at school any more. They'll be off any time soon. I can't think why you haven't married again. It must be nearly ten years since poor old Bob got written off in that awful crash.'

'You know why I don't,' she says calmly. 'I told you once before that I lose my half of his naval pension if I marry again and I haven't met a man yet that's worth it.'

'Haven't you?' he asks, watching her. 'I've sometimes wondered if that's absolutely true.'

She turns her back on him, washing her hands at the Belfast sink, drying them on a towel and hanging it back on the Aga rail.

'Don't tell me. The famous Callaghan intuition at work again?' she asks lightly. 'Doing your Mystic Meg thing?'

He pulls out the chair and sits down in it. He looks serious, even anxious.

'Are you sure you're OK, Jules?' he asks. 'I've been worried about you this last couple of months.'

She leans back against the Aga, smiling at him. 'Perhaps you're right and it's empty-nest syndrome. Ollie going off to uni this term. Laurence joining his regiment. It's odd here without them. Don't know what I'd do without Bertie.'

At the sound of his name the big golden retriever, lying in his basket, thumps his tail a few times, and Davy shakes his head.

'Isn't that just what I'm saying?' he asks irritably. 'That's why I thought you'd be pleased. The timing of this new production is perfect.'

'Don't go on, Dave,' she says.

Her voice has changed, not light-hearted now, and he looks at her quickly.

'OK,' he says. 'Forget it. Now. I'm taking you out to lunch. No arguments.'

'No arguments,' she agrees. 'We'll go up to the Church House at Holne. But first, have some more coffee and tell me all the goss!'

As she watches and listens to him, smiling in all the right places, Julia's thinking of Martin: of his quick wit, his sense of fun, his readiness for a jaunt. She wishes that she'd told Davy about Martin way back so that she could have the relief of talking about him now, but she and Martin agreed that nobody should know. Martin was protecting El and she was protecting her boys. Ollie and Laurence would have been shocked to think of another man taking their father's place. They idolized their father. There were photographs everywhere of him in uniform, on the aircraft carrier, beside his helicopter. And she sympathized with Martin about his reluctance to tell his daughter that there was another woman in his life. He was honest about the reasons for his divorce: how he'd been unfaithful to Felicity on one brief occasion with an old friend. She was grieving, her husband far away, and he was lonely. Although this moment of mutual comfort and affection was immediately regretted by both of them, it was enough to show Martin the emptiness of his marriage. When, a few months later, he told Felicity that the marriage was over, his wife assumed he was having an affair and he made no attempt to deny it although it wasn't true. He moved out whilst the divorce was going through and it was at that time that he and Julia met.

'El's been so loyal since Felicity and I separated,' he told Julia, 'and I can't quite bring myself to explain it all to her. She believes that I had an affair and it was just a short-term thing. Maybe later on I'll tell her the truth . . .'

She was quick to agree with him, imagining the boys' faces if she tried to talk to them about Martin. And so the time passed. They made a pact that they would tell them all once Oliver went off to university. Then all three of them would have started their own lives and should be able to accept that their parents had needs of their own. Except that it hadn't worked out like that.

Davy is watching her, looking quizzically at her, and Julia guesses that she's missed her cue and he's noticed that she's not concentrating.

'There's something wrong,' he says. 'I know it. All I'm saying is that I'm here when you're ready to talk about it. No pressure. Just putting it out there.'

'Thanks, Dave,' she answers. 'The truth is, it's not just my secret. Maybe one day . . .'

Treacherous tears are rising, her throat is closing up. It's terrible to miss someone so much but to have no right to express her grief. They were so successful at keeping their love a secret. It almost seemed a part of its charm. Silly messages, coded texts, random meetings: it was like a game. Yet their feelings for each other were so strong: that irresistible fusion of compatibility, of being totally understood, totally known.

'It's like being recognized at last after years of being alone,' Martin said. 'And being appreciated. It's like I'm being allowed to be me, even encouraged, instead of living in an atmosphere of permanent disdain. Like sunshine after years and years of rain.'

'I know.' She held him tightly, wondering how she would cope with the boys, with everyone knowing.

He let her go and smiled at her. 'Felicity has wanted to move back to Dorchester for a while and now she has the perfect excuse. But she'll never forgive me. If I'm truthful I don't want her to. We should never have married. She knows that. Secretly she despises me. But she would hate to stay around here and face the reaction of her friends. Felicity hates failure.'

'So what is she going to do?'

'Her mother died last year. She's going back to Dorchester to be with her father, who isn't terribly well. Freddie's at uni and El is at boarding school, so I hope it won't be too traumatic for them.'

Now, aware that Davy is watching her, Julia blows her nose and tries to smile at him.

'Don't say anything,' she says. 'I promise that when I feel ready to talk it will be to you. I know it's girly and boring being like this but . . .'

'OK,' he says. 'But remember I'm always here if you need me.'

His kindness touches her and quite suddenly she gives in.

'Oh hell,' she says. 'OK. There's been this man for years now but we had reasons for keeping it secret. He died a couple of months ago, unexpectedly.'

It's odd that now she's spoken the words she feels calmer. Davy, on the other hand, is looking horrified.

'My darling girl,' he says, stretching a hand across the table to her. 'How unutterably bloody. And you haven't said a word. For Christ's sake, surely you could have told me?'

She squeezes his hand and lets it go. 'I could have, but when I found out, Laurence was just back from Sandhurst and Ollie was around all the time and I just didn't dare let myself go. I knew if I told you I'd be all over the place. I've been here before, remember, and I know how hard it is for other people.'

Sensing the change of atmosphere, Bertie heaves himself up and comes across to lean against her chair and Julia digs her fingers into his thick ruff. She knows that Davy is one of the few people she could confide in without risking the pitfalls that go with sharing the pain of bereavement. He won't over-emote or do that awful competitive grieving thing, he'll just be there, but even so she needs to feel strong. It's odd that it's so easy to feel even weaker after sharing these feelings than before, and it's perilously difficult to get the timing right.

'It's complicated,' she says. 'Nobody knows about us. I didn't even know he was dead until I saw his obit in the *Western Morning News*.'

Davy buries his head in his hands. 'Jesus!'

'I know.' She sits in silence for a moment. 'I went to his funeral in Tavistock.'

Davy raises his head and stares at her. 'Seriously?'

She nods. 'All the details were in the paper. I just slipped in at the back of the church when a group of people were going in and sat behind a pillar. I had to, Dave. I just needed to say goodbye, I suppose. And even then I could hardly believe it. It happened so quickly. We'd made a plan to meet and he didn't turn up, but even then I wasn't too worried. He didn't get much time off except at weekends and I just thought something had cropped up. You know?'

'I'm trying to imagine it,' he answers.

'I know it sounds bizarre,' she says, 'but we both understood it. To begin with we were both in the same boat with children to think about and then it kind of morphed into a pattern.'

'And nobody recognized you? At the funeral?'

She shook her head. 'It's not like I'm famous or anything. I've only done very local stuff.'

'*Cakes and Ale* was very popular.'

'Yes, but luckily it was nearly a year ago and my hair's shorter now. It was a very hot day so I could wear dark specs. Afterwards I waited till nearly everybody had gone before I came out of church and then I just slipped down the side path and vanished away into the town.' There's a little silence. 'Sorry,' she says at last. 'Honestly, Dave, I didn't mean to drain down on you.'

He shakes his head. 'It seems to me that some people get all the shit.'

'You've had your share, too. When Phil walked out on you.'

'Yes, but that was different. Phil and I were like an ongoing sitcom. Everyone knew about it. They were taking bets about how long we'd last.'

She turns to smile at him. 'You're better off without him.'

He gets up, walks round the table and holds his arms out.

'Come here,' he says. Bertie gets up, too, and butts his head against their legs. 'You, too, Bertie. Group hug. Are you sure you're up for the pub?'

She nods. 'We'll give Bertie a walk in Hembury Woods on the way.'

But she holds on to him for a moment longer, feeling comforted by his presence. It's impossible to think she won't see Martin again, share the jokes, talk about books, walk together on the moor. It's different somehow from Bob's death. He took risks, accidents happened, and she was always braced for the news of disaster. Martin was a country solicitor: a gentle, quiet, scholarly man. This sudden dramatic ending seems so out of character for him.

She lets Davy go but she can see that he is wrestling with what she's told him. His thin eager face is alive with speculation.

'So are you telling me that you have no contact at all with anyone? Not a single soul? You must have phoned him? Texted him? It'll be there in his phone.'

He's hit on her one real anxiety. She thinks of all the texts: plans to meet.

'Even with that we were careful,' she says. 'We kept it brief, almost in code. They might have been from anyone.'

'But the number,' he insists. 'Your number and your name will be in the phone. So no one's contacted you?'

She shakes her head. 'We just used our initials. Martin had a work phone. I know that. But I don't know what happened to his private one.'

'So what if you get the call one of these days and somebody says, "Hello. I've got your number here. Who are you?" what will you say?'

She groans. 'Don't. You can't imagine how awful it is. The terrible finality of it and having no rights. Sometimes I just long to hear from his daughter. He loved her so much. Part of me thinks that she'd understand how it was, but another part of me fears that she might be upset that he kept our relationship a secret. Or perhaps she might be jealous. I have no idea how this works. But the silence is odd because I assumed that she'd contact everyone in his address book. I've been on tenterhooks.'

'It's a reasonable assumption,' agrees Davy. 'My poor old darling. This is hell for you.'

'Oh, don't, Dave,' she says. 'Don't be kind or I'll start crying and then I might never stop. Let's go for that walk.'

He begins to clear the coffee things, stacking them on the draining board, and she feels a rush of affection for him, and gratitude. Now she doesn't feel quite so alone. She knows she can trust Davy and, even more importantly, she has someone to whom she can talk about Martin.

CHAPTER ELEVEN

That evening, after Davy has gone back to Plymouth, Julia puts their tea things in the dishwasher and comes through to the front of the house and into the drawing-room. It's an elegant room with tall sash windows and comfortable sofas. Taking the matches from the high mantelshelf, she kneels down before the brass fender and lights the kindling and twigs that she laid there earlier. As the wood catches and flares she builds a little pyramid of logs above them and sits back on her heels to watch the fire burn into life. Kneeling there on the rug she's glad now that Martin never came to the house. It's odd but somehow she misses him less here because there is no memory of him. They both agreed that no risks should be taken. There must be no chance of being surprised by a friend dropping by or a child coming home from school unexpectedly early. Holidays were especially difficult with her boys at home for weeks at a time. How strict their love has been; how hedged about with rules.

Except, she thinks, for that very first time, when they met and their normal rules of behaviour went up in flames just as this fire is burning in front of her now. Her experience with

Bob hadn't prepared her for this kind of conflagration. That had been a romantic attraction kindling slowly into a warmth of love that sustained her as he made his busy, noisy progress through life, and supported his devotion to his career, his aircraft, his promotion, until that flight that had gone so disastrously wrong. His sons are very like him: Laurence already passed out from Sandhurst, Ollie a keen sportsman. They strove to emulate him and were so proud of him. Even his death was glamorous in its terrible tragic way.

Slipping sideways a little, tucking her feet beneath her and supporting herself on one hand, Julia allows her memories more freedom. It was strange that she should meet Martin at The Garden House on a blowy March day. She can remember the journey across the moor: daffodils growing in the ditches and along the dry-stone walls on the road to Princetown; creamy curds of blackthorn blossom in the hedges; a sheep with one small black lamb. The tawny grasslands flowed away to high bony outcrops of rock that looked like sleeping dinosaurs.

The sun was shining as she got out of the car at The Garden House, looking around with pleasure at the camellia blossom, smiling at the woman who greeted her at the visitors' entrance. Julia walked along the paths, glancing across the cloudy treetops in the valley to the distant hills of Cornwall, delighted by the unexpected display of purple tulips in the Walled Garden. She resisted the little wooden seats, placed in secret, sunny corners, and decided that she needed coffee. It was chilly, too cold for the terrace, but when she went inside she saw that the coachload of people she'd been avoiding on her walk had the same idea. She stood for a moment looking around at the chattering groups and then her gaze lighted on a man sitting alone at a small table for two. It was clear that he saw her plight and with a smile and a slight tip of his head, he gestured towards the empty chair. She went towards him gratefully.

'I didn't expect it to be so busy,' she said. 'Thanks. I thought for one terrible moment that I might have to go without my coffee.'

He laughed, shaking his head in mock horror at such a prospect, and she sat down opposite, liking his friendliness. A young woman came to take their order, assuming they were together, and looked slightly surprised when neither knew what the other was having. Julia shrugged herself out of her coat, feeling rather pleased to have such agreeable company, but it was he who moved it a stage further.

'It's difficult to enjoy a cup of coffee with a complete stranger,' he said. 'Shall we introduce ourselves? My name's Martin Haynes,' and he offered his hand across the table.

She hesitated for a moment and then decided to use her married name rather than her professional one. It was possible that he'd read some of her articles and she wanted to keep this on a private basis.

'Mine's Julia Grant.'

She took his warm hand in hers and he gripped it for a moment and then sat back in his chair.

'That's good,' he said. 'I'm feeling ridiculously light-hearted. I was on my way to see a client at Yelverton and halfway there I had a text from the office saying that the appointment had to be cancelled, so I have a whole morning to myself. It's like having an unexpected half-holiday from school.'

She laughed at his enthusiasm. 'So why did you choose The Garden House? Are you a keen gardener?'

He shook his head. 'Not so's you'd notice, but I love visiting gardens, especially this one. The atmosphere here is wonderful and, anyway, it was just down the road from where my client lives.'

She guessed that, although he was ready to give his name, he wanted in every other respect to remain anonymous; to keep this moment as something odd and special between two strangers. She understood this and decided to play along with it.

'My mother was a volunteer here,' she said. 'After she died I was given permission to dedicate a bench to her. Do you have a favourite place?'

He sat back to allow their coffee to be put on the table before he answered her.

'Oh, it's got to be the seat by the *Nancy Fortescue*,' he said. 'Down by the lake.'

She smiled. 'Clearly you're a *Swallows and Amazons* man,' she said.

'Definitely,' he said, putting sugar in his coffee, 'except that I get seasick in the bath. But I love Arthur Ransome.'

She fell silent, looking around her, suddenly shy. She was oddly attracted to this stranger, so quickly at ease with him. Yet she didn't want to exchange the intimacies of their lives. She didn't want to hear about his wife and children, or to tell him how Bob died, and see his inevitable awkward embarrassment and listen to his expressions of sympathy. She just wanted to go on sitting with him, happy in his company. It was extraordinary, and the odd thing was that she knew he felt the same way: totally at ease, discussing the Charlotte Marlow paintings on the wall beside them, a film they'd both seen recently; she at the Barn Cinema at Dartington, Martin at the Wharf in Tavistock.

'So which is your favourite part of the garden?' he asked, watching her across his coffee cup, his brown eyes bright, interested.

'I like all of it at different times,' she answered. 'I'm fickle. I don't have favourites.'

He finished his coffee, still watching her. 'Good,' he said, as if approving of her answer. 'In that case, let's go and look at that amazing view across to Buckland Monachorum church, shall we? It gets me every time.'

Julia leans forward to place another log on the fire and kneels upright. She's stiff and as she stands up she flexes the hand on which she's been resting her weight. Bertie is stretched out just behind her and she steps across him, kicks off her shoes, and sits down in the corner of the sofa, curling her legs under her.

How strange that day was: strange and life-changing. They walked away from the tearoom after a slight wrangle about allowing him to pay for her coffee.

'But why should you?' she asked. 'After all, I interrupted your solitude. I should be paying.'

'It was so nice to have the company,' he said as they headed into the gardens. 'It's such a waste to feel happy all on one's own.'

She laughed, shaking her head. 'You're crazy.'

'Yes,' he agreed. 'This morning I am crazy. I'm not sure if it's the sunshine or that ephemeral rainbow over there. But spring does that, doesn't it? New life, new hope.'

He glanced at her, almost anxiously, as if suddenly visited by a doubt that she might not be as much in tune with him as he believed. It was a strange look: confident but tinged with doubt.

'Absolutely,' she said. 'I have this mantra: "I can do anything as long as the sun is shining." Add into that primroses, bluebells and daffodils, and what can go wrong?'

His smile was full of relief. 'It's nearly bluebell time. Where's your favourite place for those? Mine's all around Burrator Reservoir.'

She shook her head. 'Holwell Lawn. Above Widecombe-in-the-Moor. Spectacular.'

'Never been there,' he said.

She decided to test him a little. 'You must check it out. And afterwards you'll need coffee or a drink at the Moorland Hotel.'

'Is that what you do?'

She nodded. They walked in silence for a short while until they reached the Summer Garden and then he stopped and gestured across the Wildflower Meadow valley towards the old church tower set amongst the trees. As they stood together, she knew that she must go. She guessed that he hadn't picked up on her very gentle hint about meeting for coffee at the Moorland Hotel because he was married and instinct warned her that it was best to leave before he started to explain why the morning couldn't continue along these delightful lines or why there shouldn't be other meetings. She felt strangely desolate but she was smiling as she turned from the contemplation of the view.

'I must go,' she said. 'I've got a three-year-old golden retriever waiting patiently in the car and I've promised him a walk on the way home. I mustn't push my luck. Great to meet you, Martin.' She held out her hand. 'Thanks for my coffee.'

She hated the look of disappointment on his face; the surprise. He held her hand longer than he should have done and she wanted to say: 'Come with us. Follow us in your car.' But she knew that there was an impediment to the continuation of this strange meeting. Turning away from him, she hurried back the way they'd come, towards the car park, huddling herself into her coat as a sudden heavy shower of icy rain crashed all about her.

In the car park she stripped off her wet coat and jumped into the car. Bertie was on his feet in the back, tail wagging, and she was glad of his large welcoming presence.

'Good boy,' she said, putting up the windows. 'Good fellow. Away we go then. Lucky we had a walk coming over because you might not get one on the way back if this carries on.'

Hail battered against the windscreen, stopped suddenly, and the sun shone out as she drove away.

CHAPTER TWELVE

The logs collapse inward with a little explosion of flames and sparks. Bertie stirs, raises his head and then drops back into slumber. Julia uncurls her legs and gets to her feet. Taking up the poker, she pushes the embers together, piles more logs on top and goes back to the sofa.

How strange that next meeting was; how hoped for and yet how unexpected. During the next few weeks she thought about Martin often, analysing that odd moment of time, recalling their conversation and her reaction to him. Several times she went back to The Garden House but she didn't see him. Spring was blossoming all around her, and as she walked Bertie at Cross Furzes and watched the lambs in the field, she heard the cuckoo down in the valley and was caught up in the beauty and the melancholy of the cold, sweet April morning.

Now, as she pulls cushions around her, tucking her legs beneath her again, Julia is remembering the late April morning when she drove again to The Garden House, pulling in through the gateway, parking the car. She paused to gaze in amazement at the yellow magnolia in full, glorious flower at the entrance and then headed towards the Walled Garden. She strolled along, noticing the precision of the mown pathways, enjoying the beautiful stone buildings, and passed under the archway into the Jubilee Arboretum. Martin was sitting on the bench beside the lake. Kingcups were in glorious golden flower and the *Nancy Fortescue* was moored near by. The old wooden rowing boat rested quietly on the still water whilst Martin sat gazing at nothing in particular, at ease, as if he were waiting for her. She walked calmly round the lake, across the stone bridge, until she was standing beside him. She was planning some light-hearted remark, a jokey comment, but when he raised his head and looked at her, the words remained unspoken.

'I was so afraid that I would never see you again,' he said.

His words, his look, totally disarmed her. She sat beside him, half turned towards him.

'I've been here several times,' she said, 'wondering if I might see you.'

She paused, not knowing how to continue, and he spoke again as if continuing his train of thought.

'Even though I had no right to hope for it.'

In the following silence Julia wondered how to voice the things that needed to be said, but Martin was there first.

'I'm separated from my wife, you see, while our divorce goes through.' He continued to look at her. 'When we met last time it was like a gift from the gods. One of those magical moments that happen rarely and are never forgotten. And that was the problem. I couldn't forget it. It was as if a curtain had been pulled aside showing me a whole new landscape.' He shook his head as if unable to find words to describe it. 'And I wanted it more than I've ever wanted anything in my life.'

He looked away from her, watching the *Nancy Fortescue*, his face bleak. Julia reached out and lightly touched his hand.

'I felt like that. It was very odd. As if I'd known you forever.'

He turned quickly to look at her. 'Did you really feel that?'

Julia nodded. 'Truly. I wanted it to go on and on but I guessed you were married. I'm a widow. My husband was a navy pilot. He died in an air crash five years ago. I have two sons.'

She saw the quick flash of relief in his eyes quickly replaced by an expression of confusion. Julia waited. She knew that she should get up and walk away, just as she had on that first occasion, but this time her willpower failed her. By waiting she was being complicit in his decision, but still she could not move.

Martin sighed, a long deep breath, and when he spoke his words filled her with a mix of elation and fear.

'Shall we go and have some coffee?' he asked.

Abruptly, as if this recollection is too much to bear, Julia sits up and feels about for her shoes with her toes. Bertie struggles into a sitting position and looks at her.

'Supper-time,' she says. 'Please remember that you've had yours.'

He gazes at her with a wounded expression, as if she has misjudged him, and she relents.

'Maybe,' she says, 'just maybe, one small treat.'

He follows her down the hall and along the passage to the kitchen, his tail wagging expectantly. The kitchen, thanks to the Aga, is always warm, unlike the passages and bedrooms, and Julia opens the fridge and stares into it, hoping for inspiration. The lunch at the pub was good and she isn't particularly hungry. Perhaps a mug of soup and a sliver of Sharpham brie will be enough. She sets the soup to warm, slices the cheese and cuts a hunk of bread.

Bertie drinks from his bowl and then goes to the door and Julia takes him out, along the passage, switches on the outside light and opens the door into the garden. Leaning against the door jamb, arms crossed against the chilly evening air, she watches him disappear across the grass into the dark shadows of the rhododendrons. Her mind slips back to those early days with Martin, the impromptu meetings: walking in the watercolour magic of the Wildflower Meadow in spring, the scarlet and orange and yellow glory of the Acer Glade in autumn. His first text was enigmatic:

```
Crosby, Stills, Nash & Young. Woodstock.
```

Julia stared at it, baffled, trying to remember any conversation they might have had that related to it. Amused, curious, she was determined to crack this code. She googled the names and then listened to several of the tracks on YouTube. Joni Mitchell. 'Woodstock'. She was getting it now and began to feel excited. She read the lyrics on the screen as she listened, oddly moved, and suddenly there it was: 'We are stardust, we are golden . . . And we've got to get ourselves back to the garden'. She replayed it, laughed aloud, punched the air triumphantly as though she'd passed a test. And then she texted back:

```
Yes we do. When?
```

His reply was swift.

```
Monday afternoon? The Magic Circle?
```

So it began, this silly, wonderful time of texts and codes, swift meetings: how precious they were.

Bertie comes padding out from the shadows, trots across the grass towards her. Julia is surprised to feel tears on her cheeks. She scrubs them away, lets him pass her, then shuts the door behind them, locks it and switches off the light.

*

She sits at the old farmhouse table, with its odd assortment of wooden chairs, caught up now in this act of remembrance. Ever since Martin's funeral she's been in denial – getting through the holidays with the boys, working on some assignments, writing a few articles – but now the door has swung open to the past and she can't slam it shut. Martin is with her, sitting at the end of the table, talking, gesticulating, getting up to reach for a book, searching for a reference. He is here with her now, in her kitchen, as he never was in real life, and she is woefully aware of how much she has missed and gloriously alive to what they shared.

'Have you heard . . . read . . . seen?'

Their absences from each other are filled with things to be shared once they are together again. Those snatched moments at The Garden House, in quiet moorland pubs and on deserted coastal paths and beaches, were like sips of champagne.

'Not champagne,' he said. 'Champagne goes flat and loses its savour. No, we shall be like Kubla Khan, "For he on honey-dew hath fed, And drunk the milk of Paradise".'

She laughed at him when he 'declaimed', as she called it.

'Do I hear a declamation coming on?' she'd ask, and they'd laugh with the sheer craziness of it.

Julia sips her soup, breaks off a crust of bread. From the beginning they both could see how impossible it would be to live together. How would they do it? There was no room in the Pig Pen for Julia and her boys, nor could Martin move in with them. He talked about the difficulties and resentments El and Freddie were experiencing when their mother remarried, and Julia couldn't begin to imagine explaining the situation to Laurence and Ollie. She couldn't risk losing her widow's pension, and the house was to be the boys' inheritance.

'Perhaps the right moment will come,' Martin said tentatively.

There were so many complications and it was too early to take risks. Other people managed it, clearly, but neither of them wanted to rock the boat. And somehow it was working. Martin was in his office all through the week and she had the boys to look after, to ferry to clubs and entertain their friends. At Easter and Christmas, and during the summer holidays, El would be staying with Martin. Time together was rationed.

Crumbling her bread, Julia remembers those shared lunches and walks; a few days snatched when the boys were on school trips or staying with their grandparents. Each kept clear of the other's territory.

'It's crazy,' Martin said, recently, as they sat together in the Stables café at Killerton House near Exeter. 'I'm divorced and you're a widow. Why don't we just throw caution to the wind and get together?'

Even now she can remember the feeling of panic. How would she tell the boys or explain to Bob's elderly parents? She couldn't imagine how the two families could be merged without the same kind of resentment and awkwardness that he'd told her that El and Freddie had experienced.

'Soon,' she answered. 'Now that Laurence is already on his way and El is in her last year at university. Ollie goes next year. That's the time to make changes, once they're all moving on.'

Part of her knew that it was irrational but at the same time she simply couldn't face the upheaval. She'd done it all before when Bob died and she simply couldn't face it again. And it was working. She and Martin's relationship was so special, perhaps because it didn't have to stand the warp and weft of family life.

There was something exciting about the secrecy, impromptu meetings, and those magical days at the flat.

Julia gives a little gasp as she thinks about those special moments in Bristol. Martin had a cousin who lived in a remote cottage in North Wales: a man of his own age, a bachelor, a writer. He owned the flat, enjoying regular fixes of city life, but when he wasn't staying there he was very happy for friends or relatives to use it. Central to the city's cafés, galleries, docklands, it had all the anonymity that Julia and Martin needed. Perhaps without the flat they might have been more inclined to change the status quo, but the flat gave them that extra dimension for privacy and intimacy.

The flat was their home, the place where they could be a couple, and it was within easy reach for both of them. Julia caught the train from Totnes, Martin drove, meeting her from Temple Meads Station and driving them to the flat. It was clearly a bolt hole: small but functional. Martin's cousin was a minimalist but there was everything at the flat that enabled him to lift and shift between Wales and Bristol with very little luggage. He always left the bed stripped and visitors brought their own sheets and towels.

Julia finishes her soup, thinking of that first day, driving through the traffic with Martin, parking in the reserved place in the small car park, climbing the stairs to the flat. Once inside she was fascinated by its compactness, the glimpse of the cathedral from the window. Her excitement was suddenly swamped by shyness, by the close proximity of Martin moving around, putting overnight bags in the bedroom and unpacking clean sheets. She was relieved by his pragmatism – he'd remembered to bring milk and bread – and by his suggestion that they should go out to explore and find some lunch.

'We shall need a name for it,' he said, as they strolled across College Green and began to climb Park Street, and she laughed and at once felt easy again.

'For Bristol?' she asked. 'Or for the flat?'

She could see he was thinking about it whilst at the same time taking in his surroundings. He looked happy, alert, and she slipped her arm into his and he pressed it closely to his side.

'Either,' he said. 'Both. Give me time and I'll find it.'

Now, slicing some cheese, Julia's heart aches with the loss and loneliness of being without him. The Bristol days were the best. At the most they could generally manage two whole days, three nights. Usually it was two nights with one whole day to be free. Maybe its scarcity value was a gift: the relationship never staled. There were no rows or falling out. Nothing challenged their happiness. Martin was relieved when Felicity married her childhood sweetheart.

'She should have stuck with him,' he said. 'Maybe he would have made her happier than I did.'

'But then,' Julia pointed out, 'you wouldn't have had Freddie and El.'

She knew how guilty he felt about his children, how hard he worked to maintain contact. El responded readily but Freddie, already at medical school, withheld his understanding. He was polite, friendly, but there was no real closeness. Julia felt guilty, too, however many times Martin assured her that his marriage was over in all but name long before they met.

The Bristol days gleamed in her imagination like sunshine after rain.

'I know what we should call it,' Martin exclaimed, raising his glass of Shiraz to her in what was to become their favourite wine bar. 'It's obvious, isn't it? The flat is the Play Pen.'

She laughed with him, still on a high after their first whole night and day together. To wake up next to him, to feel his warm skin under her fingers, to hold him close, was still a marvel to her. She hadn't realized how lonely she was for a man's touch, his companionship. At the flat she felt free, happy.

'To the Play Pen,' she said, touching her glass to his.

So the name moved into their foolish code along with all the others that would baffle anyone who might pick up their phones. And now the boys are gone, El has inherited the Pig Pen, and Martin is dead.

Five years, thinks Julia sadly. We wasted five years that we might have been together.

Yet even as she thinks it she knows that back in those early days, trying to make it work in one house with El and the boys all together, would have been very different from the five years she and Martin shared. She wonders how El is coping, where she is, and whether it would ever be possible to have some kind of relationship with her. How would it work? Julia tries to imagine the conversation they might have about Martin, but fails. Would El be hurt to know that her father kept such a secret: that he shared so much with another woman? How would a twenty-one-year-old react to such a situation?

Julia wonders what happened to Martin's phone. Maybe it got mislaid. Davy put his finger on her greatest fear: a call from El asking whose number it is. Yet she can't bring herself to block the number or to delete Martin's messages. They are all she has, apart from the Charlotte Marlow painting he bought for her. She turns her head to look at it, hanging on the wall at the end of the table: a pretty, impressionistic watercolour of a flower. They saw it during one of the artist's exhibitions in the café at The Garden House. A few months later, she bought a similar one for him. It was an astrantia – Moulin Rouge. There was one planted outside a small stone and slate building up above the Bowling Green Terrace where they sometimes met if it was raining.

'For those times,' she said, 'when we can't get ourselves back to the garden.'

She wonders where it hangs and whether El likes it. A text pings in and Julia reaches for her phone, her heart quickening, half imagining that it might be from El: that by allowing this luxurious indulgence of her memories she has somehow conjured her up. It's from Davy.

`Thanks for a great day. Are you OK? Dx`

She stares at the text. Am I OK? she asks herself.

She's glad now that she's told Davy about Martin. It has unlocked the memories, and the pain of bereavement, though she's used to that.

`I'm OK. How about you? x`

He texts back quickly.

`Missing Phil. I've got to move out of the flat. Can I come over on Sunday?`

Julia heaves a sigh of relief. By sharing his own misery Davy has made them equals and she can allow herself to accept his kindness, his affection and sympathy. She texts back.

`Yes please. Whole weekend if you like. x`

She holds her breath, hoping he'll accept. The house feels empty and quiet without the boys and she longs for company. Davy's text pings in.

`Thought you'd never ask! x`

Julia lets out her breath. She can get through until Friday night.

CHAPTER THIRTEEN

In the bar of the Bedford Hotel, Kate sits with Plum discussing the pros and cons of naval quarters and hirings.

'I know Dad thinks it's foolish to rent somewhere when we could live quite easily with him,' says Plum, 'but I'm not sure Ian's terribly keen on the plan. He and Dad get on really well but I don't know how it would work in the long term.'

Instinctively both women glance at the tall, angular figure ordering their coffee at the bar. Kate remembers a former conversation here at this very table when Angus told her and Cass about his hope that Plum and Ian might use his house for a base when Ian comes ashore. It might seem an obvious solution but Kate can also imagine how Ian would feel, home from weeks at sea, to spend his leave with his father-in-law.

'Although we shall keep the flat in London, we need to have a base near to Devonport,' Plum is saying, 'and . . . you know what it's like when they come back from sea?'

Kate nods. She knows what it's like. The trouble is that visiting in-laws is one thing and living with them is another. She tries to think of some kind of compromise but she knows there isn't one.

'The thing is, Kate,' Plum is saying, leaning forward, slightly lowering her voice, 'I know your cottage is empty. You have to admit that it would be perfect for me and Ian. Ten minutes' walk from Dad's, plenty of room when the girls want to come home.' She pauses. 'You haven't found a tenant yet, have you?' she asks anxiously.

Kate's heart sinks, imagining how she'll feel when Angus realizes that she is the cause of his disappointment, but she shakes her head.

'No,' she admits. 'No, I haven't got a tenant yet. The cottage isn't quite ready.'

'Oh, that's great.' Plum sits back with a little gasp of relief. 'Will you give us first refusal, Kate?'

'Of course,' says Kate, trying to look pleased, hating herself. 'But have a think about staying with Angus. I know he'd love it.'

'Yes,' says Plum wretchedly. 'Don't think I don't feel an absolute traitor but I have to think about Ian first, don't I? I think your cottage might be the perfect compromise.'

Kate thinks that there is no such thing as a perfect compromise, that it is a contradiction in terms, but she nods understandingly and smiles at Angus as he comes back to the table. She searches about in her mind for a distraction.

'I've been into Book Stop to see El,' she tells them as Angus sits down. 'It's her first day. Of course she's worked in bookshops before, which must be a help, but she was looking very competent.'

Kate is aware that Plum sits back, almost as if she is distancing herself from the conversation, but Angus is delighted.

'I shall go and buy a book from her,' he says at once. 'Now what shall it be?'

'One of Bruno's,' says Kate at once. 'I have to read them so why shouldn't you? He's written several about Bazelgette but you need one of what he calls his wolf-scarers. What we used to call a ripping good yarn, back in the day.'

'I shall do that,' says Angus. 'Is Cass joining us?'

'I left her buying something rather nice at Brigid Foley's but she's on her way.'

Even as she talks, Kate wonders what it is that is distracting Plum. Perhaps she is gathering up the courage to announce her new plan to her father, now, whilst they are all together. As Kate braces herself for this possible new development she sees that Plum is staring beyond her and Kate glances round to see what or who has caught Plum's attention. A woman has come into the bar and is looking around her. She is smart in a casual sort of way, about Plum's age, very attractive, and as she sees the group at the corner table by the window, her face breaks into a wide smile.

'Hi,' she cries, advancing towards them. 'You know, I had a feeling that you might just be here.'

She's beaming at Plum, who gets to her feet and, as the woman embraces her, Kate gets a glimpse of Plum's expression, which is less than delighted. Angus is already on his feet.

'Issy!' he exclaims. 'How good to see you. It's been too long. How are you? This is our friend, Kate. This is Issy, Kate. She and Plum were at school together.'

Issy hugs Angus and extends a hand to Kate, who is aware that she is being summed up.

'Hi,' Issy says. 'Great to meet you.'

Kate smiles, shakes Issy's hand, aware of various vibes resonating around the table and wondering why this old school chum should make Plum react so negatively. Angus re-arranges chairs and goes to order more coffee just as Cass appears and, as the whole group forms and reforms, Kate sits back a little, pours herself some coffee and watches and listens.

Isla is delighted. Instinct guided her here this morning and now she looks at them all, sizing them up: Plum's family and friends. Even as she watches them, responding to a question from Cass (very pretty woman, very elegant), dear old Angus (enjoys a little flirtation, absolute pushover) is talking about going to the bookshop to buy a book from El.

Isla shoots a glance at Plum, so beloved by this particular group of people, but just at this moment Plum is not looking quite so sure of herself and Isla guesses just how much poor Plum must be regretting that moment of confidence. Isla remembers how she comforted her, made light of it, whilst privately she marvelled at sensible, reliable Plum being capable of such an act.

'It was one of those awful moments,' she said, 'when grief just hits you. I'd found all the baby toys the girls had packed into a trunk and I just suddenly thought of my baby, and then I heard the doorbell ring and there he was . . .'

Isla accepts a cup of coffee from Angus, listening to the conversation, and wonders if any of these people know what it's like to have spent all your formative years coming last. Big, clever, elder sister: beautiful, intelligent, firing on all cylinders. Small, cute, little sister: funny, endearing, loved by everyone. And Issy, pig in the middle, not belonging, never in the right place, nothing special to commend her. Always fighting for attention, for the right to be loved, never fitting in.

At school she learned how to cultivate the other girls, to befriend them by amusing them with her quick wit whilst being swift to sympathize, encourage. She learned to manipulate, too, which was amusing but it didn't make her feel less lonely. This loneliness makes her long both to draw people close to her whilst, at the same time, punish them for the love and happiness they enjoy.

As she sips her coffee she wonders how this group of people would react if she were to say: 'I'm glad to hear that El is doing so well. Wasn't it her father you had that fling with, Plum?'

She's aware that the woman across the table (Kate, is it? Bit of an enigma, bit of a challenge) is watching her almost quizzically, and for one panicky moment Isla wonders if she's guessed Isla's own secret, that somehow she knows how much she loves Plum. But it's most unlikely. Isla takes control of herself and turns to Angus.

'How are those amazing dogs of yours?'

Immediately the conversation turns on dogs and Isla sees Plum relax and she smiles at her. The smile carries a subliminal message: You see? No need to worry. You can trust me.

And she knows by the way Plum returns the smile that she's feeling very slightly guilty that, just for a minute back there, she doubted her old school chum: feared that she might give her away somehow.

Isla sits back in her chair. It's always like this, feeling like she's on the outside looking in. She'd like to change that but she wants to draw Plum closer, not alienate her. She needs time to think about things.

El comes out of Book Stop on a high. It's been a great first day: learning the computer system, how the till works and all the usual jobs that happen in a bookshop. Unpacking books and shelving them, checking wholesalers' next-day deliveries, and meeting the friendly customers like Trudy and Vanessa, who recognize her; some who knew Pa and like a chat. Simon and Natasha are kind, really helpful, and El feels on top of her new job. She wishes there was someone she could tell it all to; with whom she could share a bottle of wine and talk through her day.

As she drives home she thinks about those texts in Pa's phone: odd, random texts, which seem to be in code. El wonders why she doesn't simply phone the number, explain who she is and ask the question: who are you? Several emotions are preventing this. First, she is oddly confused by her reaction to the fact that Pa had someone in his life with whom he clearly had an important friendship but had kept a secret from her. This hurts. She knows it's foolish. After all, she hasn't told Pa about all her friends and relationships. The second problem is that the person at the other end – and El's pretty certain that it's a woman – might not know that Pa is dead, though it seems fairly unlikely.

As she parks the car and climbs out, El wonders if Cass and Kate and Angus know about this woman and whether she dare ask them. As she lets herself in, hangs up her coat and climbs the stairs, she decides what she's going to do. She's going to text Will, describe to him how her day went and then tell him about the phone. At this moment El feels quite relieved that Will is gay, and her stepbrother, because it won't look as if she is coming on to him. Texting him will seem like a continuation of his last visit when he packed and took away Pa's clothes. She can explain how she found the phone in Pa's gilet pocket and then read him some of those texts.

As she switches on the kettle, finds the tea, there's a bang at the back door, which is then opened slightly. A voice shouts: 'You OK there, El?'

El smiles. 'Hi, Andy,' she shouts back. 'Come on up.'

He runs up the stairs – Andy does everything at speed – and grins at her.

'How are you doing, maid? Thought I'd best check on you. See if there's anything we can do.'

'Sweet of you,' she says. 'But the truth is that the baby's screaming his head off, you forgot to buy the bread and Trish is seriously not happy.'

Andy laughs out loud. 'You're too sharp. Mind you don't cut yourself. Your old dad would have poured me a beer and we'd have had a good old chat about liver fluke.'

'You are such an unconvincing liar. My old dad wouldn't have known the first thing about liver fluke. And if Trish thinks you're sitting here with me, having a drink while she deals with the baby and gets the supper, what d'you think my life would be worth?'

Andy sighs regretfully, still grinning. 'Worth a try. Sure you don't need any logs fetched up?'

El makes tea. It would be very helpful to get the log basket stocked up but she doesn't want any trouble with Trish, who can be sharp-tongued.

'Come on,' he says, suddenly serious. 'It's a cold old night and you don't want to be stumbling about in the dark. Trish suggested it herself.'

El is touched by their kindness. 'OK. Actually, that would be great. Would you like a cup of tea?'

He shakes his head. 'It won't take long. I'll get in enough to keep you going for a few days. Trish says come over some time.'

As she lights the fire and Andy brings in the logs, El thinks back over her day. Natasha has told her to look out for *Book of the Week* on Radio Four. It will be El's responsibility to write a link for the *Western Morning News* and she feels excited about this. It's giving her ideas about how she might start writing her own book, but so far she's only got as far as making copious notes. Yet, all the while, at the back of her mind, she continues to think about the texts and, once Andy has gone, she curls up on the sofa, reaches for her phone and wonders how to describe it all to Will.

Angus is making a curry. As he chops ingredients and stirs and mixes he's aware of Plum, sitting on the sagging old sofa, a dog at each side of her. He can feel tension but he can't quite see the reason for it. Each time she makes one of her little dashes from London he hopes that she'll ask if she and Ian can make this their Devon base, and he's having to make a huge effort not to ask outright. He remembers what Cass and Kate said in the Bedford – that he should give Plum and Ian time to come to their own decision – and he's trying to stick with that. But it's hard. As he puts plates to warm in the bottom oven of the Aga he remembers that Plum became even more tense when her old friend suddenly appeared.

'It was good to see Issy,' he says rather randomly. 'Haven't seen her for a long time. Fancy her remembering Blossom and Dearie.'

'You've always had dogs,' answers Plum. 'It was a pretty safe guess. I don't think she mentioned them by name.'

Angus is taken aback by this retort – not Plum's style at all – and he straightens up and turns to look at her.

'Are you all right, darling?' he asks. 'You seem to have been a bit on edge today.'

Plum gathers the dogs more closely to her, as if she is using them as a defence.

'There is something,' she says quickly. 'It's about where we live when we're down here. I know you'd like us to be with you, Dad, but I'm not sure that it would work. Ian's not the easiest person to live with when he's just back from sea, and the girls are so random these days, turning up with friends. I feel really mean about this but I asked Kate this morning if we could rent her cottage.'

Briefly, Angus is filled with terrible disappointment. It's so good to have Plum here: to hear her about the place, talking to the dogs, turning on the radio, making breakfast.

'After all,' she's saying, 'Chapel Street is only a ten-minute walk away so we shall be in and out all the time . . .'

How can he explain that, however conveniently close Kate's cottage is, it's not the same as having Plum and Ian living in the house with him, providing companionship? He gets a grip on his emotions, swallows down his disappointment, and nods.

'I can quite see that,' he says. 'Ian will need his own space when he comes ashore. Perfectly reasonable.' He hesitates. 'So what did Kate say?'

'Well, she says the cottage isn't quite ready but she's given us first refusal.'

Angus feels a little spasm of gratitude towards Kate. She knows what he's hoping and she's probably just trying to buy some time for him.

'Well, that's all good then,' he says. 'Supper's nearly ready. Shall we have a drink?'

*

Plum struggles out from between the dogs, stands up and goes to the fridge to find the wine. She feels utterly miserable. It was such a shock to see Issy standing there, in the bar at the Bedford, and she felt suddenly very vulnerable. It seems impossible that her old friend should drop her in it, yet ever since Plum met her in the Pannier Market, she's felt that Issy is in a slightly volatile state and might easily say or do something a bit crazy. Just for a minute, when Dad mentioned her, Plum was taken off guard again and talked about Kate and the cottage so as to deflect him away from Issy.

Plum takes out a bottle of Pinot Grigio, stands it on the kitchen table and finds glasses. She knows perfectly well that it's her own guilt that is at the root of the trouble. All the while she's been away she's been able to cope with it, but now, back here amongst her friends and family, it's getting more difficult. She was horrified when she heard that Martin and Felicity were divorcing. When her father told her, on the telephone, she'd held her breath with shock and dismay. It was a year since she and Martin had been caught up into that mad, brief moment of shared affection. Martin, whom she'd known since she was a teenager, her father's junior partner, family friend. He often dropped in to see them if he was passing their naval hiring in Roborough, but on this occasion she was alone and very miserable, missing Ian, who was at sea, thinking about the baby, James, both girls staying with grandparents. Martin was so sweet, comforting her, encouraging her. They had a drink, and then another. Even now she can't quite remember how they'd finished up making love . . .

'Martin is getting divorced. He tells me that the marriage is finished,' her father told her during that phone call a few months later, after she and Ian had moved to Portsmouth. 'Felicity is accusing him of having an affair and he's not denying it. Very sad, but it seems that he's made up his mind.'

'Having an affair?' Plum asked faintly.

'He tells me he's not and I believe him. They've separated. To be honest he seems happier than I've ever known him but that's between me and you . . .'

Now, as she pours the wine, Plum wishes she could tell her father the truth. She will never know now if Felicity found out about her and Martin but she can't believe that she did. Felicity would never have kept silent about it. Nevertheless, Plum feels responsible for the break-up and guilty every time she sees El.

'Are you sure you're OK, darling?'

Her father slips his arm around her shoulders and Plum longs to turn and bury her face into the warmth of his jersey and hold him tightly. Instead, she smiles up at him and passes him a glass of wine.

'I'm fine,' she says. 'Let's eat.'

CHAPTER FOURTEEN

Will stands by the old stone cross, one hand on its rough, cold surface. He feels the lichen crumbling beneath his warm fingers and once again he experiences the sensation of release: the melting of the icy lump of misery that he's pushed deep into his heart since his mother died, smothering it with other emotions, other sensations, denying it.

He stares around at the valleys and hills that flow away into infinity, the overarching sky streaked with cumulus, and his fingers tighten on the granite as if he is communicating his pain into the cross. Here he can allow that pain to dissipate as he has never been able to do; not with his father, or his friends, or even with Christian. He has no idea why this distorted lump of granite should have produced such a reaction in him but he welcomes it, offers his misery back to the cross, allows this strange sense of eternity to free him.

The sun gleams out, touching rocks, distant woodland and tors with its light. Will feels hopeful, anticipatory, but he has no intention of trying to analyse his feelings. It's enough to be experiencing this new lightness of spirit. He turns to go, crossing the granite slab over the gully, getting back into the car. As he drives towards Tavistock he thinks about El. She's phoned him to say that she's found her father's phone and some odd texts, which she can't make out. They seem to be a kind of code, suggested meetings. The name and number mean nothing to her and when he asked if she couldn't just phone the number El became confused, reluctant to explain why that was difficult for her. A moment's thought showed Will several reasons why this might be the case and, cursing his tactlessness, he said that he'd like to see the texts. She took him up on this at once and suggested that he should pay another visit to the Pig Pen. They worked out when they both had time off and made a plan.

And now here he is, hoping that he'll be able to help, guessing how much El must be missing her father and that she's slightly fearful of this unknown texter. Will's immediate reaction is that Martin had a woman friend, a lover, although clearly El knows nothing about her. It will be hard for El to discover that her father had a very close relationship, kept secret, but there might be several reasons for that.

Even as he broods on these things, he's aware of the moor all around him: a pony grazing, sheep trotting across the road ahead of him. Unexpected shafts of sunshine light up a distant plantation of pine trees, a little stream, and cloud shadows pass across the bleached grasslands. He tries to imagine this land-scape under snow or in high summer, and he hopes that he and El will be able to have another walk, leaving the car and striding out into unknown territory. It's clear that she knows the moor very well, that it was almost like a back garden to El and her father. She seemed glad to show it to him, to share with him its mystery and its magic.

Already, as he drives, he's remembering landmarks, but at the same time he's beginning to feel apprehensive about this second visit. He knows what it's like to miss someone very dear to you, to adjust to the terrible finality of death, and he wants to try to help El through it. He knows she hated their parents marrying just as much as he did. He saw how her mother tried to manipulate El into conforming to her own ideas and how El stood up against the coercement and remained loyal to her father.

Will wishes he'd known Martin. It might have helped to get a handle on this new development. Clearly there must have been a woman who'd been the reason for the divorce, but El believed that this was a very short affair and hadn't lasted beyond the separation. Knowing El as he now does, Will feels it very unlikely that she would have resented her father finding companionship and even love in the last five years. What was odd was that he'd never talked to her about it. Maybe the woman was married . . . Or maybe he's wrong and Martin feared that El would be jealous; that after all the loyalty she showed him she'd feel threatened and displaced. Human relationships are never straightforward.

Will glances at his sat nav to confirm his route and turns off into the lanes that run between Tavistock and the farm. He shakes off his apprehension and prepares to enjoy the visit. El has promised to show him Tavistock, to explore the moor, and he wants to hear all about her first week at the bookshop. Maybe the texts can be easily explained away; maybe they're from some old friend who enjoys codes and puzzles. They might simply be a bit of fun between two old friends arranging to meet up for a lunchtime pint or an evening at the pub. Will drives carefully down the track and pulls in beside El's car. He sits for a moment, then shuts off the engine and climbs out.

El watches from the window. She's been waiting for him. Learning to live alone is not as straightforward as she imagined it might be. She's always had school friends, family, or her friends at uni. It's especially odd to be alone here, at the Pig Pen. Pa's death is too sudden, too unexpected, to grasp. He should be here, sitting at the table calling out a clue to a crossword, making coffee, wandering out on to the little terrace outside the door where he has his favourite tubs and the birdfeeders. It's all so silent, so empty, without him.

During these last few days, when the westerlies came rolling in, bringing soft grey curtains of rain that shrouded the moor in mist, she'd begun to wonder if she could actually make it alone, if she could endure long, dark winter evenings. The sight of Will's big car, so totally unsuitable for a Devon farmyard, sliding gently to a halt below her fills her with relief and she has to prevent herself from running down the stairs and outside to greet him. He gets out, looking around him, and El steps back from the window lest he should see her watching. She tries to think of something casual she could be doing but nothing comes to mind. Quickly she opens her laptop so that when he bangs on the door, opens it and calls out, she can shout back and be sitting at the table when he appears at the top of the stairs.

'Hi,' she says, pleased to hear herself sounding cheerful. 'You've made good time.'

She realizes that she doesn't know how to greet him, whether she should get up and hug him, but he solves the problem by walking across to the window and looking out.

'You've got good views here,' he observes. 'I couldn't remember them clearly from last time.'

'It's the advantage of being upside down,' she says, and suddenly she's calmer. 'It's really great in the summer with all the sunshine pouring in. Would you like some tea?'

'That sounds good. I didn't stop on the way down.' He turns back into the room. 'I dropped my bag in the bedroom. Hope that was OK?'

'Yes, of course.' She's glad to have something to do, to fill the kettle, find two mugs. Even though he was here to help clear out Pa's things, for her to be here in the Pig Pen with him still feels slightly bizarre. 'I'm glad you could get down again. To be honest I was totally thrown by finding Pa's phone. And those messages.'

She has her back to him as she makes the tea but she hears him drag out a chair and sit down at the table.

'Well, I totally get that,' he replies. He hesitates and then goes on. 'It was a bit like that after my mum died. I'd open a book and find in it a card she'd sent me or a letter from when I was at school. It really shredded me. Like I could hear her voice.'

El is touched by this disclosure. She can imagine that it must really cost Will to share this with her, and suddenly all her anxiety, this discomfiture at his presence, is done away with. She carries the two mugs to the table and then fetches a plate of chocolate cookies.

'It was a bit like that,' she admits. 'It's the whole thing. Not just seeing these weird texts but feeling like I'm spying on something private. You know what I mean?'

Will raises the mug to his lips. He looks thoughtful.

'It's a tricky one, isn't it? In the old days people had address books and at times like these they could be checked through so as to let everyone know what has happened. But these days everything's in your computer or your phone, isn't it? So when you check it out you're always going to come across texts and emails.'

'Pa had a very comprehensive database of friends and business acquaintances on his laptop,' El said, 'and I checked right through it to make sure everyone was informed. The thing was, I couldn't find his phone and then I kind of forgot about it.'

'Well, that's fair enough. You've had a lot on your mind.' He reaches for a cookie. 'So you found it in his jacket pocket?'

She nods. 'His fleece gilet. I forgot his coats when we were doing the packing up because they were hanging in the hall, and there it was in the pocket. It was out of charge, of course, but when I'd got it charged up I thought I should just check it.' She hesitates. 'There were these unanswered texts, you see. It was awful, really. I felt I was spying but I didn't know if there were people who still hadn't heard about what had happened.'

'And were there many?'

She shakes her head. 'Only this one that I didn't recognize. The others were on his database. Just close family and friends.'

He's watching her across the table, compassionate but slightly challenging too, which oddly gives her courage to admit her fears.

'I know I could just phone the number and ask the question,' she says. 'It's the obvious thing to do. But the texts have made me . . .' she shrugs. 'I don't know. They've made me wary.'

He nods. 'OK. So shall I have a look at them?'

As an answer she picks up the phone lying beside her, unlocks it and pushes it across the table to him. He takes it and looks at the screen, reading the last text and then scrolling slowly upwards. El watches him, seeing his expression change from interested, to puzzled, and then slightly amused.

'Yes,' he says at last. 'I see what you meant now when you talked about codes. Was your father into that?'

El thinks about it. 'I can see that it would have amused him,' she says at last. 'He was a solicitor so you might say that it was part of his work to assemble facts, sort out truth from lies, see his way through things. You notice that I'm not using the word "devious"?'

Will smiles at her. 'Don't think I can't see how hard this is for you.'

She stares at him, slightly taken aback. 'Yes,' she says. 'OK. Yes, if you want the truth I'm finding it really hard to think that he's had this kind of fun relationship with someone that he never told me about. I know most of his friends, but this is different.'

Will looks at the screen. He begins to scroll up again, making comments as he goes.

'So you don't know Nancy Fortescue? . . . Some of these are just initials and a time . . . Almost businesslike, isn't it? . . . The magic circle sounds interesting . . . the wisteria bridge . . . Sophie's place. Do you know anyone called Sophie?'

'Only a school friend who lives miles away.'

He shakes his head, puzzled. 'So all we know is her mobile number, a voicemail, and an initial J. And you really feel you can't just phone the number?'

'I don't want to admit to whoever might answer that I didn't know this obviously important part of his life because he's kept it secret from me.'

'Would you like me to do it?'

'No!' She reaches across the table and pulls the phone back towards her. 'No. Not yet, anyway.'

'OK,' says Will pacifically. 'So what do you want us to do?'

'Sorry,' she says, feeling foolish. 'I know I'm probably over-reacting here, but what I wondered was whether we could perhaps follow up some of the clues.'

Will sits back in his chair and drinks some more tea. 'OK,' he says. 'I'm cool with that. Where do you want to start?'

El sighs with relief. She has her answer ready.

'I thought we'd start with Nancy Fortescue,' she says.

CHAPTER FIFTEEN

'So what's the plan?' asks Davy at breakfast on Saturday morning, buttering toast, reaching for the marmalade. 'What excitements do you have in store for me?'

Julia smiles. Davy always likes to have some jaunt planned, though nothing too strenuous. Not for Davy a yomp across the moor or the cliffs. He likes something more civilized, which might include a gallery or a National Trust property, but which definitely includes some kind of sustenance. Julia has an idea, though. She wants to go back to The Garden House, to revisit those places she went with Martin. The prospect of going alone fills her with a kind of dread, yet she's got to get herself back to the garden.

'I was thinking.' she says casually, 'that we might go over the moor to The Garden House. It's the most amazing garden and the acers will be really spectacular just now. There's a café and they make delicious cake. I think you might enjoy it. What d'you think? It's a lovely morning now all the mist has blown away.'

'Perfect,' Davy answers, contentedly. 'I haven't the least idea what an acer is, but I trust you utterly, darling.'

Julia laughs at him. 'You'll love it. That's an order, as dear old Bob used to say. I'll give Bertie a quick run up the lane now and then we can give him a walk on the moor on the way back home.'

Davy waves his piece of toast in acknowledgement of the plan. 'Sounds good to me. I am so enjoying this, Jules. Thanks for rescuing me this weekend. I've been feeling pretty low and sorry for myself, and now I know what you've been going through for these last few weeks I'm quite ashamed of myself.'

'Well, don't be,' she says swiftly. 'Nobody has a monopoly on feelings and it's not a contest. I'm really glad I told you, Davy. And, OK, The Garden House is somewhere I first met Martin and it's a pretty special place for me. It would be really good to go back there but somehow I don't want to go on my own.'

Davy puts down his toast and stretches a hand to her across the table. 'My dear old darling,' he says feelingly, 'what complete and utter shit life is. We shall go together. I'd feel very privileged to share this with you.'

She takes his hand and holds it tightly. Davy is exactly what she needs right now. Someone who is not afraid to show his emotions, to enter into her loneliness and grief without uttering platitudes or pulling a sad face.

'Thanks,' she says. 'The gardens open at eleven so we've got plenty of time. It's about a forty-minute drive.'

Davy, who is still in pyjamas with an ancient fleece jacket over the top, glances down at himself.

'Why do I feel that there's a tiny hint there?' he muses as if to himself. 'Just one more piece of toast then, and perhaps half a cup of coffee, and then I shall rush away and get ready.'

'It's open till three,' says Julia. 'We could have lunch there.'

She feels a mixture of excitement and apprehension. How odd it will feel driving the familiar road, parking the car and walking in, remembering which code he's used. *Nancy Fortescue*. Sophie's Place. Moulin Rouge. They each have a special significance. The Garden House was always a bit of a risk, being so close to Tavistock, but after all, anyone might meet an old friend by chance in a garden – and even have a cup of coffee together. After *Cakes and Ale* was aired there was a little more danger of being recognized but she always wore shades or a hat, and since she and Martin arrived and left separately nobody seemed to be aware of the relationship.

Julia sighs. Today will be different: no Martin, no codes, no meeting. She's aware that Davy is watching her and she shrugs and makes a little face.

'Ghosts,' she says. 'I'll take Bertie up the lane.'

She gets up from the table and Bertie, who has been keenly observing the progress of Davy's toast, ambles out of the kitchen behind her. Kicking off her shoes and stepping into her wellies, Julia pulls on a jacket and opens the back door. The morning is mild and a blackbird is singing in the shrubbery. As she and Bertie set off together, Julia is humming: 'We are stardust, we are golden . . .' There are no sheep with their lambs in the meadow, no cuckoo calling down in the valley – spring seems a long way off – but the early November day is mild and the sky is clear. It will be a good drive across the moor to The Garden House. She knows that Davy will not be blown away by the immensity of the landscape or even by the charm of the gardens. Davy is a city man but he enjoys a little change. He enjoyed producing *Cakes and Ale*, visiting the small pubs and cafés on the cliffs and in small villages perched around the Cornish peninsula, and talking to the people whose livelihoods depended on tourists visiting these wild, spectacular places.

As she walks, Julia's fingers grip the phone in her pocket. She knows she should block Martin's number but can't quite bring herself to do it. It would be like killing him all over again: blotting him out. And supposing El might need to get in touch? They'd always talked about the children: her boys and El and Freddie. Occasionally they showed each other photographs they'd taken on their phones. Photos of Freddie were rare but there were a few of them, and Julia sometimes wondered what might happen if all four of the children were to meet. Right at the beginning, after the divorce, they were both determined that it was foolish to risk any kind of upset, then, after Felicity married again, it seemed important to allow a period of quiet whilst El and Freddie came to terms with the new situation. And so it continued, probably because there was no obvious, pain-free way where they might all come together happily. So they'd made the pact: when Ollie went off to university a plan would be made.

How odd it is, thinks Julia, as she turns for home, calling to Bertie, to miss someone so much when I saw him so little.

The thing was, of course, that there has always been the prospect before them, something to anticipate: a meeting, a lunch, a visit to Bristol. And now there's nothing but her Charlotte Marlow painting and his texts.

CHAPTER SIXTEEN

Will and El are in the Pannier Market. Nothing has come out of their exhaustive talking or searching the internet apart from a portrait of Nancy Fortescue of Devon painted by Thomas Hudson, hanging in the Yale Center for British Art.

'And don't tell me,' Will said, 'that they popped over to Yale for a quick cup of coffee. Although there's another here that says "Moulin Rouge. Midday". I mean, Paris? Seriously?'

Glancing at El he realized that his amused incredulity was misplaced. She looked bemused, unhappy, and he cursed his tactlessness whilst feeling unsure about how to play this.

Now, as he follows her along the aisles between the market stalls he wonders exactly what Martin and the mysterious J were really doing. There was never anything romantic in the texts between them. And they weren't even very regular. If they were lovers then they were having a pretty hard time of it. Will stops suddenly beside a stall selling hand-painted Mediterranean pottery. He picks up a bowl, scarlet and blue with splashes of thick cream paint, and grins to himself. He's seen something similar on the dresser at the Pig Pen and

wonders if El or her father bought it from this stall. It's definitely not his scene but he knows that Christian would love it.
El, who has wandered on, glances over her shoulder and comes
back to him.

'These are fun,' he says, showing it to her. 'Christian's
birthday is coming up and I think he'd like this.'

He talks to the stall-owner, looking at the other plates, whilst
El stands silently beside him. Luckily she's brought a linen bag,
folded in her coat pocket, and she offers it to him silently whilst
he carefully packs the bowl and a plate away. Before he can
speak, a voice hails El, calling from across the stall, and he sees
a tall man, probably in his early seventies, waving at them.
Will glances down at El, who is already waving back.

'It's Angus,' she says to him. 'Pa's senior partner and oldest
friend. We'll have to say hello.'

Will can't see why this should be a problem but understands
as soon as El introduces him and clearly can't quite find the
words to describe their relationship. As Will shakes Angus's
outstretched hand he realizes that it's a tricky one. Since El is
reluctant to call him her stepbrother, Will simply smiles.
Angus, however, seems to grasp the situation. Perhaps he recognizes the surname; maybe Martin has mentioned him to his
old friend. Angus is exclaiming that they must have coffee,
that he and Plum were meeting at the Bedford and Will and El
must join them. Angus clearly isn't considering that 'no' might
be an answer – he reminds Will of his former headmaster –
and it's clear that El is very fond of this old boy with his mop
of white hair and wide, angular shoulders. Will smiles and
nods, and follows them out of the Pannier Market, across the
square and into the big hotel that stands across the road from
the church.

'Nice old town,' he says to Angus as he follows him into the bar. He has to make an effort not to call him 'sir'.

Angus beams at him, as if he is personally responsible for Tavistock's good qualities, and hurries forward to a table by one of the windows. A pretty, fair-haired woman who is sitting there glances up from her phone as Angus approaches.

'Look who I found in the Pannier Market,' he says happily.

He stands aside to allow El to come forward and Will sees an odd expression cross the woman's face: surprise, even alarm. El is already squeezing past the chairs so as to give her a hug.

'Hi, Plum,' she says warmly. 'This is great. I didn't know you were down.'

She turns and Will braces himself for another ambivalent introduction. He stretches a hand towards this woman – can she really be called Plum? – and smiles at her. Whilst they mill about deciding who should sit where and what everyone should drink, Will is aware that Plum is not relaxed. Her hands flex, she picks up her phone and puts it down again. Angus goes to the bar to order while El sits next to Plum and begins to ask her questions about her family. Angus returns and then the coffee arrives. Angus, to Will's surprise, knows that he is a pilot, and they talk about that, but all the while Will is conscious of some kind of distraction on Plum's part. A thought occurs to him. Nobody mentions Martin. Moreover, if Plum and Angus are surprised that Will is staying at the Pig Pen they give no sign of it. Presently the party breaks up with promises that they must meet again.

As they drive back in El's car – 'Your flash car is just so not appropriate for Tavistock,' she said, laughing – he's still following a train of thought.

'I suppose,' he says tentatively, 'that Plum couldn't possibly be J, could she?'

Glancing sideways he sees that El looks first incredulous and then amused. 'You have to be kidding,' she says. 'I told you, Angus is Dad's oldest friend. We've known Plum for ever. Apart from which, she's been abroad for the last two years. Her husband's a naval commander and they've only just come back from Washington.' She shakes her head. 'Why would you think that?'

He shrugs, staring out of the window. 'She just seemed as if she'd been caught off balance.'

'I haven't seen her since Pa died,' El says, as if that explains it. 'They weren't back in time for the funeral and I missed her when she was down last. Some people find it hard the first time they see me. They don't know what to say.'

He nods; that could be the reason, although he's not totally convinced. By the time they get back to the Pig Pen, El is in an odd mood.

'Don't forget Christian's present,' she says, almost waspishly, holding the bag out to him. 'You'd better pack them carefully so that they don't break. And I want my bag back.'

As she goes ahead of him into the house, he opens the boot of his car and stashes the pottery away, wrapping them carefully into a coat he keeps there, folding El's bag. He guesses that she's finding this whole business of the texts harder than he thought, not to mention meeting people she hasn't seen since her father died. Though he was only twelve when his mother died, he can still remember how difficult that whole process was. He locks the car and follows her into the house.

*

El stands at the table, staring at nothing, furious with herself for behaving like a prat. She was surprised at her reaction when she watched Will choosing the pottery, smiling to himself, taking his time over deciding which pieces Christian might like. It was almost as if she was jealous, which is crazy. And just now she'd been really snide about telling him to wrap them properly. After all, it's precisely because Will is gay that she can be so easy with him, that he can stay here without being any kind of threat to her. The stepbrother and -sister thing is a bit thought-provoking, but actually that's not really a problem. It's surprising, though, how difficult she's finding it to introduce him to her friends. She knows that Angus, as Pa's friend and her own legal adviser, knows all about the remarriage, and it's clear that he remembered who Will is, which made it easier. Not so easy with Plum, but El guesses that she was much more concerned with concentrating on how to be tactful about Pa than to wonder about Will.

As to Plum being the person who sent the texts, El almost laughs at the thought of it. Plum, who is so good and kind, such a lovely mother, and a devoted wife following Ian around on his naval postings. On the other hand, it's simply not fair to snap at Will, who is being very patient and kind about all this. She breathes deeply, gets a grip on the emotions that threaten to overwhelm her, and by the time Will arrives upstairs she's in control again.

'Not quite what I planned for your introduction to Tavistock,' she says, 'but never mind. I'm glad we'd already been to Book Stop and you met Simon and Natasha.'

'It's a great bookshop,' he says, putting El's bag on the table. 'And I loved the Music Room upstairs. I'd like to have a really good browse around there.'

'Pa loved it, too,' she answers, relieved to be back on a calm footing. 'He once found a remastered Miles Davis CD and I thought he was going to die of joy.'

She stops abruptly, realizing what she's said, and sits down at the table, dropping her head into her hands.

'Sorry, she says, muffled. 'Honestly. I'm all over the place today.'

'Don't beat yourself up,' Will says gently. 'Think of everything you've got through so far. You've sorted out the funeral, the house, your pa's belongings, you've moved in and got yourself a job. I can't think of anyone else I know who would have achieved all that so quickly. Be proud of yourself. Pa would be.'

His kindness, mentioning Pa like that, is too much for her. El folds her arms on the table, puts her head on them and bursts into tears. He doesn't touch her, or make soothing sounds. He walks to the fridge and opens it, she hears the clink of glasses, liquid pouring, and then something set on the table beside her. She fumbles in her pocket for a tissue and wipes her eyes.

'Thanks, Will,' she says. 'Perhaps it was trying to decipher all those texts.' She takes a sip of wine and sets the glass down. 'I wasn't sure where we might have lunch. I was thinking we might go for a walk and have lunch in a pub but instinctively I just drove straight back here.'

'Well,' he says, 'perhaps we could have a sandwich and then go for a walk. Do we need to take a car to have a walk?'

She shakes her head. 'We can go down the lane and then cut up on to the moor. That's not a problem.'

'Good. In that case,' he raises a glass to her, 'here's to Nancy Fortescue.'

El laughs. 'I'll drink to that,' she says. 'To Nancy Fortescue.'

*

Julia pulls into the car park, gets out and looks around her. Nothing has changed. As usual someone is waiting at the visitor reception to check membership cards or to take the entrance fee, there are plants for sale, leaflets. Davy is beside her and she shows her membership card and waits whilst Davy pays his entry fee, then she slips her arm into his and they walk away into the garden.

He looks around, interested, glancing back over his shoulder towards the old house.

'So this is where you used to meet?' he asks. 'Why? Why here? I can see the point in the summer but,' he shakes his head, 'all year round?'

'I think it's because it's where it all started,' she says, steering him towards the Acer Glade. 'We met by chance in the tea-rooms and then again by the *Nancy Fortescue*.'

'Who?' Davy sounds startled.

'The Fortescue family created this garden about forty years ago,' Julia tells him. 'They bequeathed it to a trust, which still looks after it. Nancy was a member of the family. On the lake in the Jubilee Arboretum there's a lovely little wooden rowing boat named after her. That's where I met Martin the second time, also by chance. He was sitting on the bench there. We used to go to other places but this was our favourite. Martin used to make up crazy names for places in the garden. He was a complete nutter in some ways, but that's why I loved him.'

Davy presses her arm closely against him. 'I can get that.'

'I know,' she says. 'That's why I knew I could tell you. I wish I'd done it earlier but somehow we seemed to set this vow of secrecy on it. It sounds a bit silly now but that way we felt that nobody could be hurt.'

She guides him along the paths, past the Summer Garden and the Quarry Garden, and he glances at the little stone structures, slate-roofed, trying to imagine what this must be like in all its summer glory. Because it's been such a calm, mild autumn, the Acer Glade is still a blaze of colour: red, crimson, orange.

'Wow,' says Davy. 'Seriously wow.'

She smiles, pleased with his reaction. 'This was one of Martin's favourite places. I bought him an acer in a pot for his birthday one year. I hope El looks after it. I suppose she'll sell the cottage.'

Davy glances at her. 'Couldn't you phone and ask her?'

Julia frowns, shakes her head. 'The thing is, she doesn't know about me. How do I explain myself? Especially if she's found Martin's phone and all our texts. I simply can't decide whether it's best if I come blasting out of the woodwork or stay where Martin wanted me, incognito. What would you do?'

Davy thinks about it, frowning, as she guides him on through the Rhododendron Walk, then he shakes his head.

'I honestly don't know,' he says.

'They were so close, you see. El stuck with him through the divorce and after it, despite her mother's annoyance with her. Felicity thought Martin should have been cast out, but El was faithful and I think Martin found it impossible to tell her about me. He feared she might be hurt that he'd found someone else and then, of course, the longer it went on the worse it got. And, to be honest, I didn't really want to explain to the boys. It all sounds crazy now.'

'But you're still worrying that she has his phone and your texts?'

Julia nods. 'Our texts were deliberately short and to the point. After all, the boys were around and anyone might see a text pop in. Even so, she must wonder who they're from. Especially as they were kind of cryptic. I should have done it straight away, I suppose, but I didn't have the courage. I kept thinking that Martin might not want her to know, especially as he died so tragically. She must have been out of her mind, even without me showing up.'

'And the longer it goes on the more difficult it gets,' says Davy thoughtfully.

'Exactly. I'm hating it, and I can't bear to think she's distressed about it, but how do I explain myself? How do I text? "Hi, El. My name's Julia. Your dad and I were lovers. How about meeting up for lunch?"'

Davy lets go of her arm and puts his own around her. 'Stop it,' he says. 'You're tearing yourself to pieces.'

Julia swallows down her distress. 'Sorry,' she replies. 'But can you see what hell it is? I don't feel I even have the right to mourn him, yet I loved him so much.'

He holds her tightly. 'I get it, sweetie,' he says, 'but stay tough. Don't give in now. We'll try to see a way through this together. So where's this *Nancy Fortescue*?'

She smiles, takes a deep breath and shakes her head. 'You won't find her,' she says. 'She's always taken out of the water for the winter so it's no good looking for her. Come on, let's go and have some coffee. And then I'll show you where she'll be next spring.'

That night El has a nightmare. She dreams that she is with Martin in a big garden but she is small, a child again. She holds on to his hand and jumps along, and they laugh and he swings around. Suddenly he disappears and she can't find him. She shouts to him but there is no sign of him. Now she is much older, running through the garden, calling out to him. 'Where are you, Pa? Come back,' but her voice makes no sound. It seems that he's a little way ahead of her and shouting something she can't hear. Something about Nancy Fortescue, about meeting her there. She can't hear or see him now, and suddenly she wakes, heart thumping, tears on her cheeks and she remembers that Pa is dead. In despair, she buries her face in her pillow, learning all over afresh that she will never see him again. It's unbearable and on an impulse she slides to the edge of the bed. She will go to Will. He will be kind and she will no longer be alone. She thinks no further than that: she cannot bear, at this moment, to be alone. She stumbles across the hall and opens his door.

'Will,' she says, still unable to stanch the flood of tears. 'Will, I've had a terrible dream about Pa.' She scrambles up on the bed just as Will struggles up and she bumps her head against his arm and begins to weep again. She curls against him, her cheek against his bare chest. Will lies still, trying to pull the duvet from beneath her so as to cover her in it. He speaks soothingly as if she is a child or an animal but still the tears come and come. He doesn't turn on the light but allows her to be there, letting her cry, sharing his warmth, his closeness.

Gradually this terrible outpouring of grief subsides and she simply lies there, taking great breaths. Sensing that the worst is past, Will gently eases the duvet up, wrapping it more warmly around her, and she relaxes into it, exhausted.

'Listen, El.' His voice comes from some way above her head, infinitely calm and gentle. 'If you're OK I'm going to make some tea.'

He waits as if she might make some protest, but although she doesn't want him to go away, she is much less stressed and a hot drink sounds comforting. She turns her face into the pillow as she nods: yes, she is OK. Will touches her lightly on her shoulder and then she can hear him shifting to the edge of the bed, standing up.

'I shan't be far away,' he says, and presently the hall light clicks on and she can hear him going upstairs, water running into the kettle, mugs clinking. Slowly El rolls on to her side. Her pyjamas are twisted and uncomfortable. She straightens them out, rubs the warm flannel sleeve across her eyes. Her hair is a curling mass, strands sticking to her cheeks, and she drags her wet fingers through it. Gradually she hauls herself up, piling the pillows behind her, glad that it's still dark in the bedroom.

She can hear Will coming back down the stairs, his shadow stretching before him into the room, but he still doesn't turn the bedroom light on and she's grateful. By the light from the hall she can see him put a mug on the small chest beside her before going back to his own side of the bed.

'Thanks,' she says. 'It's clearly my destiny today to make a complete fool of myself.'

'In that case,' he says, 'if I were you I should just go with the flow. No good fighting destiny.'

She can hear the smile in his voice and feels a huge gratitude. She reaches for the mug and sips the hot strong refreshing tea.

'I put some sugar in,' he says. 'Just a little bit. It's supposed to be good for shock.'

'Have I had a shock?' she asks, propped against the pillows, sipping gratefully.

'Yes,' he says, and this time his voice is unusually serious, almost grim. 'You've had one of the biggest, bloodiest shocks any of us can have and you don't get over it in one go. Or even in a series of small goes. It'll come back unexpectedly and hit you when you least expect it. So don't feel guilty about it. And if you really want to know,' he goes on, 'coming down here, being with you, is really helping me to come to terms with my mum's death, and that was fifteen years ago. So shall we agree that somehow this is helping both of us and then neither of us need feel grateful or guilty?'

Somehow these strong words restore El's sense of balance and she smiles.

'I'll go with that,' she says. 'But am I allowed to say thanks for the tea?' She swallows the last drops and sets down the mug on the chest. 'I'm fine now.'

She swings her legs off the bed, stands up, and hesitates.

'I was just about to say thank you again,' she says, 'but I won't. But I hope you manage to sleep for what's left of the night. See you in the morning, Will.'

She crosses the hall, switches off the light, and feels her way to her bed. Climbing in, she prepares to feel shock or guilt or just embarrassment for what has just happened but instead, as she curls against her pillow, dragging the duvet over her head, she topples suddenly into a deep sleep.

CHAPTER SEVENTEEN

Angus folds his newspaper and glances at his watch. Kate should be arriving any time soon and he looks around the kitchen to make sure all is clean and comfortable. Marina never quite grew used to having visitors drinking tea and coffee – or even having lunch and supper – in the kitchen, but Angus is growing accustomed to it.

'Much cosier and less formal, Dad,' Plum says. 'I know that Mum was so good at all that stuff but that was then and this is now. You've got to keep up.'

And so now, when his friends drop in, he's ready to dispense hospitality here in the warm kitchen with the dogs stretched out by the Aga or in their beds. If he's honest he rather likes it. Plum is right. There is an informality about it that puts his guests at ease and seems to provide the right atmosphere for confidences.

Angus wonders why Kate has asked if she can have a chat with him. It sounded rather more than the usual meeting, and he was with her and Cass in the Bedford only yesterday, so his curiosity is roused. As he takes one more glance around, he hears the ring of the doorbell, and he goes out to greet her.

'This is good,' he says, giving her a hug. 'Come on through. Ah, here come the dogs to greet you. Where's Flossie?'

'I left her at Chapel Street and walked over,' says Kate, following him into the kitchen. 'She's fine. I gave her a run on Plaster Down earlier.'

She bends to greet Blossom and Dearie, murmuring endearments, whilst Angus pushes the kettle on to the Aga and smiles at her, hoping that she'll make the first conversational move so that he knows where he stands. Kate drops her bag on to the floor and sinks down on a chair at the table.

'I'm in a bind, Angus,' she says, 'and I need your help.'

He is surprised at her directness but pleased that there's to be no beating about the bush. His instincts were right and this is not a casual visit.

'Always glad to be of help if I can,' he says. 'What's the problem?'

'Actually, it's who is the problem,' answers Kate. 'And it's Plum *and* Cass *and* Tom.'

Angus leans his weight on the back of the old wooden Windsor chair and stares down at her.

'Really?' he asks. 'All of them?'

Kate sighs and pushes her fingers through her short grey curly hair. 'Yes. All of them.'

Angus turns back to the Aga. 'Coffee?'

Kate nods. 'Thanks. That would be great. Sorry, Angus. I don't mean to talk in riddles. I'm hating this, actually. When we were all together in the Bedford recently, Plum was talking about finding a place for her and Ian. She asked me about my cottage. I know what you said about hoping they would stay here with you so it was just a tad tricky.'

Angus makes coffee, his back to Kate, imagining the difficult position she's in whilst trying to hide his own disappointment.

'And what did you say to her?' he asks.

'I told her that the cottage wasn't quite ready yet, hoping that she might give it some more thought, but she asked me if I would give her first refusal.'

Angus turns, puts the mugs on to the table and sits down. Kate looks at him anxiously and he smiles reassuringly at her.

'I can see why that put you in a difficult position,' he says, 'after what I'd said to you.'

'Well, it did,' she admits. 'I think Plum feels that Ian needs space when he comes home . . .'

Angus knows that she's trying to be tactful and he nods. 'And privacy,' he suggests. 'Please don't be upset, Kate. I understand and I was expecting it, anyway. So you agreed to give her first refusal?'

Kate nods reluctantly. 'But there's worse to come.'

He raises his eyebrows. 'Really?'

'You know that Cass and Tom have been having the great downsizing debate? Tom really wants to get on with it but Cass is finding the prospect hard to come to terms with. Well, apparently a friend's son and his family would be very interested in buying the Rectory and Cass has really got a battle on her hands now. So Tom has had the bright idea that they should move into my cottage so as to make the whole transition less traumatic, and to give themselves time to look around to find what they might like to buy. Cass is thinking about it. It takes the pressure off having to find what they want quickly.'

Several different thoughts cross Angus's mind. Clearly it's difficult for Kate now, caught between her oldest friend and Plum, but at the same time he wonders if this might make Plum rethink her decision not to make a base with him, even if it's temporary to begin with.

'I don't know how to handle it. For the first time Cass is really beginning to waver about downsizing and, to be honest, I think it's right that they should do it. But, having given Plum the option, how can I back out?'

Angus smiles at her. 'It's a difficult one for me to answer. I declare an interest.'

Kate begins to laugh. 'I do see that. And I know that Plum will understand, but it doesn't really make it easier.'

'Poor Kate.' Angus sips his coffee. 'But even if Plum can't have Chapel Street it doesn't mean that they'll come here.'

'No,' agrees Kate, 'but they might start off here and then find they're too comfortable to move. Personally, I think we all need to get through Christmas before making any life-changing decisions.'

'But if you let your cottage to Cass and Tom,' says Angus, 'where will you stay when you come up from your Cornish rock? With all their stuff, you'll be a bit cramped in Chapel Street with Tom and Cass.'

Kate smiles at him. 'With you, of course,' she says. 'Simples.'

He laughs back at her, pleased at the prospect. 'I shall hold you to that. But it's a bit of a thought, isn't it? The last Christmas at the Old Rectory.' He shakes his head. 'How tiresome getting old is. I should be thinking about downsizing, too.'

'But at least you're right here in the town,' argues Kate. 'And you don't have all that land to worry about. You can walk everywhere you need to go. Tom and Cass have to get into the car for every little thing.'

'Will you come up for Christmas?' he asks her.

Kate thinks about it. 'For some of it,' she says. 'That's the thing, you see. Our families, Tom and Cass's and mine, are mostly all living half an hour away down on the Tamar now, so they don't need to stay over Christmas any more. They're having a big Boxing Day thrash down there so I'll certainly come up for that.'

'Plum suggested that they come down from London,' says Angus. 'We might have a drinks party on Christmas Eve if we can get enough chums together and then go to Midnight Mass. It's good that we can walk to church from here.'

'Sounds fun,' says Kate. 'And what about El? Has she mentioned Christmas at all?'

Angus shakes his head, thinking of how he met El recently in the Bedford with Will. He seemed a nice boy and he and El were getting on very well. Angus is pleased: El needs all the friends she can get during this period of bereavement.

'I shall invite her, of course,' he says. 'I'd hate to think of her all alone at Christmas. Even with the family here there will be room for her. And you,' he adds, smiling at her.

'I might take you up on that,' says Kate, 'though I can't quite see Tom and Cass being out of the Rectory before Christmas. Thanks, Angus. I was having a panic.'

'I think Plum will completely understand your dilemma,' he reassures her. 'Don't give it another thought. Now, I've had a rather nice idea. Tuesday is one of El's days at Book Stop. Shall we stroll down and see if she'd like to have lunch? Would that fit in with your plans?'

'It's a great idea. I'd love it,' she says at once.

His heart lifts at the prospect of company. 'Good,' he says. 'That's settled then.'

As they walk into the town, Kate thinks of times past when she lived here in Whitchurch, not far from Angus: walking to the shops, to the Bedford to meet Cass, to St Eustachius for the end-of-term school service. Perhaps Tom is right and it will be good for him and Cass to be in the town, though Kate is still wondering how she will put this change of plan to Plum. As they wait to cross the road opposite the church an old brown Morris Minor pulls up and Father Steven leans out of the driver's window to hail them. Angus raises an arm in salute, gives a cheery shout of greeting and they cross in front of him.

As they approach the bookshop, Kate wonders if El will be pleased to see them. It's been good to talk things through with Angus, and Kate's glad that El has someone like him in her corner.

El is alone in the shop, working at the computer screen and, as she glances up and sees them both, her reaction is one of pleasure. Yet Kate notices that she looks tired and her eyes show signs of soreness, as if she has been weeping.

'I'd love to have lunch,' she says. 'Simon will be back in a minute and then I can join you. Where will you be? I often go over to Church Lane. They do really good sharing boards.'

Kate hides a smile at Angus's faintly baffled expression. 'Sounds good,' she says. 'See you there.'

'El looks tired,' Angus says, following Kate into the café, glancing round at the bright modern interior set in this old Georgian house. He smiles at the white bicycle hanging above an original fireplace and at the bar with its high wooden chairs. 'I like this place,' he says unexpectedly. 'And please, before El arrives, tell me what a sharing board is so that I don't show my ignorance.'

Kate laughs as they sit down at a long table with benches on either side. 'You have to keep up,' she agrees. 'My grand-children love this place. I'll go through the menu with you now.'

He chuckles when he sees that the pizzas are named after famous cyclists, agrees that he and Kate will share a seafood board, and by the time El walks in he's enjoying a glass of Plaza Bonita Tinto.

'You look well settled,' says El, sliding in beside Kate. 'This is nice. It's been a busy morning. I can't believe Christmas is only six weeks away.'

'Speaking of which,' Angus says, 'I was telling Kate that Plum and Ian are coming down with the girls. We're hoping to have a little party on Christmas Eve and then go to Midnight Mass. Does that appeal to you, or do you have other plans?'

Kate can see from El's expression that Angus has caught her unprepared. She hesitates, clearly at a loss for words, and then recovers her composure.

'That sounds a really nice idea.' Another hesitation. 'I must admit I haven't really thought about it yet.'

'Of course you might decide that you want to spend Christmas with your family,' Angus says, 'but the offer is there.'

Watching her, Kate thinks that there's something more here than not having thought about Christmas yet. It's as if Angus's invitation has suggested the possibility of something else that El also hasn't considered yet: a new idea that has taken her off guard. To give her space, Kate begins to talk about her own plans. She describes the chaotic lives of her family and their sailing school down on the Tamar.

'It must be odd,' says El to Kate, 'your son marrying Cass's daughter.'

Angus laughs. 'At least they can't slag off their in-laws.'

'It's been a bit of a roller coaster,' Kate admits, 'but would it be too much of a pun to say that it seems to be all plain sailing at the moment?'

Their food arrives and Kate begins to instruct Angus in this new form of eating.

El sits back and watches, amused by these two old friends and their easy, affectionate relationship. Is this how Will and she might be in fifty years' time? It's difficult to know how she feels about him, partly because her sadness about Pa is colouring everything, along with the effort needed to stay strong in the new life she's making for herself. She's really grateful to have the job in Book Stop. Natasha is encouraging her, so that El is trying new things: planning a visit to the local primary school as well as making an effort to keep up with recently published books so that she can discuss them with the customers. The time she spent working in a bookshop during her gap year is really paying off. Then there are the ideas for her novel, which are beginning to make a very satisfactory pattern. She makes notes, jots down ideas and wonders if she can really make it work.

Yet all the while, this new relationship with Will is there at the back of her mind. She knows that because of his own grief for his mother he's able to empathize with her – and she was very touched by what he said about his visits being helpful to him, too – but she's still feeling embarrassed about the way she'd gone into his room in the middle of the night. He'd driven away early the following morning to get back to work and by now she feels so tired, unable to catch up on sleep, that she can hardly concentrate.

When Angus asked her about Christmas it suddenly made her wonder if Will might come down for it. This idea filled her with pleasure, and then she wondered if instead he might spend it with friends, with Christian. She realizes that she actually knows very little about Will's life and yet he's being so kind to her, trying to help her. It occurs to her that there is nobody else with whom she could discuss the texts on Pa's phone, which is odd, given that until recently she's hardly known Will at all. And supposing he were to come for Christmas, would he want to go to a drinks party and then Midnight Mass? It's becoming increasingly difficult to explain his visits and their relationship. Of course, Angus knows their shared family background, but she still occasionally has a problem with how to introduce Will to her friends.

Angus is asking her a question about her work, and she tells them that a local author has a new book published and that he will be coming into the shop to do a signing session.

'There's lots to learn,' she tells them, 'but I'm loving it. It's good that I've had some previous experience, which certainly helps, but I've a long way to go yet.'

They talk about books as they eat and suddenly Kate asks: 'Oh, by the way, have you found out who Nancy Fortescue is?'

El is startled by the question but before she can answer, Angus has picked up on it.

'*Nancy Fortescue*?' he asks, beginning to smile. 'Surely you know about *Nancy Fortescue*, Kate?'

Kate shakes her head, looking puzzled. 'Should I?'

'Never been to The Garden House?' he asks. 'Surely you have? The *Nancy Fortescue* is the little wooden dinghy on the lake. She's named after a member of the family who created the gardens.'

El can hardly believe it. 'A boat?'

'Mmm.' Angus smiles at her surprise. 'Of course, Marina was a real garden person, so we often went to The Garden House. She used to do some volunteering there quite a few years back. So who was asking about *Nancy Fortescue*?'

'I can't quite remember now,' says El, prevaricating, confused by this revelation. 'It might have been a customer. So where is The Garden House?'

'Over at Buckland Monachorum,' answers Angus. 'Out of Tavistock on the Plymouth road and turn off at Yelverton. Amazing place. You must go and see it. Or I could take you. We could all go.'

El feels bewildered by all this information and unnerved by Angus's suggestion. Her whole instinct tells her that she needs to go to this place with Will – he must be the first to go with her – but how can she explain this? Unwittingly Kate comes to her rescue.

'I shouldn't think they'll be open in November, will they?' she asks.

El feels a huge relief coupled with great disappointment. She doesn't want to visit these gardens for the first time with a group of people, but she can't bear to think that she can't go there with Will very soon. Angus is frowning, trying to remember.

'I think that they might be open at the weekends through the winter,' he says. 'But actually, this probably isn't the best time of year for your first visit. Maybe we should go in the spring.'

They all agree that this is a better plan and the party begins to break up. El hugs them both, promises to stay in touch, and hurries out. She can't wait to get back to the shop and google The Garden House.

CHAPTER EIGHTEEN

Julia walks in the lanes above Buckfast, glimpsing the pale stone of the abbey walls, surrounded by bleached wintry fields and bare-twigged hedgerows. She watches the squirrels, those high-wire acrobats, launching themselves from branch to branch, leaping, climbing, racing each other, as they swing high up in the beech trees. The low November sunshine burnishes the holly berries into fiery crimson and their prickly leaves into shining emerald. A cock pheasant breaks cover, running stiff-legged across the lane, scrambling awkwardly between the bars of a gate and launching suddenly into clumsy flight, whilst Bertie stands disconsolate, his head thrust through the lower bars, watching its escape.

'You wouldn't have liked it, anyway,' Julia tells him. 'Think of all those feathers.'

She walks on, hands in her pockets, thinking of her visit to The Garden House with Davy. How strange it was to be there with him and not with Martin. How odd to be showing him the places where she and Martin met, having coffee in the café again. At least the spell was broken: that sense of being unable to return. She knows now that she can go back to wander the familiar groves, and no longer feel that in some way she's been barred from Paradise.

'We've got to get ourselves back to the garden.'

She remembers that was Martin's very first text clue: Crosby, Stills, Nash & Young. He loved crosswords, puzzles, Sudoku, and she'd had to sharpen her wits to keep up with him. How she misses that. Deliberately she turns her mind to more positive thoughts, glad that she's told Davy, who is encouraging her, keeping in touch. And soon the boys will be home for Christmas: her heart lifts at the prospect. She's got a little plan at the back of her mind that she might invite Davy now that he's on his own. Of course, she'll need to check with Laurence and Ollie, but she knows that they're very fond of Davy. It's something to think about, to plan for . . . However, as she turns for home, calling to Bertie, Julia is thinking about El. She wonders if she's sold the Pig Pen, the cottage Julia has never seen, and where El's living and working. How proud Martin was of her; how he loved her.

'I wonder how they'd get on,' he mused once. 'Your boys and my girl and Freddie.'

She had no answer for him. It seemed impossible that they could merge into one family, yet other people did it. Why should it seem so impossible for her and Martin? They both knew he would find it difficult moving into her house, and he wasn't prepared to present El and Freddie with a second family of stepbrothers, and there certainly wasn't room in the Pig Pen. But the prospect of selling everything, finding some new place for them all, with Julia's boys in the middle of exams, was too daunting to contemplate. Now Julia is glad that they didn't attempt it. At least she is still in her own home, her boys' home, and if they were to leave it, then they will all three decide together what might happen after that. As she strides home, Julia wonders why it should be her luck to lose both the men she'd loved. Then, once again, she deliberately turns her mind away from grief to an article she's researching for *Devon Life* about wedding venues on the south-west peninsula. It's an interesting prospect and she's glad of the distraction. Work is a good antidote to sadness. And then there's Davy's new project, which might just be worth considering after all.

It's odd that the visit with Davy across the moor to The Garden House seems to have unlocked some kind of paralysis in her mind. Ever since she read of Martin's death she's been in a strange sort of limbo, only just able to hold herself together. Now she is able to think more clearly, to begin to allow the past its place in her life. Sometimes she's felt like a fly in amber, stuck, unable to move, but since that trip back to the garden she's begun to free herself up.

Is it possible that one day she might be able to make some overture towards El? Instinctively she shakes her head. The question comes to mind: what do you hope to achieve? She can't see the answer to that. No one can bring Martin back and what advantage could it possibly be to her or to El to attempt some kind of conversation? Yet she longs to know that El is recovering, even happy. She would give much to know that El is moving forward. Julia remembers her at the funeral, surrounded by her friends, and she knows that they will be supporting her.

Julia turns into the driveway, Bertie just ahead, his tail waving as he anticipates a treat. She opens the back door, lets him into the passage and they go together into the warm kitchen.

As she makes some tea, gives Bertie a biscuit, checks his water, Julia thinks again about her Christmas plan, determined to make it a good one for the boys but knowing, too, that the inclusion of someone who isn't very close family can keep arguments at bay, add a different and interesting dimension. Her own parents are spending Christmas with her brother in Scotland and her mother-in-law is going to Hong Kong to her daughter's family, so Julia is able to make up her own guest list without fear of upsetting anyone.

Julia leans back against the Aga, her hands around her favourite Cath Kidston mug, sipping her tea and remembering how much Bob loved Christmas. All the aspects of it – the tree, the decorations, the food and drink – brought out his generosity, his love of hospitality. The little Georgian house was filled with lights and noise and tantalizing smells – and people. After he died it was almost impossible for Julia to recreate the atmosphere. Bob was so much larger than life, and though the three of them did their best, his absence was palpable. They got better at it, adapted, and Julia is determined to do everything she can to make it a special time this year.

She has no memories of Christmases with Martin. They were never together. Julia sips her tea, remembering that strange sense of unity, of intimacy. How to explain that feeling of belonging, of anticipation before each rendezvous? She wonders if it could have survived ordinary day-to-day living, imagining how it might have shrivelled and dwindled under the sceptical gaze of their children. The whole point of it was that it was something apart, something rare and secret. Perhaps each of them, instinctively knowing this, had connived at keeping the status quo, neither asking too much of the other or putting any strain on this special relationship they shared.

As she looks around the kitchen, her glance drifting across the cyclamen in their pots along the windowsill and fixing on the Charlotte Marlow painting Martin gave her, Julia reflects on how little she'd known him. She'd never seen him under stress, with the flu, in a bad mood. He'd never seen her in a panic with a looming deadline, shouting at the boys as she tried to muster them for school in the mornings, grumpy with a cold. They were at their best with each other and now Julia is glad of it. They talked briefly about the people that were the framework of their lives – she told him about Davy and her workmates, and he mentioned names: Angus, who was his senior partner, and other friends, Tom and Cass and Kate – and they talked about their children, but they also discussed books and music and plays. Martin went to the Wharf cinema in Tavistock, whilst she went to the Barn Cinema at Dartington. Each knew what the other was going to see, each kept the other aware of new productions, so that they could discuss them, exchange ideas and laughter. Neither of them ever said: 'What a pity we can't go together.' Even here they kept to their codes: no regrets, no complaining. The secrecy was absolute. And it is this aspect of it that makes it almost inconceivable to imagine describing it to El. What would it be like for her to know about something her father had kept totally hidden from her? Surely she would feel hurt, betrayed? Her own loyalty to him was such a strong, vivid thing, and for it she'd risked her mother's displeasure.

How lucky we were, thinks Julia, that we never bumped into any of those friends of his while we were at The Garden House.

That was their greatest risk, yet they couldn't resist the gardens. And they were always careful. Anyone seeing them might have assumed that they were two friends who had met by chance whilst walking in the gardens, having coffee on the terrace. Only in Bristol at the flat were they able to be totally free.

'It's odd,' Martin said one evening as they had supper at The Florist in Park Street, 'how flowers seem to follow us around.'

It amused them that not long after they'd begun to use the flat, this restaurant, which hitherto looked rather like a gentlemen's club, should suddenly have a new name and a whole new décor.

Now, a sudden twist of pain to the heart causes Julia to hunch over her mug, eyes tight closed. However can she manage without those moments, without him? But she knows the answer. Work will get her through, as it got her through after Bob died: the discipline of work will keep her focused. And she has her boys to think about, to plan for.

Bertie nudges her leg and she smiles down at him.

'And you,' she says. 'Don't worry. I'm not forgetting you.'

It was Davy who looked after Bertie on those rare dashes to Bristol. He and Phil loved Bertie and were happy to manage him between them at their little house in Plymstock. They teased Julia about her secret lover and she laughed back, pretending to go along with the joke, although she told them that she was going to see an elderly godparent. She didn't care if they believed her or not and Bertie enjoyed his little holidays. It's sad for Davy that he and Phil have split up and, on an impulse, Julia takes up her phone from the kitchen table and texts Davy.

How about Sunday lunch at the pub? Xx

Perhaps by then she might have had a chance to speak to the boys about inviting him for Christmas. Davy will be the perfect guest, entering into the spirit of it all, ready to have fun.

'And you'd like it, wouldn't you?' she says to Bertie, stroking his head, gently pulling his ears.

The short winter's day is fading, the wind is rising. Julia pulls down the blinds at the windows and turns on a lamp. A text pings in. It's from Davy.

Great idea. Thanks xx

Julia feels relief. It's something to look forward to, a little light shining in the lonely days ahead.

CHAPTER NINETEEN

Cass and Kate come out of Brigid Foley's boutique in Paddons Row and head off towards Chapel Street.

'That was rather fun,' says Cass contentedly.

Brigid is celebrating twenty-seven years in Tavistock with special offers and a glass of bubbly, and Cass is carrying several bags. Looking at her, Kate wonders if her old friend might be thinking that living in the town could have its advantages.

'I'm sure that Tom will totally agree that you need several special outfits for Christmas,' she says. 'Or will you just pretend that you've had them for ever, like you usually do?'

'The day that Tom notices what I'm wearing I'll get me to a nunnery,' answers Cass.

'You say that,' says Kate, 'safe in the knowledge that there aren't any left. None that would have you, anyway.'

They walk in silence for a short way and then Cass says: 'I can't bear to think that this might be our last Christmas at the Rectory.'

Kate tries to think of comforting words but can only come up with platitudes, so she says nothing.

'I know they're true, the things that everybody says,' Cass says. 'That it's better to do it whilst we're still fit. That it's better to jump than be pushed. All that stuff. But it doesn't make it any easier.'

Still Kate remains silent as they turn into Chapel Street, but Cass continues her train of thought.

'The thing is, we can't afford to refuse this offer. They're really keen, the money's there, we'd be crazy not to accept it.'

They stop outside Kate's gate where Cass's car is parked and she loads her parcels in and then pauses.

'I need the loo,' she says. 'OK if I just dash in for a minute?'

Kate unlocks her front door and Floss comes to meet them as they go into the cottage. Cass goes upstairs and Kate takes off her coat, thinking about how her old friend must be feeling, trying to imagine what it must be like to live in the same house for forty years.

'At least,' she says as Cass comes back downstairs, 'this place isn't strange to you. That might help a bit while you're deciding what you want and where you want to be.'

Cass glances around her. She bends to stroke Floss and looks a little less bleak. 'It's a dear little cottage and totally different from the Rectory, which is probably a really good thing. But what about you, Kate? Without the Rectory, or this place as a bolt hole, where will you go when you need a break from your rock? Not,' she adds hastily, 'that you couldn't stay here with us. We can all fit in. That's not a problem.'

Kate smiles to herself as she imagines them all squashed into her little cottage.

'Remember that I was always going to let it,' she reminds Cass, 'so it wasn't going to be an option for me anyway.'

She doesn't mention Plum. There's no need to give Cass an excuse for backing out.

'And anyway,' Kate adds, 'Angus has told me I can stay with him.' She makes big eyes at Cass. 'Rather good, eh? Bruno down at St Meriadoc. Angus here in Tavistock. What's not to like?'

Cass begins to laugh. 'Another FWB?' she asks.

'It'll be fun,' says Kate. 'Now if you didn't have to drive home I'd offer you a glass of wine but, as it is, after your bubbly with Brigid, I shan't.'

'I suppose that's one advantage of living in the town,' says Cass, preparing to leave. 'You can walk everywhere.'

'As long as you're not too drunk to stand up,' agrees Kate. 'Sure you've got everything?'

Cass nods. 'Are you sure you won't come back with me for lunch?'

Kate raises her eyebrows. 'Are you kidding me? And have to watch Tom's face when he sees no less than three Brigid Foley bags? Give me a break.'

Cass laughs. 'Traitor. OK then. See you soon.'

As they hug, there's a knock at the door and Kate opens it to see Plum on the doorstep. Her stomach gives a little lurch of apprehension but luckily Cass shows no intention of stopping.

'Sorry, sweetheart. Got to dash,' she says to Plum. 'Tom will be wanting his lunch. Be seeing you.'

She hurries away to her car and Kate leads the way back into the cottage.

'I didn't know you were down.' she says. 'This is nice,' though it isn't nice at all. She doesn't quite know how she's going to explain to Plum that she'll be letting the cottage to Cass and Tom. But Plum forestalls her.

'I got down last night,' she says. 'Dad and I were talking and he told me about Cass and Tom and how you've been put into a dilemma about the cottage. I just wanted to say that you mustn't worry, Kate. Cass is your oldest friend. I quite see that you've got to let them have it. Dad says they've been given an offer they can't refuse and they won't want to make some rash decision about buying. It's the obvious thing to do.'

Kate is taken aback by Plum's generous understanding, though not surprised. Plum is a good girl. And Kate is very grateful to Angus for dealing with it for her.

'That's amazingly kind of you, Plum,' she says. 'I have to say I was in a complete two and eight, especially as I'd promised you first refusal. I feel really bad about it.'

'Well, don't,' says Plum swiftly. 'Dad said you were in a state about it, which is why I came round. Actually, it's good to see you.'

She looks around her with a strange expression as if she's reminding herself where she is and Kate realizes that, ever since she arrived, Plum has been looking rather stressed; not at all her usual calm, happy self.

'Are you OK, Plum?' she asks, concerned. 'Look, let's have a drink. Would you like some lunch? I'm about to have something. Sandwich? A bowl of soup?'

Plum shakes her head and then suddenly changes her mind.

'Actually, I'd really like that,' she says. 'Dad's out at one of his meetings. Are you sure? It's a bit much just to rock up uninvited.'

'Don't be silly,' says Kate. 'Let's have a drink and then we'll decide what we're going to eat. I've got a very nice Shiraz. Are you OK with that?'

Plum crouches to stroke Flossie, hugging her, putting her cheek against the soft coat and closing her eyes.

'Her coat is so soft,' she murmurs. 'Much softer than a Lab's coat.' There's a little pause. 'I'm in a bad way, Kate,' Plum says, casually. 'And if I don't talk to someone I shall go mad.'

Kate stares down at her, alarmed. Then she continues to fill the two glasses and picks them up.

'Come on,' she says. 'Let's go into the sitting-room and you can talk to me.'

Plum sits down in a corner of the sofa with Flossie beside her. Kate doesn't tell Flossie to get off the sofa because she can see that just at this moment Plum needs her warmth and comfort. Flossie settles herself close to Plum and Kate puts a glass of wine on a small table beside them. She doesn't attempt to encourage Plum to speak, she simply sits opposite and waits.

Plum hugs Flossie and sips at her wine. Her gaze is inward, as if she's marshalling her thoughts, and then she takes a deep breath.

'I've just seen El,' she begins, almost conversationally, putting her glass on the table. 'Up near the bookshop. I see her now every time I come home.'

A pause. Kate, slightly puzzled, desists from pointing out that this is probably because El lives and works here, and waits.

'The thing is, you see,' Plum raises her head and looks at Kate, and her expression is strained, almost fearful, 'the terrible thing is, Kate, that I'm the reason for Martin's divorce.'

Nothing could have prepared Kate for this. It seems quite unbelievable that Plum, of all people, should be the cause of anyone's divorce. But now is not the moment to say so. Kate nods, as if to encourage Plum to continue, and after a moment she does.

'We had a . . .' She hesitates over which word she should choose, then shakes her head. 'It's difficult to know how to put it. It wasn't an affair. Or a one-night stand. Not really, though it was just once . . . not long after I lost the baby.'

'Maybe,' Kate says, taking a chance as Plum remains silent, 'it was just one of those moments that can happen. Some action – kindness, for instance, mutual comfort – can just tip over into something more. Especially if you've had a drink . . .'

Kate sips at her own wine, wondering what she's saying, totally at a loss. But Plum is gazing at her in amazement.

'Yes,' she says. 'That's just exactly what it was like. Martin dropped in to see us on his way home from a client. D'you remember that naval hiring we had at Dousland? Well, Ian was at sea, the girls were away at school, and I was having the most terrible low. Martin was so sweet. Well, you remember how kind he was? I think he wasn't particularly happy at the time and we were trying to cheer each other up. Felicity was away so I invited him to supper.'

She stares at Kate almost beseechingly, willing her to understand, and Kate smiles at her.

'Darling Plum,' she says, 'occasionally these things happen. We all know they shouldn't but there are times when life is so completely awful that the physical comfort of another human being is the most wonderful and necessary thing in the world.'

'But it was wrong,' mutters Plum, hugging Flossie. 'It wasn't just comfort but . . . more than that.'

'Let him who is without sin cast the first stone,' says Kate. 'So you comforted each other and it got a bit out of hand. It happens.'

Plum is silent for a moment. She takes another sip of wine.

'But what I can't understand is how Felicity knew about it,' she says. 'Nothing happened after that one . . . moment. Ian was posted to Portsmouth, and then I heard that they'd separated – Dad always kept me up with all the news – then about a year later that Felicity was divorcing Martin. I didn't know what to do. By then we were in Washington. I suppose Martin refused to tell her that it was me.'

'Probably,' says Kate gently, 'because it wasn't you.'

Plum sets her glass down on the table and stares at her.

'Wasn't . . . ?'

Kate shakes her head. 'It was too long afterwards. Think about it. Anyway, I saw Martin with another woman. Once down on a beach in Cornwall and once at The Garden House.' She hesitates. 'And then she was at his funeral.'

Plum looks thunderstruck. 'But who was she?'

Kate hesitates. She recognized the woman, Julia Braithwaite, from a local television series but she's reluctant to name her. Nobody has ever mentioned her in connection with Martin. And Plum suddenly understands this.

'It doesn't matter,' she says quickly. 'But do you mean he was seeing her all along?'

Kate thinks about the time frame of events: Martin's moment with Plum before she moved away, followed by his separation, and then after some months, his divorce. She shakes her head.

'Probably not. I'm not certain when this other woman came into the frame but I saw them at The Garden House before he was divorced.'

Plum's whole body slumps with relief, she closes her eyes and she hugs Flossie tightly. 'So you really believe that I wasn't the cause of it?'

'I shouldn't think so for a moment. I have no doubt at all that Martin was seriously involved with this woman.'

Briefly, Kate sees the scene in her head: Martin and Julia Braithwaite walking across the deserted beach, a cold wind whipping the waves into little peaks. Arm in arm, tightly linked, heads close together they were laughing. She called Flossie to her, clipping on her lead, and then walked quickly away in the opposite direction. They didn't see her, locked into their own private world.

Plum is watching her. She looks calmer, as if a weight has been lifted from her.

'I really want to believe you,' she says.

'I'm certain that Felicity knows absolutely nothing about you and Martin. She would never have kept quiet about it. Try to see it in perspective, Plum. There was no follow-up, no ongoing affair. OK, I'm not saying that it wasn't wrong, but remember your own situation at that time and the fact that Martin's marriage was a non-event and cut yourself some slack.' She pauses. 'You didn't tell Ian?'

Plum shakes her head. 'Oddly, though, I suspect that Ian might understand. I was in a pretty bad way that year after James died and he was away a lot.'

'Well, let's not test him at this late date,' says Kate lightly. 'Good, so nobody knows . . .'

Plum is shaking her head again, looking as if she might burst into tears.

'Oh, for Christ's sake,' says Kate, irritable in her concern. 'Who did you tell?'

'Issy. I told my friend Issy. We were having one of those girls' nights out and I drank a bit too much and, you know how it is, I just blurted it out.'

'Issy,' repeats Kate slowly. 'Issy? You mean that woman who was in the Bedford?'

She remembers the clever, watchful face and her heart sinks. Plum looks contrite, embarrassed.

'Yes. I was at school with her. God, I am a fool.'

Kate is inclined to agree with her but manages to control her impatience.

'I suppose,' she says thoughtfully, 'with Martin dead and Felicity remarried, it's all rather water under the bridge . . .'

'No, no,' says Plum quickly. 'I couldn't bear for Dad to know, or our friends. And then Ian might get to hear now that we're moving back. But the person I feel most badly about is El. I can hardly bear to talk to her as it is, I feel so guilty.' For a moment Plum seems about to dissolve into tears. 'I dread to think that she might find out. And Issy is a bit, well, she likes a bit of a drama. And when I was with her the other day I just got this feeling that she was rather enjoying it, as if she were, you know, kind of holding it over my head?'

Sitting there in her jeans, her fair hair looped back behind her ears, clutching Floss, Plum reminds Kate of a younger Plum. Way back she wondered if one of her twin sons, Giles, and Plum might make a match of it. She and Giles were alike: gentle, kind, loving people. Then Giles met Tessa and Plum met Ian and they went in different directions. Kate is very fond of Plum; she can't bear to think of her labouring under this sense of guilt or fear of exposure.

They both hear a phone ping. 'Mine, I think,' says Kate, and gets up and goes into the kitchen to find it. When she gets back Plum is still sitting in a huddle.

'It's your old dad,' Kate says. 'The meeting finished early and he wonders if you want to go home for lunch or if you have other plans?'

'No,' says Plum quickly. 'I don't want to go back just yet. Or is that pathetic?'

'Of course you can stay. Look, shall I invite him to share the soup? That way you can normalize a bit whilst we're all together.'

'That's a great idea, Kate,' Plum says gratefully. 'Are you sure?'

'Sure I'm sure,' says Kate. 'By the time he's walked over here you'll be a bit calmer and then we can all talk about Cass and Tom downsizing.'

'Maybe Ian and I can bunk in with Dad, after all,' Plum says thoughtfully. 'Just to begin with. It would give me time to look around and see what's going.'

'Sounds like a plan,' agrees Kate. 'And you can always escape to London when things get tough. So finish that drink and I'll heat the soup.'

'And thanks, Kate,' says Plum, looking up at her, still hugging Flossie. 'Really, thanks. There's nobody else I could have talked to like this. I can't tell you how grateful I am.'

Kate smiles at her. 'Don't be a twit,' she says.

In the kitchen she takes a deep breath and begins to prepare some lunch.

CHAPTER TWENTY

The Garden House – El tries to imagine it as she drives out of Tavistock towards Yelverton. She's told Will about Angus's throwaway comment in Church Lane.

'The *Nancy Fortescue* is a boat,' she said. 'It's a little boat on a lake at some sort of garden.'

She'd texted him, her excitement making it impossible to wait until his next visit, and he FaceTimed her straight back.

'A boat?' He sounded disappointed. 'Really? So where is this garden? Is it National Trust?'

'No, it's called The Garden House and it's run by a trust and volunteers. The trouble is, in the winter it's only open on Fridays, Saturdays and Sundays.' She hesitated. 'I suppose you can't get down?'

When she first thought about going to find the *Nancy Fortescue* it seemed perfectly natural that she should ask Will to accompany her. He's been down to see her, between flights, several times now and somehow it has become their quest. Now, as she talked to him, she could hear noises and voices behind him, and suddenly Christian's face appeared beside Will's and he called out 'Hi, El!' Will shooed him away, laughing, but somehow El felt inhibited.

'I can't get down this weekend,' Will said. 'I'm flying. Where is it, this place? Is it far from you?'

'No,' El answered, feeling disappointed, as well as inhibited. 'About ten or fifteen minutes.'

Christian and someone else were still making a noise, laughing and talking, and El suddenly couldn't bear having this conversation with them able to overhear what Will was saying. Up until then this whole thing about Pa's phone and the texts had been private, and she was unwilling to say any more.

'Never mind,' she said cheerfully. 'I'll go over and have a look round to see what it's like. I'll let you know if I find anything. See you later.'

She cut him off and then felt as if she'd behaved childishly. She realized that it wasn't simply the privacy issue that was niggling her, it was listening to their voices and their laughter. She remembers, on a drive to Chagford in Will's car, picking up a Kylie Minogue CD. She held it up, eyebrows raised, and he gave a quick glance sideways at it, grinned and shook his head.

'Not mine. Christian's.'

Now, she thrusts the memory away. She doesn't want to think about it, or to examine her feelings for Will or his for Christian; she wants to concentrate on the texts: to crack the code. As she drives out towards Yelverton on this bright, late November Sunday morning, she knows, at least, that Angus and Plum and Kate won't appear unexpectedly in the gardens. They'll be in church and she is free to explore. In Horrabridge she turns up on to the moor and heads towards Buckland Monachorum. Up here cars are parked. Families are walking their dogs, whilst ponies graze, ready to kick up their heels and canter away if the children or dogs come too close. El drives slowly, looking for a signpost, and here it is: The Garden

House. The wide gateway leads into a car park, half empty, and El pulls into a space near to the entrance where she can see a small group of people. She switches off the engine and looks around.

Did Pa come here? He loved to visit gardens, and he enjoyed his pots of plants and shrubs, especially the really big tub with the acer tree in it. Perhaps this is where he bought them. As she gets out and walks across to the visitor reception she can see that there's a plant sales area right next to it.

El pays her entrance fee, takes a map from the friendly volunteer and walks out into the gardens. She sees from the map that the lake is near something called the Jubilee Arboretum, so she heads off that way, seeing the old house amongst the trees, noticing signs to the tearooms. The garden is quiet, deserted, the borders empty of flowers, yet here suddenly is a bright gash of colour: a bush of bare rods, shining scarlet in an unexpected gleam of sunshine. She turns into a walled garden that, even at this time of year, is beautiful, and wonders what it must look like in the summer. A stone arch is ahead and she looks through it eagerly, hoping to see the lake and the boat. The water lies still, reflecting the grey skies, skimmed with silvery pond weed, but there is no sign of a boat. El is surprised at the depth of her disappointment. After all, what would it prove: what could it show her? She walks slowly round the lake, seeing the bench, wondering if this is where Pa met the woman who sent him texts, whose voice said that she and *Nancy Fortescue* were waiting for him.

The stab of jealousy takes El by surprise. It hurts her to think that Pa had this other friendship, one that used codes and jokes, about which he'd told her nothing. She knows she's being childish, but the pain is real, mixed as it is with her grief and all the regrets and this new knowledge of the terrible finality of death.

A chill breeze ruffles the surface of the lake and El jams her fists into her coat pockets and walks quickly towards the tearoom. She needs coffee, and she wishes that Will was here with her. It would have been different with Will; he would have kept her balanced, focused on the clues, on the code. She makes her way to the house and into the hall, and looks around her. She sees that there are two rooms, the second of which opens on to a terrace where picnic tables are set out. A young man appears behind her and asks if she would like some coffee and she follows him into the first room where a few people are sitting at tables and there are some delicious-looking cakes set out.

El chooses some cake, orders a latte and sits down by the tall sash window. She surveys the other groups, glances at a little exhibition of watercolour paintings on the wall and stiffens with surprise. They remind her of the one hanging in the big room at the Pig Pen. She stands up to look more closely, notices the artist's signature, Charlotte Marlow, and wonders if this is where Pa bought it. Another mystery. She eats her cake, drinks her coffee, trying to imagine Pa here. Her relationship with him has been based on a shared passion for the moor and literature, and she struggles with this new revealing of her own character. She tries to analyse these unexpected feelings of jealousy, first with Will and now with Pa. She's never felt like this before and she doesn't like it. She's believed herself to be a generous, liberal-minded person. Now, it seems that she can't come to terms with Will's easy-going relationship with Christian, or Pa's with the mysterious J of the texts.

She wonders if she should walk round more of the gardens, but somehow not finding the *Nancy Fortescue* has confused her.

She'd pinned her hopes on it, as if in some way this would help her. She eats the last crumb of cake and swallows the remainder of her coffee feeling dispirited, but she smiles at the young man as she pays her bill and walks back to her car.

She's hardly got home before she gets a text from Will.

Did you go? What was it like?

El stares at this text, trying to regain those former feelings of excitement at the prospect of another clue, comforted that he should ask. She replies briefly:

N F wasn't there.

She can't quite understand her lethargy, her lack of purpose. His next text surprises her.

Send me the photographs.

El feels perplexed: what photographs? Then she understands him. Knowing his interest, his frustration that he couldn't come to find *Nancy Fortescue* or to see the gardens, he would have expected her to have taken some photographs, even spotted some clues to the codes. She's filled with annoyance that it never occurred to her to do this: that she just walked in and walked out again. Feeling inadequate she texts him back.

Didn't take any.

Almost instantly her phone rings.

'Didn't take any?' he demands, as if he is continuing a conversation. 'Seriously? What were you doing then?'

'I don't know,' she says feebly. 'It kind of threw me, the boat not being there. I'd worked myself up to seeing it and there was nothing there.'

'Nothing?'

'Well, the lake was there,' she says irritably, 'covered in a kind of weed, but no boat.'

'And you didn't ask anybody where it was, or if that's where it usually is?'

El has an odd feeling that she might burst into tears. She can't understand this volatility, that change from expectation and excitement to complete desolation.

'No,' she says wearily. 'No, I didn't think to do that.'

'Are you OK?'

Will's voice is gentler now, which somehow makes it even worse. She wants to shout at him: 'No, I am not OK and I don't know why,' but remains silent.

'Listen,' he's saying, 'I can get down next Thursday after-noon, but I'd have to go back early on Saturday morning. How would that be for you? Are you working those days? Didn't you say The Garden House is open on a Friday? Perhaps we could go together. I might spot things you've missed.'

El closes her eyes tightly and tries not to sound too grateful or too keen.

'I'm working on Saturday this week,' she says, 'but other-wise that would be good. I wasn't thinking clearly. I was just so sure *Nancy Fortescue* would be there.'

'I can imagine that,' he says. 'I'm really looking forward to seeing this place. So you just went and looked at the lake and came out again?'

'Not quite,' she answers, her spirits reviving. 'I went into the tearooms and had coffee and cake. It was good.'

'I like the sound of that,' he answers, and she can hear the smile in his voice. 'We need to get our priorities right. So I should be with you by about four o'clock on Thursday. I'll text you just to confirm. Look after yourself, El. 'Bye for now.'

El puts her phone on the table and as she turns away her glance is caught by the watercolour hanging above the sofa.

She goes closer to look at the signature. It's the same artist: Charlotte Marlow. It hangs amongst a small group of water-colours. Pa liked to support local artists, and she hadn't particularly noticed any one of them before. It's a small painting and El lifts it from its peg and turns it over. The label reads: Astrantia. Moulin Rouge. El stares at it, remembering the text. She can hardly believe it. Moulin Rouge is a shrub and almost certainly is at The Garden House. She's delighted to have cracked one of the clues and instinctively she reaches for her phone and sends a text to Will:

I've found Moulin Rouge and it's not in Paris, it's at The Garden House.

Then she hangs the painting back in its place and goes into the kitchen to make herself some lunch.

CHAPTER TWENTY-ONE

Christmas in the town: Dickensian evening with the town crier, the Christmas lights switched on at six o'clock. The main street is pedestrianized and shops are open until nine in the evening. There are some stalls set up along the pavements, and in the bookshop there are wine and nibbles for the regulars. El is busy serving customers, recommending books, pouring drinks, when Angus and Kate come in together, but she is able to spend a few moments with them before she is required to serve another customer.

'This is fun,' Angus says to Kate. 'I like to see everyone getting the Christmas spirit. It's a pity that Plum's gone back to London. She would have enjoyed this.'

He still feels slightly guilty that he pre-empted Kate by telling Plum that Cass and Tom were downsizing and might like the cottage, but Kate has been very calm about it all.

'I hated the thought that Plum knew that you and I were talking about her plans behind her back,' she told him, 'but in the end it worked out very well. She's been very good about it and, to be honest, I think this is the best solution. After all, Ian won't be ashore that often and they'll spend his long leaves at their flat in London. I can't see that they really need to rent anything, with you in that great big house on your own. And I think that it will be just the boost Cass and Tom need to make the crucial decision to sell. Anyway, they might find something to buy quite quickly and then the cottage will be up for grabs again, and if Plum still wants to rent it, she can have it then.'

Angus sips his wine reflectively. He supposes that his guilt springs from the fact that it seems he has got his own way and will be seeing more of his family. After her visit to Kate, Plum was much more cheerful than she's been of late, more like her old positive self, and he was relieved though slightly puzzled. He expected her to be irritated by losing the opportunity of renting Kate's cottage but she was unconcerned by it; other things seemed to be occupying her mind. He raises his glass to Kate, who grins at him. The other plus to the plan, of course, is that in the future Kate might stay with him when she comes up from St Meriadoc. That will definitely be a bonus.

He watches El dealing with a young mother with two excited small children in tow, and is glad that she's managing so well. She's clearly loving working here with Natasha and Simon, and he can see that she's getting a lot of support from the customers who knew Martin. Mentally he raises his glass to his old friend and partner. Life – and death – is so random; so indifferent. Turning to the shelves behind him, Angus begins to read the titles of the books, to think about Christmas presents, deciding to ask El's advice when it comes to choosing for his grand-daughters, who are much the same age as she is. He thinks about his drinks party; his family at home with him on Christmas Day for the first time for three years. Reasons to be cheerful.

*

Kate watches his tall, stooping figure with affection. She's very fond of Angus and is very glad to see him getting his own way. It will give him so much joy to have all his family visiting him, staying with him, even if those visits are random and therefore not necessarily all of them together. To be their base when the ship is in will please him immensely. And, if Kate's honest, she admits it will be rather nice to stay with him occasionally, to go to the cinema at the Wharf with him, when she comes up from St Meriadoc. Somehow she can't quite see herself sharing the only bathroom in the cottage with Tom, who has definitely become a very grumpy old man, fond though she is of him. The cottage will seem cramped enough as it is, after the Rectory, without adding guests to it.

She thinks about Plum. From childhood upwards there has been a sweetness of temperament, a generosity of spirit that has made her much beloved, and it seems hard that one small act has caused her so much pain. Kate can imagine that losing a child is devastating. Coping with your grief alone whilst your husband is at sea must be very hard, and Kate can't bring herself to judge Plum or Martin for their brief moment of shared comfort. She wonders too about Issy and whether Plum's guilt is magnifying her fear of her old friend. Watching Issy that morning in the Bedford, Kate could see that she might well be a bit of a loose cannon – someone who simply cannot help putting the cat amongst the pigeons for the sheer hell of it – but she wonders just how much of a threat Issy is and how much harm she might do. She suspects that Issy simply hoped to draw Plum closer to her: to bind her into a conspiracy rather than to expose her. Now, as Kate watches El, busy and happy, it seems inconceivable that she should hear about her father and Plum from a stranger. Briefly, Kate thinks about Martin walking on the beach with Julia. How well he kept his secrets, but what if El should discover them?

It's with relief that Kate sees Ruth, her old friend and neighbour in Chapel Street, come into the shop with her little dog, Scrumpy. Kate waves and goes to greet her, glad to be distracted from her thoughts.

Finally Cass and Tom arrive. It's become a tradition on the night that the Christmas lights are switched on to meet in the town, pop into Book Stop, and then go across to the Bedford for supper in the bar.

'It's such fun on Dickensian evening,' says Cass, kissing Kate and giving El a hug. 'On these occasions I can see how much easier it might be to live in the town and walk everywhere. Tom got the last space in the Bedford's car park. It's such a pity you can't come and have supper with us, El, but I suppose you'll be busy for a while yet.'

El explains that the shop will be open until nine o'clock and thanks Cass for the offer, but secretly she knows that by the time the shop closes she'll be more than ready to drive home, have a shower, then listen to her music and read for a while. It's been a long day and she's very tired. Nevertheless it's worth it. She's loved the friendliness, the party atmosphere, this new sense of belonging. She's tried to explain it to her mother, who clearly thinks it's crazy to waste her talents in a small community on the edge of Dartmoor.

'You could be working in publishing,' she said, 'or in a literary agency. Lucy has got a job with the BBC.'

El is sad that her mother is unable to enter into her feelings, to feel any pride in what El is trying to do. Even Freddie, who tries to understand but clearly would rather she sold the Pig

Pen and embarked on a career more worthy of her qualifications, is unconvinced that any good can come of her endeavours. But she is determined to keep on with her plan, to try to make a go of things here. She's grateful to her father's friends who support her and praise her efforts. And to Will, an unexpected ally.

She rather wishes he could be here this evening, seeing her in her new environment, amongst her friends. Quickly she gets out her phone and sends him a text. Then a customer claims her attention and she puts her private life to the back of her mind and concentrates on the job in hand.

CHAPTER TWENTY-TWO

There is nothing to see but the infinite. The flight deck is dark. There is no moon. The sea is invisible beneath the black sheet that stretches out from the nose cone to the horizon. Will is leaning forward in his seat, looking up through the windshield, through the atmosphere, to the familiar comforting guardians in his sky. He smiles. On a night like this he could find his way home without a compass. To his right the Plough, on the nose the Little Bear, stretching down from Polaris, the Pole Star: the ever steady, ever north. Tonight, from here, at thirty-six thousand feet over the North Atlantic, one hundred miles off the coast of Portugal, Polaris will take Will home. Christian is sprawled back in his seat. He is 'taking a moment', leaving Will to monitor the aircraft. Will can feel it talking to him in the quiet hiss of the flight deck. The engines powering them north are whisper-quiet from up here in the pointy end. Will knows aircraft, is in tune with them, sensing them as they talk to him. It amuses him that he can often feel a problem before the computers will identify it. Tonight, across the switch panels, almost all is dark. Lights out means systems are working as they should and Will has eased the flight deck lighting lower and lower till the stars become vivid in the sky outside his comfortable cocoon and he can see Cygnus in flight above the north-west horizon.

On a night like this it is as if he can feel the warmth of his mother's hand in his; remembers them lying on their backs together on a rug, staring at those same stars: a cold chill in the air and in his heart; not a boy, yet not a man either.

He remembers her calm words: 'How will you remember me, Billy?'

He gripped her hand tighter, his response inarticulate. A long silence, then she raised her free hand and pointed to the vastness above them.

'Do you see those stars, Billy? Like a cross in the sky? That's Cygnus. She looks like a swan flying down the river. See, there is her head, there are her wings, and that bright star in her tail is called Deneb. Perhaps, when you look up and see her flying in the night sky, you will think of me?'

He looked up at the star swan, still unable to speak. He could see under her left wing another brighter star, almost blue-white, gleaming like a jewel: a beacon in the sky that marked the swan's position. And speaking both to the stars and to his mother, he said: 'I will, Mum. I will always.'

Will looks away from Deneb and the blue-white of Vega, glancing to the left, to the only other part of the aircraft visible from his seat. Out in the ferocious cold the glowing red navigation light on his port wing etches the winglet into the darkness. His eyes lift and move forward across the sky, arching up from the horizon, Libra, Taurus and, further towards the north, Cassiopeia reclining in her chaise longue. If only he could share all this with El . . .

This longing floors him for a moment. There was a time, not so long ago, when the idea of sharing this with anyone would not have occurred to him. There were times of quiet, of beauty, when his thoughts would stray to his mother, but no one has ever intruded into his solitude the way El does. He recalls with renewed embarrassment his exchange with Christian earlier in the flight on their way south to Tenerife.

'So how's your sister doing?'

It was well meant, casual, and undeserving of the tetchy reply.

'She's not my sister.'

He was even more irritated by Christian's explosive, involuntary laughter.

'Yes, my captain, as you say, my captain.'

'Oh, shut up, Chris.'

'Yes, sir.' And Chris was laughing again.

Will didn't intend it, didn't mean to reveal his feelings to Chris. If he's honest, he hasn't even allowed himself to consider those feelings, to consider openly what is so obvious in retrospect.

He has feelings for El, and they aren't in the least brotherly. And therein lies 'The Problem'. Are you allowed to feel that way about your stepsister?

He knows full well what his stepmother would have to say on that subject, but what about a reasonable person? Whilst he isn't sure that Christian would consider himself a 'reasonable person', he is someone Will can trust, someone whose opinion he values. And so, when they reached a natural pause in the business of operating their aircraft, he broached the subject again.

'The thing is, I rather like her . . .' His voice trailed off. Then he looked at Christian, who once more was trying not to laugh.

'Will, how many texts do you send a week? Two, three . . .
ten? Do you know how many you've sent in the last twenty-
four hours?'

Will looked sheepish.

'Seriously, mate, I'd have to be an utter idiot not to realize
you "like" El. The question is, what are you going to do about
it?'

Will was silent for a moment, and Christian stepped in
again.

'I mean, I could tell you not to fish in your own pond, but I
don't think you're going to listen to me, are you?'

And that, at least, was true.

All Will could manage in response was, 'It's difficult . . .'
before falling silent again.

'No, it isn't.' Christian sat back in his seat and pulled off his
glasses. 'Come on, Will, if you'd met El before your dad met
her mother, who would have raised an eyebrow?'

'Yeah, but can you imagine what Felicity would say if El and
I got together?'

'Felicity? Well, for starters she'd be bloody surprised,' and
both of them burst out laughing.

Will had to admit that Felicity would indeed be surprised.
She made it clear from the start that she resented so much of
the family's resources being spent on flight training. She's
never let up on her criticism of his father's continued and loyal
support, never acknowledged that it was Will's mother who
made becoming a pilot possible by insuring against the possibility of her own early death. He isn't sure if it was his relief at
finally gaining his professional licence, at that certainty of
independence that he no longer needed to rely on his father, or
perhaps a bloody-minded rebellion against Felicity's constant

disapproval, but either way he and Christian had put on quite a show at her New Year's Eve party, and she has despised him since then and has worked hard to avoid him as much as possible.

Christian was watching him, still waiting for Will to speak. Will looked away again.

'It's difficult,' he repeated lamely.

Chris nodded, sighed, and said: 'Is she worth it? Because if she's worth it the rest is irrelevant.'

And that's Christian: intuitive, direct, logical. He's always had the uncanny ability to see through Will's façade, to understand the underlying issues, and to help resolve them. Will knows that Christian has nailed it although it's the advice he was hoping to hear. El is worth it. Whatever 'it' is or would be, she's worth it. And maybe Christian's right: maybe this is all a problem in his own head. After all, before their parents married, who would have cared if he'd met this girl who was not his relative?

Idly, Will calls up the ECAM display pages reviewing the various aircraft systems, looking for tiny changes that might identify an incipient problem. All is as it should be. In his headphone he hears the Lisboa controller call an aircraft in front of them, handing that aircraft over to the French controller in Brest. There are still twenty-seven minutes before Will's aircraft reaches the same boundary, at least three hours before he is in the car heading home.

It's been a long day: an afternoon departure from Bristol, south to the Canaries. It's one of Will's favourite routes, and an unusual pleasure to be flying with Christian so soon after their last flight. It's been a long slog south to Tenerife but the arrival, routeing around Mount Teide, the volcano at the south of the island, was spectacular as usual. And yet, today, he's found this trip unusually long and irksome. He doesn't want to be here, he wants to be in Devon.

He leans forward again, looking out at the night sky, but he is no longer seeing the stars. He feels the softness of her hair on his skin, her body curled against his, small within his arms, feels her grieving, her sorrow, her loss. He has known her, the real El, for such a short time, but he yearns to be with her again, to hear her voice, to feel the casual touch of her fingers. Momentarily he considers the possibility of abandoning Christian at the airport, of getting in his car and driving straight to Devon, but he knows it isn't viable. El would not be pleased if he were to turn up at two in the morning, knocking at her door. No, he would have to go home, get some rest, but he could at least text her and see if she could get home early from the bookshop. He could be in Tavistock before lunch if she wanted him.

If she wanted him . . . ? His heart thumps. Why is he investing so much in this? Why is he presuming so much? He knows what he is beginning to feel, but how can he tell if El feels the same way? She is more than friendly towards him. She is relaxed, happy in his company and, when she was hurting, when she was in pain, she came to him, trusted him. In that moment of intimacy he felt his heart change, open, and accept her. The thought almost frightens him and leaves him unsettled and uncertain.

Beside him, Christian stirs, sits up and stretches. 'I need a cup of tea!'

Will glances at the clock. Donna, the cabin supervisor, is due to call them soon anyway, making sure that her flight deck crew are still awake. Will knows that most of his passengers will be asleep by now, so at this point in the flight the team won't be too busy and he needs the distraction. He reaches down to the comms panel.

'I'll see if they're free.'

He presses the call button to contact the cabin behind them and starts the complex process of getting tea delivered to the locked flight deck.

CHAPTER TWENTY-THREE

El and Will are driving to The Garden House. They are feeling happy this morning, in a kind of holiday mood, hoping to solve some of the clues and codes. Will arrived in time for supper, not long after El got home from the bookshop, and he came up the stairs to find her kneeling in front of the wood-burning stove, crumpling brown paper to make spills.

She grinned up at him. 'The wholesalers wrap the books in this,' she told him. 'It's great for getting the fire going. What was your journey like?'

'Pretty good. The moon's up already. It was quite eerie seeing it hanging over the moor. It was pretty icy on the roads, though.'

'Luckily the forecast is good for tomorrow,' said El, shutting the wood burner's door and standing up. She was looking forward to showing Will The Garden House. 'I've made a proper list of the texts on Pa's phone.'

On the table was a sheet of A4 with the letter J and the telephone number at the top, and underneath a list of the clues, as well as the watercolour painting, which had the words 'Moulin Rouge' on the back: another clue.

'There must be one of these plants in the garden somewhere,' El said, 'though we might need to ask one of the gardeners where it is.'

There are several texts that begin with the initials NT, which they've already decided are National Trust properties, but others are more difficult to decipher.

Will studied it. 'Well, we know *Nancy Fortescue* is there but the others could be anywhere. Still, it's a good place to start. We'll take this with us.'

And here they are, driving out towards Yelverton in the pale winter sunlight. There's been a chill wind from the east and the high moors are dusted with snow.

'I've googled some of the clues,' El says. 'It's really odd, this passion for cryptic codes. I mean, I know Pa loved his cross-words and Sudoku, but the more you look at the texts the more they look like he's just enjoying the game.'

'Well, perhaps he was. And obviously J was on that same wavelength.'

El is silent for a moment. It's still difficult for her to imagine this other life Pa was leading.

'I mean,' Will adds, 'that it might have been golf. Or darts. Or a choir. People have hobbies, passions, that they do with like-minded people.'

'Yes, but they still discuss them or refer to them, even if it's only casually.'

She knows that Will is trying to reassure her, to try to remove the feeling that she was shut out from a part of Pa's life, and she's grateful to him. It's so good to be with him in this easy unforced way, able to be completely relaxed with him. Coming to terms with Pa's sudden death, moving to the Pig Pen, starting her new job, all these things are keeping her emotionally in a whirl. It's such a relief to have him here – calm, thinking along the same lines – without having to wonder more deeply about the oddities of their relationship, about his being her stepbrother, or being gay.

'Have you got the piece of paper?' she asks suddenly, as she turns on to the road to The Garden House.

'Yes,' he answers, automatically feeling in his jacket pocket, 'although I copied it to my phone as well, just in case.'

'Good idea,' she agrees. 'It's just down here,' and she pulls in through the gateway. 'We have to pay, I'm afraid. I found Pa's membership card in his wallet but obviously I can't use that.'

'I'll do this,' says Will, opening the door and getting out. 'After all, you're putting me up and feeding me. And driving me around,' he adds, slamming the door.

She smiles at that last remark as he walks across to the visitor reception. It's become a bit of a tease about his big smart car, that she'll be embarrassed to be seen driving around in it in these country places. But he seems perfectly happy to let her drive and, since she knows the roads and where they're going, it's quite sensible. El pulls on her jacket and locks the car, wrapping her scarf around her neck. It's such a cold morning that Will has borrowed Martin's fleece gilet, which he's slipped on under his jacket. He's coming back with a leaflet, which he shows to her.

'It's the map of the gardens,' he says. 'I didn't like to say we already had one. Where did you go last time?'

'I went straight to the lake,' El told him. 'I was on a quest for *Nancy Fortescue* so I didn't bother about anything else. And then afterwards, when she wasn't there, I kind of lost my nerve.'

He slips an arm around her shoulder and gives her a quick hug. 'I know. But I think today we'll go right round and check everything we can. Then we'll have some coffee in the tearoom.'

They study the map together, then set off, looking around them, pointing out the small stone buildings; places where people might meet. Will pulls out the sheet of paper and El slips her arm through his. This is so much better than being here alone. He smiles down at her.

'I can't wait to see Sophie's Place,' he says. 'Or the Moulin Rouge. Thank God it's not raining.'

Ever since her visit to The Garden House with Davy, Julia longs to go again. The inhibitions she experienced after Martin's death, the reluctance, have all disappeared and now she longs to walk the paths they'd loved, remember their conversations and silly jokes, have coffee in the tearoom. This time, though, she'll go alone. It was good to have Davy's company but now she's ready to think about the past, to allow her memories to surface.

There has been a spell of wet and windy weather but the forecast for the next Friday looked promising and Julia made her plans. An early walk for Bertie, then drive across the moor to arrive not long after The Garden House opened at eleven o'clock. She is quietly excited, pleased that she is able to face up to it at last. It means that she is making some kind of progress, beginning to move forward a little.

The morning is bright and clear as she drives up out of Holne and on to the moor. She can see for miles; the swoop of landscape down into the wooded valleys and up again to the bony rocks of the tors, which gleam with a faint covering of snow.

Black skeletons of twisted thorn trees, a sudden blaze of flowering gorse, the glittering river-water flowing under the old stone bridge at Hexworthy.

'If only I could write poetry,' Martin once exclaimed, gazing round him at the glory of the Wildflower Meadow in all its painterly beauty.

'Have you ever tried?' she asked him.

'No, no.' He shook his head in horror at the thought. 'I know my limitations. My legal mind is a real handicap when it comes to any kind of creativity.'

Remembering, she smiles, but her heart aches at the thought that there will be no more exchanges. She turns on to the Princetown road, heading for Yelverton, well into Martin's territory. They'd considered meeting at the Prince Hal or the Two Bridges Hotel but both were risky.

'More risky than The Garden House?' she challenged him.

'Anyone might meet a friend by chance in a garden,' he answered.

The truth was, they simply couldn't resist it. It was their place.

'And if we meet anyone I know I shall simply say that you are a client,' he added.

'And if I meet anyone I know?' she asked.

'Then you can tell them that you are interviewing me for an article.'

'Actually, that's not a bad idea,' she said thoughtfully.

Luckily the problem never arose, although they were both more cautious once *Cakes and Ale* was aired. Several times she was recognized, but on these occasions Martin was able to slip away unobtrusively and, since they always arrived separately, he often simply drove away, phoning her later to apologize for abandoning her. Sometimes she wondered if subconsciously she was hoping that their cover might be blown and that they would have to go public, but each time she thought about the consequences, the difficulties of creating a joint life with four young people, her spirit failed her.

'What cowards we were,' she murmurs aloud, as she drives through Princetown and on towards Dousland. 'Or were we right?'

Still her heart speeds with anxiety at the thought of El reading those texts and she is just so thankful that they kept them very brief and to the point. She still wonders why El has never been in touch, whether somehow Martin's phone was lost. She can imagine no way in which she can describe their relationship to his daughter; to try to explain why he kept it secret from her. She might not be able to understand that he was trying to protect her from any kind of hurt so soon after the divorce, and might simply see it as a kind of betrayal. Even if Julia were inclined to try to find some way through, the fact that Martin had wanted it to be a secret continues to prevent her. She feels she would be breaking his trust.

Driving through Yelverton, pausing at the roundabout, she feels everything is so familiar and yet so different. This time she won't be checking out the car park to see if Martin's arrived, nor glancing at her phone to remind herself where they're supposed to be meeting. There was nothing regular about these meetings and, anyway, they depended on the weather, so it was doubtful that even the volunteers had suspected any kind of liaison. They always staggered arrival and leaving times.

Perhaps, she thinks, as she drives in through the gateway and parks the car, we simply enjoyed playing an elaborate game. Perhaps, deep down, we knew it would never survive in the tohu-bohu of real family life, but we didn't want to give it up.

Julia puts all the windows down an inch or two for Bertie, although the weather isn't warm, and gets out of the car.

It's Will who spots the first clue. They've walked around the gardens, examining small structures built of stone or wood, where two people might meet, but none seems to match with any of the codes. It's only when they've passed through the Walled Garden and are approaching the stone archway that leads through to the lake that Will stops suddenly and begins to laugh. El looks at him and then around her, puzzled.

'Look,' he says pointing to the plaque on the wall of the arch. 'Sophie's Place.'

El reads the words on the plaque that say that the Jubilee Arboretum was opened by the Countess of Wessex. For a few moments she is still puzzled, and then she sees the connection: Sophie, the Countess of Wessex.

'Do you think so?' she asks, beginning to laugh with him.

'Definitely,' he says. 'This leads to the lake, doesn't it? It's another way of saying they'd meet by the *Nancy Fortescue*. The same area.'

'This definitely needs a selfie,' says El, and they pose together whilst she takes a photograph of them both in front of the plaque.

They pass beneath the arch, still laughing, and El points to the lake.

'That's where the boat would be,' she says. 'I wonder where it is now?'

They walk around the lake, perching briefly on the bench, listening to the fast-flowing stream running behind them. But it's too cold to sit for very long and they continue the circuit of the lake and begin to climb the small winding paths that lead up towards the Bowling Green Terrace. It's El who notices the label attached to a shrub outside a small stone building: 'Moulin Rouge'. She clutches Will's arm and points to it.

'Moulin Rouge,' she says. 'Remember I told you about Pa's painting? What a pity it's not in flower.'

They look at the little building. 'Not quite Parisian,' says Will, 'but I bet this is it. A good place to meet if it's raining.'

El walks into the structure and stares around her, trying to imagine Pa here, and with whom? She's prey to the now familiar confusion and she gives a little shiver. Will is watching her.

'Coffee time?' he suggests.

'I'm just trying to imagine it,' she tells him. 'It's weird not knowing who the other person was. But then again, part of me doesn't want to know.'

She feels suddenly near to tears and he puts his arms round her, holding her gently.

'Don't be so hard on yourself,' he says. 'This grieving business is really tough and you're still a beginner. It's like being a bit crazy all the time. Sometimes you feel normal, other times you feel desolate. Sometimes, when you're having a really good time you feel terribly guilty. You get these mood swings and it's totally bloody. Just don't feel guilty about any of it.'

She rests against him, knowing that he's been there, knowing that she can trust him, and she feels him kiss her lightly on the head. Involuntarily her arms tighten around him for a moment, then she straightens up.

'Thanks, Will,' she says. 'That just about sums it up. I some-times forget that you've been through it all, too. But you were much younger, so it must have been really hard for you. You're right. Coffee sounds good. Where are we?'

He takes out the map and they study it together.

'We're not too far away, by the look of it,' he says. 'This way, I think.'

Julia digs into her bag for her membership card, shows it to the friendly lady at reception, who tells her that the skimmia and the dogwood are at their best, and then hesitates before telling Julia how much she enjoyed *Cakes and Ale*. They talk about the programme and then Julia wanders into the garden. She still can't get used to being recognized, and although she's a very minor presenter – and it doesn't happen very often – she can see how it might have begun to affect her and Martin's privacy. She reminds herself that with Ollie starting at uni this term she and Martin were going to go public, that it wouldn't have mattered, but somehow she can't believe in it. Perhaps it was, after all, like one of those holiday romances that flourish in a rare and particular atmosphere but wither in the face of reality. She walks the familiar paths, passing their meeting places, pausing beside the lake. At the circle of standing stones – the Magic Circle – she stands gazing down across the gardens to the house at the far end of the avenue, and then walks more briskly back through the arboretum to the tearooms. Perhaps coming here alone wasn't such a good idea after all, especially now with the garden dressed for winter, and a chill breeze. She's glad to be inside. There are only a few people and as she looks around she has a sudden memory of that very first time, standing just here, listening to the chatter and laughter of the coach party, and seeing Martin sitting by himself, their glances meeting and his little smile, his hand lifted to indicate the empty chair.

She stands still for a moment, realizes that a couple at a nearby table are staring at her as if they recognize her. They begin to get up, still staring at her, and suddenly she can't bear it. Grief threatens to overwhelm her and she turns swiftly away, almost bumping against a young man who has just come in, and who looks at her curiously as she hurries out into the cold winter morning.

Will watches the tall, attractive woman disappear into the gardens and turns back thoughtfully. Her face was familiar and he tries to remember where he might have seen her before. A couple jostle past him, following her, talking together, and he catches a fragment of their conversation: '. . . Braithwaite . . . television presenter . . . cakes and ale . . .' The friendly waitress is hovering, smiling and asking if Will would like some refreshment and, as he chooses a table, El appears in the doorway, looking around, and he raises a hand to her, forgetting about the woman.

'You won't believe this,' she says, as she joins him, 'but the gardener was telling me that the *Nancy Fortescue* is taken out of the water and laid up for the winter. That's why it wasn't here when I came last time.'

'That's a pity,' he says. 'I'd love to see what it looks like.'

'Well, I can show you,' says El triumphantly. 'He told me there are postcards for sale so I went back to the visitor reception and had a look.'

She holds out a postcard to him: a blue-painted wooden dinghy floating on the lake, with the words *Nancy Fortescue* painted in white on her bows.

'Did you ask when it goes back into the water?' he asks.

'Not till the spring,' says El sadly, 'though he doesn't know when. But he's told me roughly where the Magic Circle is. Maybe we could look for it.'

As they order coffee and choose cakes, he thinks about El. She needs either some kind of resolution to this mystery in her father's life, or to be able to make the decision that it's none of her business and to move on from it.

As he looks across the table at her, at her pretty face with her red-brown curling hair piled high into a knot, her blue eyes bright at the prospect of their walk in the gardens, he feels that he would like to protect her from all these unknowns. He remembers how she was in the little building beside the Moulin Rouge, her distress and confusion, and he wants to say: 'Look, why don't we give all this up? Let's just move on with our lives. Show me Dartmoor and all the places that you love, but let's leave all this to them.' But how can he do that?

'OK,' he says, smiling at her. 'So where shall we start?'

CHAPTER TWENTY-FOUR

In Tavistock, Kate and Angus are already in the Bedford when Tom and Cass arrive. Cass makes a face behind Tom's back as he gives Kate a hug and she grins back at her old friend. The face indicates that Tom is in a grumpy mood and will need a bit of jollying along.

'Plum's down,' Angus is telling them as they settle around a table. 'She'll be along in a minute. I think we'll commandeer this next table and two more chairs or there won't be room. Shall I get an order in?'

'I'll come and help,' says Kate. 'Isn't the little Christmas tree pretty? Did you notice the big tree out in the hall, Tom?'

Tom shakes his head: no, he hasn't noticed the Christmas tree. Clearly he isn't yet in Christmas mode. His mood is in direct contrast with Angus's cheerfulness and Kate smiles at him as they wait to order at the bar. There's something so comforting about Angus, so dependable.

'I hope you're coming to my party,' he says to her. 'No excuses. Drinks and bit of supper, then off to Midnight Mass. Plum and Ian and the girls will be down. And probably El. Now don't tell me that you're going to stay down on that old rock of yours with what's-his-name.'

'His name's Bruno,' says Kate, 'as you know perfectly well. And yes, that's probably exactly where I'll be. Though I'm coming up for the party with all the kids on the Tamar on Boxing Day.'

Angus shakes his head, guying profound disappointment. 'Won't be the same without you.'

Kate reaches up to put an arm around his bony shoulders. 'But think of all the fun we'll have when everyone's gone home and I come to stay with you, just the two of us together.'

Angus gives a great shout of laughter, surprising Lynn behind the bar, and Kate has to remind him about the order.

'What are you up to?' asks Cass when Kate gets back to the table. 'I saw you making up to Angus. Not getting fed up with Bruno, are you?'

'You know what you always used to say to me,' says Kate, sitting down beside her. 'It's always good to have a reserve. Where's Tom gone?'

'He's in the loo,' says Cass. 'Do you mind if we come back to the cottage afterwards, Kate? He'd like to have another look. Maybe he'll think it's too small.'

Kate notices the faint note of hope in Cass's voice and shakes her head.

'You know that you've got to do this, Cass. You're just not managing there any more. Go while you're ahead. You needn't be at the cottage for long,' she reminds her. 'It's just a resting place so you don't have to be rushed into buying something. It'll give you time to think without pressure. And think of all the lovely money you'll be getting for the Rectory.' Kate pauses. 'Sorry,' she says. 'I know this is making me sound heartless, but I'm not really. I'm trying to be realistic.'

'I know that,' says Cass. 'And I'm coming round to it slowly, although it's such a massive upheaval I simply dread the thought of it.'

'The boys will help you,' says Kate encouragingly. 'Everyone will rally round.'

'Here's Plum,' says Cass. 'I'm so glad she and Ian and the girls are coming down for Christmas.'

'Angus is like a schoolboy,' says Kate affectionately. 'He is just so happy.'

She stands up to hug Plum, thinking of their conversation, and they pull up another chair. Tom joins them and greets Plum whilst Kate watches them, remembering all these friends when they were young and wondering where all the years have gone.

She's sipping her coffee, listening to Tom telling her a dit when she notices Plum straighten in her chair, her expression changing to an odd mixture of surprise and anxiety. Instinctively Kate glances round. Standing just inside the entrance to the bar is Issy.

Isla gives a little inward chuckle. Here they all are, as she suspected they might be. These are creatures of habit, seeking reassurance in the little routines of their lives. Plum's old dad in his white Aran jersey and cord trousers, the couple whose names she is struggling to remember; pretty woman, and the man is one of those who still likes to be thought a bit of a rake, despite his age. Kate – she remembers Kate's name. She has a tiny sensation of disquiet when she remembers Kate's assessing look. And there is Plum: pretty, darling Plum. Her hair is pushed back behind her ears, just like she used to wear it at school, although back then she would have worn a velvet Alice band. Even as Isla looks at her, Plum sees her. Isla waves at her and crosses towards them all.

'Hello,' she cries brightly. 'I just wondered if you might be here. I've been buying Christmas presents in the Pannier Market and I decided to take a chance and walk over to see if any of you were around.'

She smiles round at them all, holding her big heavy bag, noting their reactions: Angus and the other man getting to their feet, the pretty woman smiling in a welcoming manner, Plum recovering from her surprise and getting up too. Only Kate remains still and watchful, with that odd expression that Isla mistrusts, though she doesn't quite know why. She makes all the right noises as they shuffle around to fit her in and Angus goes to order coffee for her. 'That's so kind,' she says to him, and, 'Oh, thank you,' to the other man, as he offers to relieve her of the heavy shopping bag, and then a kiss for Plum. She sits down beside her, asks about Ian and the girls, doing the old school chum act whilst glancing around so as to include them all. Angus comes back to the table and squeezes into the chair beside her so that she is able to start a conversation with him about Christmas, and in the talk that follows she is able to discover that the other couple are called Cass and Tom. When her coffee arrives, Isla raises the cup in a toast to them all, crying, 'Happy Christmas. Only two weeks to go,' and watches them all respond, smiling, happy, talking about their plans, and she wonders what they'd say if she said, 'It all sounds great. How about if I were to come and join you?'

She has to stifle a moment of bitterness as she imagines their expressions, how they would respond, which, she is pretty certain, would be in a very predictable and polite way whilst feeling dismayed inside. Instead she smiles at Plum, noticing that she hasn't asked her dear old friend Issy what she's doing for Christmas, and asks if she's found anywhere to live yet.

Plum looks slightly awkward and shakes her head. 'I think we'll just stay with Dad to begin with,' she says. 'Just to see how it goes.'

Isla raises her eyebrows fractionally, as if she's questioning whether this is wise, and Plum hurries in to explain that there's the flat in London and the ship won't be in that often, and Isla smiles at her. It always amuses her that people need to rush to justify their reasons, defend their choices. She listens to Plum's explanations and nods understandingly.

'What are you doing afterwards?' she asks. 'Could you manage lunch?'

Plum hesitates, glancing around as if hoping someone will come to her rescue, but the others are talking together and she nods, though not very enthusiastically.

'Great,' Isla says. 'I'm just going to dash to the loo. Shan't be long.'

She gets up and goes out of the bar, along the passage to the ladies' lavatories. She's washing her hands when Kate comes in behind her. They look at each other through the mirror over the basin and for a moment Isla stands quite still, allowing the water to trickle over her hands, staring at the older woman. Kate smiles at her.

'She's such a pretty girl, isn't she?' she asks.

Isla's stomach contracts and her heart speeds a little.

'Plum,' says Kate, as if in explanation. 'I could see by the expression on your face when you first arrived how very . . . how shall we say, how very fond you are of her.'

Isla knows that in some oblique way she is being threatened, that Kate has guessed her true feelings for Plum, and she might not keep her conjectures a secret. Kate nods, as if she knows what Isla is thinking, and then goes into one of the cubicles and locks the door. Isla grabs a tissue from the box and dries her hands and then she hurries out.

When Kate comes out of the loo, Issy has gone. Kate washes her hands and dries them, frowning to herself, wondering if she has judged the situation correctly, and if she has done enough. She walks back into the bar. Tom and Angus are at the bar, Cass and Plum are sitting together. Kate raises her eyebrows.

'Where's Issy?'

'Well, it was a bit odd,' Cass says. 'She came back saying she'd had a text and had to rush. So she picked up her bag and fled away.'

'What a pity,' says Kate, glancing at Plum. 'So you won't be having lunch then?'

'No,' says Plum.

She looks puzzled but relieved, and Kate sits down beside her. Cass has taken out her phone and is checking for messages.

'So now you can have lunch with us,' says Kate cheerfully. 'Much nicer.'

Cass puts away her phone and begins to ask Plum about Alice and how she's enjoying working in a literary agency. Kate can see that Plum is distracted from her worries about Issy by this question and soon she is happily talking about her girls. Angus and Tom are coming back and Kate breathes a sigh of relief. For now, at least, the danger is over.

*

It's been a magical day for Will. Several times he's almost allowed himself to move away from the kind, reliable friend that he's been since the funeral and to push the relationship forward. He knows that he's well into being in love with El, that he'd like to make some sort of gesture to show her what he's feeling. He's inhibited by the precarious state of her emotions, doesn't want to make a false move, but all the evidence is that she's feeling the same. It shows in the way that she talks with him, sharing all her thoughts and feelings, the way she touches him so readily, putting her arm in his, grabbing his hand, leaning against him. After they left The Garden House she drove him to Meavy where they had a ploughman's lunch in the Royal Oak, which, she told him, was her father's favourite pub. Then they'd driven out to the cross, where they walked together before the short winter day drove them home to light the fire.

It was a shock, when he mentioned the cross to El, to find that she knew about it, that Martin had a keen interest in all the moorland stones and crosses, and they walked there many times. El googled it and they were amazed to see that it was called Bennett's Cross, that it was documented in 1702 as part of a boundary dispute, and re-erected in the late nineteenth century.

'It says the initials W. B. are carved into it,' she said, beginning to laugh. 'They stand for Warren Bounds but apparently they've been blasted off by lightning.'

'W. B.?' Will could hardly believe it. 'Will Bennett. Well, that settles it. I've got to take you to see it again.'

Somehow with El beside him, the cross was simply a stone, a prehistoric menhir, perhaps, Christianized at a much later date. But it was good to stand there together, running their fingers over the rough granite, trying, without success, to find the initials W. B.

Now, El is clearing up after supper and Will is piling plates together and trying to be helpful.

'So I'm thinking of going to Angus's drinks party and then to Midnight Mass afterwards. I did it last year with Pa. Angus enjoys a little party, and Plum and Ian were still in Washington then. Cass and Tom came as well. It will be fun with Plum and Ian and the girls home.' She hesitates. 'What do you usually do at Christmas?'

Will pauses, half leaning, half sitting on the end of the table, trying to decipher her words. Are they an invitation or are they simply an enquiry about his Christmas in return?

'It all depends on what my flying rota is,' he says, deciding to answer her question pragmatically. 'You won't be going . . .?'

He hesitates over the word 'home', which to El clearly means the Pig Pen, and doesn't know quite how to phrase their joint family. The last thing he wants to do at the moment is to emphasize this ambivalent side of their relationship.

She glances across at him. 'I shan't be going to Dorchester for Christmas,' she says firmly. 'Though I shall probably go at New Year. Freddie thinks he might be going then, which would be good.'

Will nods, trying to imagine them all together, telling Felicity that he is in love with El. Instinctively he recoils from the conversation, knowing just how El's mother will react: wincing inwardly as he remembers the disastrous New Year when he took Christian home to meet his family.

'Are you sure you won't have a drink?' El is asking, holding up a bottle of white wine, pouring some more into her own glass.

Will shakes his head. 'I'm flying tomorrow,' he says. 'I never drink before I fly. I need to be up early.'

She nods, smiles at him, and then suddenly looks puzzled, even sad. It's such an odd expression, so bleak, and such a sudden change from her happy mood, that it tips him over the edge of caution. He steps forward, removes the bottle from her hand, stands it down and folds her into his arms. She stares up at him, taken by surprise, and he bends his head to kiss her and when she instinctively responds he holds her even more closely, really kissing her. Just for a moment, her mouth opens under his, her hands sliding around his waist, and then she's fighting him, turning her head away.

'No,' she says, 'no. What are you doing? Stop it, Will!'

He lets her go, staring at her, shocked by this sudden rejection.

She begins to weep inconsolably, then she pushes him aside, hurrying away down the stairs, and he hears her bedroom door slam. Hardly able to believe what has happened, Will stares after her. Then, because he must, he descends the stairs until he stands, one hand resting on the door handle, his forehead pressed to the smooth white wood of the door, listening to her weeping.

'El,' he calls. 'El. Come out.'

There is no response. And he waits, confused. He wonders if he should go to her: but how can he? How could he just open her door and walk in? He is hurt by her rejection, but even worse is his shame that he has tried to force her into something she isn't ready for. He has completely misread the situation. He should have understood that she's still emotionally on a roller coaster.

Will goes into his room wondering what to do: nothing has prepared him for this. Clearly he can't stay here. What should he do? Calmly finish clearing up the supper and go to bed? Make her a cup of tea? Will shakes his head. No way could he do that. He remembers that he is flying tomorrow, that he must make an early start. On an impulse he stuffs his belongings into his bag, glances round the room and the bathroom and checks his pocket for his phone. He pauses as he takes off Martin's gilet, staring at it, wondering if his wearing it has triggered off memories for El. Then he hangs it on a peg in the hall and goes out, closing the door behind him.

El hears the powerful engine roaring into life, revving hard as the car accelerates away. She sits on the edge of her bed, her hands clasped tightly between her knees, physically preventing herself from leaping up. She wants to rush out, to call him back, although she knows that it's much too late. She's regretting her violent response but at the same time so many emotions jumble around in her mind that she needs time to separate them and think clearly.

One of her overriding feelings is shame: shame and embarrassment. She remembers going into Will's room the night she had the bad dream, climbing on to his bed. She thinks of the easy way she's behaved with him, and she cringes with horror that he might have thought that she was coming on to him. Whilst she can tell herself that she imagined that their odd relationship – and that Will is gay – was a protection against any suspicion on his part that she fancied him, in her heart she also knows that she is very attracted to him. She can recall his first morning, after he'd driven down from Bristol, when he fell asleep across his bed and she stood at his bedroom door looking at the long length of him lying across his bed and thought what a waste it was that he should be gay. She thinks of those weird stabs of jealousy when he bought the pottery for Christian, and she knows that it's cheating to be angry with him for kissing her. The stepbrother and -sister relationship has been another part of the muddle, but now a deep instinct tells her that all these emotions have been a useful shield to protect her from her own reactions to him, and she feels utterly ashamed that she's used that shield because she's wanted him to be here with her, to help her through this awful time.

But there was something much more than that. Just before that moment when Will kissed her she'd been prey to a sudden, terrible sense of guilt. She thought: Pa is dead and I am laughing. I'm having a great time with Will, behaving as if Pa's life was some sort of game, and Will and I are replaying it for fun. Pa is dead and I am happy. And it was at that moment, as Will put his arms around her, she realized that he was still wearing Pa's gilet. It was almost as if she were hugging Pa and it had taken her totally off guard. Will's kiss had completed her confusion. And now what can she say to him? How can she possibly explain her reasons? What must he be thinking of her?

El leans forward, head in hands, digging her fingers through her hair, which falls out of its knot and all over her shoulders and face. She groans aloud when she imagines how he will be driving through the evening, across the moor, alone with his thoughts. He's been so kind, so understanding, and when she thinks again of her reaction and how she's behaved she feels she might die of shame. She can see no way back; no possibility of explaining to him the complicated emotions or that childish outburst, which was a complexity of guilt about Pa and an attempt to salvage her own pride; to cover her embarrassment.

As she sits on the edge of the bed she wonders exactly what he intended. It wasn't a friendly kiss. Was he hoping that they'd go to bed? And then what? El pushes her hair back and twists it into a plait, gets up and goes slowly up the stairs. She stares at the dirty plates, the half-empty bottle of wine, and feels that she might weep with frustration and disappointment.

On the table lies the leaflet from The Garden House, the map of the grounds, and she thinks of how they walked around, laughing when Will found Sophie's Place, her arm in his, holding him close to her. Dimly she begins to see that this quest has been a smoke screen to distract her, first from grief for Pa, and then from her love for Will. It has distracted her, concentrated her mind, and she's been using it – and Will – to get her through.

It's odd that just at this moment the quest seems unimportant, that Pa's relationship with the unknown sender of the texts has lost its worth beside this loss of her friendship with Will. There was so much they were planning to do together, and now there is nothing. El can think of no way she can explain to Will the reasons behind her outburst. She feels too embarrassed.

She wanders around, putting a log on the fire, making a mug of hot chocolate, curling up on the sofa – and all she can think about is Will. Will at the funeral, helping to clear Pa's clothes, walking on the moor; his kindness, his humour, his kiss . . . In a starburst flash of comprehension, El sits aghast before the reality of her love for Will. She loves him, not just in a romantic way, nor just in a physical way – though both of these are present in her feelings for him – but in a totally overwhelming passion that encompasses everything that is generous and good and necessary. She needs him, wants him, loves him: he makes sense of everything.

El sits silently, trying to see some way forward. At this moment any kind of reconciliation seems impossible, the damage seems irreparable, but maybe things will look more hopeful in the morning. She finishes her chocolate, washes the mug under the tap, and trails downstairs to bed.

Will's hands are clenched in frustration on the steering wheel as the car surges across the dark moor. He feels the temptation to speed, to let the car have its head and drive fast and heed-lessly into the night, but it is not in his nature to be undisciplined. On this road, high in the cold blackness, any bend might reveal an animal on the tarmac, a patch of ice, a rock tumbled on to the road so as to catch the unwary.

Over and over he replays the moment in his mind, leaning forward, kissing her. She kissed him back; he knows she kissed him back. And then, in that perfect, wonderful moment, a sudden tension in her body and her hands rising and pushing him away in rejection, and her incoherent outburst of grief and confusion. He can see now that his timing was all wrong. He'd allowed the happiness of the day, their shared affection, to mis-lead him. Clearly, El is not ready to contemplate a step forward yet, and he knows he should have been aware of that. He curses himself for his lack of perception.

He passes Two Bridges and takes the road left to Moreton-hampstead. Here low stone walls line the road. Coppices of trees race left and right through the glare of his headlights. A sudden sharp shower hitting his windscreen forces him to use the wipers for a few moments and he slows a little in the reduced visibility. As the rain clears, the road narrows unexpectedly. He sweeps over a single-track bridge and on up to a long dark fir wood that obscures the view to his right. Now he is passing the sign for Postbridge and descending into the little village. There are few lights on in the houses and the village store is dark as he passes on the road that leads down to the narrow stone bridge. He does not need to slow down, there are no other cars out on the road tonight. Here are the homely lights of the East Dart Hotel on the right beside the road, then the village hall, dark and empty. He feels the double 'brmm brmm' of his tyres on the cattle grid that marks his return to the moor and he begins the climb towards the Warren Inn, which sits in lonely isolation high on the shoulder of the tor.

Will knows where he is going now. He can feel the stone drawing him, and a strange kind of turmoil building within him until he physically shakes with tension. The dark inn passes unheeded on his left and he descends, slowing, till the headlights pick out the low stones marking the entrance to the parking area. He brakes hard, turns in and to the left, and pulls up in a shower of small pebbles.

He is out of the car, slamming the door behind him. Heedless of the cold, he strides out through the marker stones on the short narrow path on to the moor. In the night sky above him, clouds are revealed by their absence, which allows glimpses of the stars beyond. There is no effective light from these solitary guardians. It is dark, so dark he can hardly see the ground, but he doesn't slow his pace. He stumbles on the uneven ground but presses on, weaving between the tufts of moor grass. And then, looming in the darkness, he perceives the greater dark of the stone blocking his path. a stooped brooding sentinel; immobile, almost human. Will can feel it, like a presence: Bennett's

Cross. It has become a symbol for him, a manifestation of his present confusion, and the grief in his past. He feels a powerful, almost pagan, connection to this stone, to the unknown craftsman who fashioned it. Tonight, he cannot perceive it as a Christian symbol, despite its name. He moves closer, reaches a hand out to the ravaged stone, to where, earlier, he and El searched for his initials, which were once carved into the west face. His own initials, W. B. – Warren Bounds. He remembers how they stood together only a few hours ago, laughing, happy; their hands sweeping over the stone, which now seems to lean towards him.

A gust of wind strikes from behind and Will turns towards it; towards the west. For a brief moment the sky above the north-western horizon is clear. Etched there in startling clarity Cygnus stretches her wings wide. In the deep darkness every star in her wings is visible and Deneb shines like the taillight of an aircraft. Another gust of wind and now the racing clouds clear from beneath her left wing and Vega flares into view, ice cold and steady. Will flings his arms up and wide, as if to mimic the stars, and shouts up at the night sky.

'Is that it? So what's next? Come on. What's next?'

With a blast of wind sweeping up from the west, a curtain of rain strikes into his face. In a second the stars fade and are gone. For a moment Will stands there in disbelief, water streaming over him, and then he begins to laugh out loud. He turns, looks again at the cross, and it is just a misshapen stone in the middle of a valley on the moor, set there for who knows what purpose, who knows when.

Still laughing at his own melodramatic foolishness and self-pity, he touches his right hand to the rock and he is suddenly aware of the cold and the wet, and the totally inadequate shoes he is wearing. He looks back along the path. In the dark he can still see the sidelights of the car. Drawing his arms about him for warmth he sets off back towards the lights. He has barely left the cross, striding into the dark, when he feels a loose stone move under his left foot, and his ankle twists outwards as his weight comes down. There is an instant of blinding pain, he loses balance, stumbles, and crashes heavily on to the ground. For a moment he lies in the wet, then rolls on to his knees, his hands supporting his weight. The pain in his ankle is ferocious. He tries to stand, but can put no weight on his left foot at all. It takes considerable effort to get up but eventually he stands, with all his weight on his right leg.

It seems a long way back to the car. He cannot hop on the uneven ground, and his left ankle will not tolerate even the briefest of loads. Nevertheless he has no choice but to get back to the car. Every limping step is agonizing, a long, sharp and repetitive torment, and he seems to be making little progress. The rain falls harder now and he is soaked to the skin. He knows that in this temperature he doesn't have a lot of time before the cold will begin to incapacitate him, and then he falls again, jarring the ankle so that he cries out in pain. He stays bent double, using his right foot, hands and knees, protecting the ankle as best he can as he crawls and shuffles towards the parking area. Metre by metre he makes progress. The little gullies and divots in the path that were of no consequence on his outward walk to the cross have become obstacles that require serious effort to pass. By the time he reaches the stone markers at the end of the path he is shaking with cold and sick to the stomach with pain. But he is able to get up, to hop the three last steps to the car bonnet. Shuffling round to the back passenger door Will wrenches it open, grabs his bag and chucks it into the front passenger seat. He pulls his sodden muddy shirt over his head and throws it to the footwell before slamming the rear door and opening the driver's door. With difficulty, trying to protect his left foot, he climbs into the car, shuts the door and with shaking hands fires up the engine. The motor is still warm and, with the heating set to maximum, it is not long before the interior temperature begins to rise. Will rips open his bag, grabs his pullover, and struggles into it before he sits with his hands pressed to the air vents, sucking the heat into his frozen body.

Eventually the shaking stops. He still feels sick from the pain and his ankle is throbbing but, at rest, it is just about bearable. His trousers are soaking, but the thought of trying to get them off over his ankle is intolerable. Thankfully, the car is automatic, so he should still be able to drive.

Briefly he considers going back to El but he rejects the thought. He decides to go on, to test how well he can drive and, putting the car into reverse, he manoeuvres it to leave the parking area.

Later, he will wonder why he didn't stop, didn't drive to the A & E in Exeter, but by the time he reaches the M5 he is fixated on getting home. The miles go by in a blur of pain but there is no possibility of stopping. If he were to stop he would never be able to drive on. There is no thought of calling for help. He is almost ashamed by his stupidity, unable to explain even to himself what he was playing at, what had driven him to go to the cross. There is within him just the primal urge to get home, to get back into familiar surroundings, to curl up, disappear and drop out.

By the time he pulls up on the drive at home he is barely able to move his foot and get out of the car. It is only then, when he can no longer function properly, slumped in the driving seat, that he calls Christian.

What follows is something of a blur for Will. Christian is opening the car door, his initial amusement rapidly turning to alarm as he takes stock of the situation, and Will yells in pain as he is helped out of his seat. Christian half carries him into the house, takes one look at Will's ankle and insists that he's going to A & E. Will doesn't protest. He's just utterly grateful that Christian is taking command, getting him out of his wet clothes into warm dry ones, and half carrying him out to the Mini.

Head back, eyes closed, he is barely aware of the journey to Bristol. Christian is dealing with reception at A & E, getting Will a wheelchair. The triage nurse arrives quickly, but Will has no idea how long they wait to be seen by a doctor, though he is aware of Christian calling Ops, reporting Will sick and signing him off his scheduled flight. In one of Will's more lucid moments Christian asks him if he should speak to El, but Will shakes his head very definitely. He has already been humiliated by her rejection, ashamed by his own insensitivity towards her, and now he feels emasculated by this injury and his helplessness. No, he tells Christian strongly. No way does he want him to speak to El. And then there is a whirl of X-rays, examinations and meds that finally begin to take the edge off his pain.

El can't sleep. She is sitting at the table in her pyjamas, staring at her phone, unable to make the decision to speak to Will. She has the contacts screen open and her thumb hovers over the top line, which reads, simply, 'Will'. It would be so easy to let her thumb drop to the glass, to activate the call, but she can't face the potential humiliation of hearing his voice sounding angry, or worse, indifferent. She presses the photo button and looks at the selfie she took at The Garden House. She and Will together, her hand forward and out of picture as she takes the photo. Will has his arm around her, his head above hers; they are embraced by the pale blue of the sky, illuminated by the sunshine.

She remembers laughing up at the plaque on the stone gate, and Will saying, 'Look! Sophie's Place!' There was certainty in his voice, knowing that he was right, that another clue had fallen into place, and she recalls his pleased grin as he looked down at her, his hair flopping forward over his eyes as it so often does.

Even as her thumb presses down and the connection is made, she has a moment of panic, an overwhelming desire to hit the red button and kill the call, but she doesn't. The number is ringing, and ringing, then there is a click, and a voice she doesn't recognize says: 'Hello, El. This is Christian. Will isn't available at the moment.'

El is silent. She doesn't know what to say. She tries to speak, but all that comes out is, 'Hi.'

For a moment Christian says nothing. Then he says: 'So, do you mind telling me what the hell is going on?'

El is filled with confusion. What can she say to him? Supposing Christian really is more than Will's house-mate?

'I'm sorry, Christian . . . I didn't know . . .'

She hesitates, because she knows that she wanted Will to make his move, welcomed it, and suddenly she is resolved to challenge her doubts and fears. She needs to ask the question.

'Christian, are you and Will in a relationship?'

There is a silence, then a disbelieving laugh. 'Seriously, El? You think Will and I are "in a relationship"?'

It seems as if he is mocking her, and she feels humiliated and regrets her brief moment of courage.

'So you think that because he shares his house with a gay man, Will must be gay?' There is humour in his voice. 'Don't you think that's just a tad prejudiced, El?'

There is a silence. For a moment El wonders if he is fetching Will, but then Christian speaks again, quickly and quietly.

'OK, just for the record, El. Will is my best friend. I love him like a brother,' he pauses, then says slowly, 'but Will is not, and never has been, gay. Trust me, El, if he was, he wouldn't be on the market. Are we clear?'

El nods: she is clear, and she knows that she has made a huge mistake.

'El?'

She realizes she has to say something. 'Yes.' She almost whispers it. 'Please can I speak to him?'

'He can't speak to you yet.'

El shuts her eyes, squeezing back tears.

'Please, will you tell him I called and when he's ready, please ask him to call me?'

She says it as a question, pleading with this stranger on the phone.

'I'll ask him,' says Christian. A pause, then, ''Bye, El.'

There is a click, the line is silent, and then there are the three beeps that signify the connection is closed.

Still clasping the phone, El folds her arms on the table, drops her head and allows herself to weep.

CHAPTER TWENTY-FIVE

Julia sleeps fitfully and wakes early. She hates these dark mid-winter mornings. She longs for the early summer sunrises when she can snatch a cup of coffee and then take Bertie out to walk in the lane; to listen for the cuckoo and hear the lambs calling. She rolls over to peer at the bedside clock – nearly ten to seven – and is relieved that it's not much earlier. After Bob died, she woke regularly at twenty past three every morning for nearly a year and then, quite suddenly, her sleep pattern changed again, returning to her normal routine of waking between six and seven. Nobody could explain the phenomenon but those long wakeful hours before sunrise, missing him, longing for him, had been devastating.

She lies for a moment, thinking how different these processes of mourning are. Back then she mourned for Bob in all those small daily routines and intimacies that couples share. This time her grief takes a different form. She misses the randomness: the unexpected text, the spontaneous meeting, the secret knowledge that at any moment the day will be brightened by the connection between her and Martin. It gave colour and excitement to her life.

Now she must learn to deal with her bereavement alone. No family or friends, this time, to comfort her, to help her through it. She must continue to keep their secret and manage on her own.

Quickly, so as to prevent that familiar slide into misery, Julia pushes back the duvet, sits on the edge of the bed, and reaches for her dressing gown, flung across the old wicker chair. She huddles into its softness, folding it around her, tying the belt. Mentally she begins to plan her day, refusing to allow herself to become depressed. After Bob died, the boys provided her with a framework. Their own commitments – school, friends, clubs – filled her waking time with activity. This time she must concentrate on work: this will be her solace.

But first comes Christmas. The boys will be home, expecting the usual routines, and she must begin to get organized, to make lists, finish writing Christmas cards, fill the freezer. Julia stands up, pushes her feet into sheepskin slippers and goes to the window. It's still dark outside but the sky is clear and there is no wind. It will be a fine day. She goes out on to the landing and down the stairs, to let Bertie out, and to make coffee.

Later that morning, Angus and Kate are walking the dogs on Whitchurch Common. He saw her coming out of Crebers and suddenly thought how nice it would be to be up on the moor in this bright December sunshine with Blossom and Dearie, and even nicer with Kate and Flossie, too. She agreed at once, told him that she'd take her shopping back to Chapel Street, pick up Flossie and meet him up on the Common. Angus hurried back to get the dogs and they arrived within minutes of each other, the dogs delighted to be together, bounding around, uttering yelps of excitement, whilst he and Kate pulled on jackets and hunted for leads.

'Not that we really need them,' says Kate, hanging Flossie's lead around her neck outside her coat collar, 'but you never know.'

They walk together over the close-grazed turf, discussing families, Christmas and Angus's party.

'I just want you to know,' Angus says, 'that I'm very upset that you've stood me up on Christmas Eve. What's Bruno got that I haven't, I'd like to know?'

Although he's met Bruno and likes him, he's rather surprised himself to find that this is true. In these last few months, whilst she's spent more time in Tavistock than usual, he's become increasingly fond of Kate and he's disappointed that she won't be there at his party with all their friends.

Kate laughs, tucking her arm in his. 'I can't just abandon poor old Bruno and my friends at St Meriadoc,' she says cheerfully. 'You can't expect me to do that. I'm coming back for the Boxing Day thrash down on the Tamar, though. Is that any good?'

He makes a face, pretends dissatisfaction, but inside he's pleased to think that she'll be back so soon and, once Tom and Cass are installed in Chapel Street, she might be a more permanent visitor with him in Whitchurch.

'How about New Year's Eve?' he asks hopefully. 'You could stay on after Boxing Day. I might give another party.'

'What a fellow you are,' says Kate admiringly. 'Well, I might have to tell Bruno he'll be spending New Year alone.'

Angus chuckles. 'I hope you know what you're taking on,' he says, 'keeping us both happy.'

'Well, you know what Cass says,' answers Kate. 'If there's anything better than one man, it's two men. *Ad infinitum.*'

'Sounds like Cass,' agrees Angus.

He feels lucky in his friendship with these two women, who make him laugh and keep him young in spirit.

'Being old is hell,' he says unexpectedly. 'I was having lunch in a pub recently with an old colleague, and there he was chomping away on a steak and all I could think was that the lucky devil must still have all his own teeth. I mean, sad or what?'

Kate bursts out laughing and hugs his arm tighter.

'If I'd paid more attention at school,' she says, 'I'd quote that thing: "To me, old friend, you never can be old."' She shakes her head. 'That doesn't sound right. I can't remember it. Is it Shakespeare?'

'It's one of his sonnets,' says Angus. He hesitates and then he says softly:

> To me, fair friend, you never can be old;
> For as you were when first your eye I eyed,
> Such seems your beauty still . . .

He pauses, feeling rather a fool, but Kate looks up at him admiringly.

'Wow,' she says. 'Get you. I'm impressed.'

Angus shrugs modestly. 'Just trying to keep up with Bruno. How many books has he had published now?'

Kate laughs. 'This is not a contest.'

He laughs with her, pauses and strikes a pose, continuing the sonnet:

> . . . Three winters cold Have from the forest shook . . .

'OK, now you're showing off,' says Kate. 'You're frightening the dogs.'

'And I haven't apologized for pre-empting you with Plum about the cottage,' he says, tucking her arm back in his own. 'I hope that wasn't embarrassing for you.'

'It actually worked out very well,' says Kate thoughtfully.

Glancing down at her, he sees that she's musing on it, as if she's remembering the talk with Plum.

'Well, I'm grateful,' he says, 'for all sorts of reasons. And Plum seems much happier, too. She went back to London in very good spirits. I think you did her good.'

'Great,' says Kate lightly. 'In that case you can buy me lunch. Why don't we drive over to the Warren Inn?'

'Love to,' he says.

They call the dogs and turn back, and he feels content. Life is good.

CHAPTER TWENTY-SIX

Nearly a week later, Will is sitting in The Florist in Park Street, drinking an espresso and musing on the series of events that have led him here. His sprained ankle is still painful and he's not flying, which has given him plenty of time to think about El. The whole thing is turning into a terrible mess. He's heard nothing from her since he drove away from the Pig Pen, and he's remained resolute in waiting to hear from her in her own time, even resisting the overwhelming temptation to text. If he's honest with himself he's still embarrassed and hurt by her rejection, yet he longs to put things right. He knew he'd been insensitive, underestimating El's grief whilst he was falling in love with her, and he knew he had been too quick to assume that she felt the same way about him. He's almost shocked by how much he wants her back in his life, how important she has become to him.

All week Christian seemed anxious that Will should make the first move. He was oddly insistent that Will should get in touch with El, and then at last, only two days ago, admitted that she phoned when Will was in A & E.

'You said you didn't want me to tell her about your ankle,' Christian said defensively when Will was furious that Christian had withheld this from him. 'And you told me not to call her.'

'But you should have told me she phoned,' Will shouted. 'Can't you see? It makes a huge difference.'

He was angry, yet the beginning of a wild hope was springing within him: perhaps he could now make an approach. The problem now was that the time gap was awkward. It would be difficult to explain to El why he hadn't phoned back before this, and the whole situation was possibly in an even worse confusion.

Still Will hesitated, looking to find the gesture that might put things right: something more than just a text or a phone call to carry them across the divide that had opened between them. All he could do was to continue to study the piece of A4 he'd found still folded in his pocket after their visit to The Garden House, hoping that through these texts he might find a way to open up a conversation with El. This was how he found The Florist.

`The Play Pen is fab. So is The Florist.`

This text was followed by emojis of flowers and glasses of wine. When Will googled the name, florists abounded and it wasn't until he remembered the wine glass emojis that he added 'wine bar'. There were several but he saw that there was one in Bristol. He noticed that the previous text was simply initials and a time.

`TM 11.25`

He puzzled over this until he heard Christian talking on his phone to a friend.

'OK. So when do you arrive at Temple Meads? Yes, that's fine. Let me know if the train is delayed.'

Slowly Will made the connections: the Play Pen, which reminds him of the Pig Pen. The Florist. Temple Meads. Perhaps all these were connected to visits to Bristol. All the while he was searching for something that he could take to El, a reason for approaching her again in a way that would be acceptable to her. He decided to drive into Bristol and visit The Florist.

Having found the place, he glanced around the bar and then climbed rather slowly and painfully up the stairs to the first floor and a series of small rooms with sofas, small bucket arm-chairs and three big windows. He ordered coffee, and now, as he sits on one of the sofas drinking his espresso, he takes the list out and looks at it again. Way down the list he sees another text that neither he nor El paid much attention to. There were, after all, a great many texts.

`Madeleines and Doom Bar. Delicious. Well done!`

'Well, obviously cakes,' El said when she read this. 'And Doom Bar is a kind of beer. Perhaps they'd been out for a meal. Odd mix, though. Cakes and beer.'

Will frowns, wondering why it sounds familiar. Cakes and beer. Idly he types the phrase into Google on his phone. The first two pages are recipes for beer cakes and he shudders at the thought. But on the third page he reads: *Cakes and Ale* or *The Skeleton in the Cupboard* by Somerset Maugham. *Cakes and Ale*? Actually Doom Bar is an ale but he wouldn't expect El to know that. *Cakes and Ale*. Will sits up straight and sets down his cup. He opens a new page and googles the phrase.

The Somerset Maugham book comes up first and then a reference to Shakespeare: *Twelfth Night*. 'Dost thou think, because thou art virtuous, there shall be no more cakes and ale?'

Twelfth Night. Perhaps that was why it sounded familiar. Maybe Martin and J had been to see a production of it somewhere. Scrolling through that reference Will finds a mention of Aesop's fables from which the phrase had originated, but he still can't make a connection.

He groans. Perhaps it was foolish to come here, to keep following the quest, but the need to open a way back to El drives him on. He hits the back icon and continues to scroll through the references.

Cakes and Ale, a BBC South West Production. Presenter, Julia Braithwaite.

Will stops, his finger hovering. He is remembering his last visit to The Garden House, that happy day with El: the garden, the tearooms, and the dark-haired woman hurrying past him with the desolate expression on her face. As he sits, holding his cup, he hears again the man's voice: '. . . Braithwaite . . . local television presenter . . . *Cakes and Ale.*'

Will sits quite still, staring ahead of him, then he re-sets the page on his phone again. It's quite easy, after all. There are the details of the programme, a photograph of Julia Braithwaite and a biog: a widow with two sons, works at the BBC in Plymouth, freelance journalist. He knows this woman.

But Will knows that he hasn't seen her on television, or read any of her articles. He is thinking furiously. And quite suddenly he remembers. He remembers the funeral: following the family down the aisle behind Martin's coffin, keeping well back, allowing people coming out of their pews to go in front of him, and as he looked around him, noticing the woman, half hidden behind the pillar at the back of the church. She was watching the procession intently with an expression that was odd; so odd that it caught his attention.

Her whole attitude was one of secrecy, as if she had no business to be there, was fearful of being caught out, and yet couldn't resist this last chance to make a private farewell. Even as he watched, she reached into her handbag, put on dark glasses and as soon as the family party were out in the churchyard she slipped outside, turning on to the little path that leads to Church Lane. By the time he reached the churchyard she was gone.

Will remembers Julia Braithwaite's face as she turned back in the doorway at The Garden House, a terrible sadness that was almost panic in her eyes, that touched him. He almost felt as if he were spying on her most private emotions, which was exactly how he felt watching her in church at Martin's funeral. Will thinks about El, trying to come to terms with her emotions, and an anger begins to rise in him. Suddenly he's had enough of these games, the confusions. He checks the list of texts again. He guesses that Julia lives within easy reach of the BBC studios in Plymouth and he remembers how he sat with El, checking the codes. After some discussion they'd decided that 'NTKH the Stables' was the National Trust property Killerton House, at Exeter.

'It's got a café called the Stables,' El said. 'Pa liked the sound of it, said it was a bit like the Pig Pen, and we went once. It's great.'

Now, Will types the number at the top of the sheet into his phone and, without giving himself time to change his mind, he taps out a message:

Hi. My name's Will. I'm sitting in The Florist. Could we meet for coffee? Is there any chance you could be at NTKH in the Stables for coffee on Sunday morning?

Before there is time for second thoughts he presses Send. He takes a deep breath, leans back and swallows the last drops of his cold coffee.

Julia stares at the text, frowning. She is utterly confused. She doesn't know anyone called Will, she doesn't recognize the number, yet she knows The Florist and that NTKH is Killerton House. These are places that she's been to with Martin – they are their special, private codes – which means that Will, whoever he is, must know about them, too.

'What is it?' asks Davy from across the table.

They've been discussing his new project, a programme very similar to *Cakes and Ale*, set on the peninsula, and the table is strewn with print-outs, maps, their laptops open.

'It's a weird text,' she answers, 'from someone called Will, asking me to meet him at Killerton House for coffee on Sunday.'

Davy stares at her, frowning. 'What?'

'I know.' She passes him her phone. 'It's where Martin and I used to meet.'

Davy reads the text. 'What's The Florist?'

'It's a wine bar in Bristol. We used to meet there, too. But nobody else knew that.'

'Well, clearly Will does.' Dave hands the phone back to her. 'How might he have found out?'

'By reading our texts.' Julia is thinking about it. 'Which means he's seen Martin's phone.'

'So you told me that El might have the phone. Could she have shown it to this Will?'

'I'm remembering now,' says Julia. 'El had a half-brother called Will. Martin told me about it because they didn't get on very well. Will's father married El's mother.'

'That's a stepbrother, not a half-brother,' says Davy.

Julia shrugs. 'OK, but there was definitely a Will. El's brother is called Freddie. Could it be him, d'you think? This step-brother?'

'Possibly. Sounds a bit odd if they didn't get on very well. So you think he's tried your number on a chance? Do you think El has asked him to?'

'I just don't know.' She looks anxiously at him across the table. 'What shall I do?'

Davy thinks about it. 'What does your instinct tell you?'

Julia tries to be calm, to think sensibly. 'Part of me would like to. I feel like I'm at an impasse. I can't quite seem to go forward. I hoped that going to The Garden House last week might help but I just felt more confused than ever.'

'Perhaps El has asked him to contact you, but it's slightly odd that he doesn't mention that.'

Julia is completely baffled by the approach, although she almost welcomes some kind of movement. At the same time she feels very nervous about meeting El.

'Supposing I were to agree to meet Will,' she says at last, 'and then El rocks up at some point?'

'But you are in the stronger position,' Davy points out. 'You know all about Will and El. Martin talked to you about them. You've seen photographs of El and Freddie. They know nothing about you. All they have is your phone number.'

'As far as we know,' warns Julia. 'We can't be totally certain of that.'

'Even so.' Davy shrugs. 'What are they going to do? Neither of you were committing a crime. You both merely decided to keep things secret from your children. You might have to tell Will that. After all, that's what Martin wanted, too.'

Julia thinks about it. Then she nods. 'OK, I'll do it, but I still don't feel ready to meet El. I can't see her being happy about it either. It's too soon.'

'It's a chance you'll have to take and trust that Will knows what he's doing. But you're not going alone. I'm sure it's all fine but I'm coming with you. Oh, don't worry, I shan't sit in on your chat but I'll be nearby.'

Julia is relieved by this suggestion. 'Thanks, Davy. I'd feel a little less vulnerable, I admit. I could take Bertie, I suppose.'

'We'll both come,' says Davy. 'Safety in numbers.'

'OK,' says Julia, and she takes her phone and begins to type a reply.

As he drives towards Exeter on Sunday morning, Will still feels the surprise at the speed with which Julia responded to his text. It was a very brief response:

I'll be at the Stables at Killerton House at 11 o'clock.

He respects her for using the proper name rather than the code he'd used. It was as if she was making the point that the codes were for her and Martin. Feeling nervous, he parks his car, wondering if Julia has already arrived and might be sitting in her car watching him. He looks neither right nor left but walks in, still limping slightly, and glances around. There are people sitting at tables, standing at the counter, but no sign of Julia and he's glad, now, that he knows who she is and she cannot take him unawares. He sits at a table where he can watch the door and at three minutes past the hour she walks in. To his irritation and anxiety he sees that she has a man with her and a large golden retriever. Julia looks around her, meets his eye and Will immediately stands up as they make their way towards him.

'I'm Will,' he says at once.

'I'm Julia,' she says, 'and this is a friend of mine, Davy Callaghan. He won't be joining us. This is Bertie.'

Will smiles. 'Reinforcements?'

'Hi, Will,' says Davy. 'I'll get the coffee in. What will you have?'

Will shakes his hand, asks for an espresso, and Davy leaves them, taking Bertie with him. Julia sits down and after a moment Will does the same. Julia is wearing jeans and an over-size jersey.

'This is very kind of you,' he begins. 'It was difficult to contact you without it coming as a bit of a shock.'

She inclines her head, agreeing with him.

'So you've seen the texts,' she says. It's not a question.

'Yes,' he says, feeling his way. 'That was how we knew about you.'

'I have to say that I am uncomfortable with it. It's like being spied on.'

'Yes.' He nods. 'I can see that. But when El found Martin's phone it was a natural act to check through in case there was anyone who might not have heard. Your texts were rather unusual, she didn't recognize your name, and she was rather at a loss as to what to do.'

She continues to watch him. 'And where do you come in?'

'My father married El's mother. We're not directly related but she asked my advice about the texts.'

'Not Freddie?'

Will's taken aback. 'No,' he answers slowly. 'Not Freddie. She decided that since Martin had kept it private she should do the same. But it's been a bit difficult for El, as you might imagine. His death was a huge shock and she needed a bit of support.'

Julia continues to study his face, and he admires her cool.

'She doesn't know I'm here or that I've been in touch with you.'

At last a response. Julia raises her eyebrows, a faint shadow of concern crosses her face.

'Why doesn't she?'

The arrival of their coffee gives Will the opportunity to gather his wits. He sees that the man, Davy, and the dog are now sitting at a table some distance away and Davy is looking at his tablet. Julia thanks the waiter and Will decides to tell the truth.

'Looking at your texts, trying to decipher them, was a kind of distraction from her grief. But at the same time she found it hard to come to terms with Martin having rather an . . .' he hesitates over the word ' . . . intimate connection with someone she didn't know about. She and her father were very close and it's been rather a shock.'

'I can understand,' says Julia. 'There was nothing wrong. I'm not married, nothing like that, but we both have children and we both decided not to rock any boats. It might sound odd but he knew that El and Freddie had already had to adapt to another family, and I was unwilling to tell my boys, who still adore their father. He died ten years ago,' she adds.

Will nods, slightly taken aback by her directness. 'I get that. I think that El is prey to quite a lot of mixed emotions at the moment and I was trying to think of a way through it all.' He hesitates and then adds, 'I saw you in the church at the funeral, and then again last week at The Garden House. Of course I didn't realize who you were. Someone at The Garden House mentioned your name and then later I began to put two and two together. And then I made the connection between you and Martin.'

She's looking interested now. 'And what was the connection?'

He smiles a little. 'Madeleines and Doom Bar.'

At last he sees her smile. It's a genuinely amused smile but hedged about with sadness. She nods.

Suddenly Will knows that he must be honest with her.

'El and I had a row,' he said. 'I've become very fond of her in these last few months and I thought she felt the same. It seems I made a mistake, she wasn't ready, and I've probably just made the whole situation worse. My text to you was sent on an impulse, hoping it might do some good. I wondered, after I saw you on those other occasions, how hard it must be for you too.'

He has her whole attention now.

'And what do you hope to achieve?'

'Closure,' he says. 'For both of you, perhaps, but certainly for El. She needs either to accept that her father had a relationship that he kept secret from her – and why shouldn't he? – and move on from it, or meet up with you and find out the truth about it.'

Already Julia is shaking her head. 'I suspect that neither of us is ready for that conversation,' she says. 'It might well be that El and I can meet only when both of us have moved forward. She needs to be strong and happy in her own life. It's very difficult for children to accept the physical relationships of their parents.' She hesitates. 'I'm not putting this very well.'

He hastens to reassure her. 'I hear what you say. But I don't quite know how to move her forward. Or even how to break this impasse between us.'

Julia smiles at him. 'Was I to be a kind of gift? A means to breaking down the barrier?'

He laughs at her honesty. 'I'm afraid there was something like that at the back of my good intentions. I admit that I want to open communications between us again for my own sake. But I really do want to help her through this.'

Julia nods. 'Go back to her. Don't ask. Just go. Turn up and tell her how you feel about her. She's probably feeling exactly the same way and doesn't know what to do either. Is she at the Pig Pen?' He nods. 'Good,' she says. 'Martin would be pleased. Look, just do it. It's nearly Christmas; buy her a present and just go.'

He stares at her. 'But you won't meet her?'

Julia shakes her head. 'Maybe one day. But not now. Not yet. Just trust me on this, Will. Forget me and Martin for the moment. Go and see El and make things right between you. For Martin's sake.' She pushes her cup aside and stands up. 'Good luck, Will. Be happy.'

She walks away, and Davy gets up from his table to join her. He raises his hand to Will, picks up Bertie's lead, and they go out together.

They drive in silence for a while and then Davy says: 'So was that OK?'

'Yes,' Julia answers uncertainly, then more strongly, 'yes, it was. I like him, Davy.'

'It certainly looked as if you were getting on OK,' says Davy.

He sounds relieved and Julia glances at him, touches his arm.

'Thanks for coming with me,' she says. 'It was surprisingly scary but as soon as I saw him I recognized him.'

'Recognized him?'

Julia nods. 'I saw him at the funeral. I was outside the church, lying low, waiting for everyone to arrive so I could slip in at the back. I saw Will arrive and the way El greeted him.' Julia hesitates, remembering that look on the girl's face: surprise, pleasure, a kind of gratitude. 'And then I noticed him again inside the church. I was trying to sort out who they all were from the photographs Martin showed me. Freddie and El are very alike but I had no idea that it was Will.'

'What did he say about the texts?'

'He said that El was puzzled that she didn't recognize the name and because the texts were so cryptic she was cautious about simply phoning the number. She showed them to Will and they tried to solve the puzzle by working through the odd codes that Martin and I used.'

'And how did they succeed?'

'Will saw me at The Garden House and he heard someone mentioning my name and *Cakes and Ale*. He remembered that he'd seen me in the church at the funeral, put two and two together. Very clever of him.'

'And what now?'

'El doesn't know he's been in touch,' says Julia. 'Apparently it all got a bit tense and they've had a row.'

'Oh, what?' says Davy. 'Why?'

'I think that during the process they've fallen in love but for some reason they've had some kind of serious misunderstanding and neither is backing down. He's upset about it and looking for a way back to her.'

'And you're his way back?'

'I think he was hoping so, in a muddled kind of way. But I told him I'm not ready for that, and I doubt very much that El is either. It's all too raw. He's just got to go back and chance his arm with her.'

'But won't that be hard now that he's seen you?'

Julia is silent. 'It's very hard for him to keep it secret,' she says at last, 'but maybe he'll find some way of telling her when the time is right. The important thing is that they take a step right away from this and build something for themselves. They need time to do that before she'll be ready to meet me. They're so young, Davy, hardly more than children. I want them to be happy.' She gives a huge sigh. 'I'm exhausted.'

'And what about you?' asks Davy. 'How has it made you feel?'

'Better,' she answers, and it's true. 'I know where I am now, and I no longer feel fearful about being contacted. I'm grateful to Will for that. I just want them to move forward as I'm doing at last, thanks to you, Davy.'

He smiles. 'Definitely made up your mind about the new production then?'

She nods. 'Can't wait. And the boys are home for Christmas this week.'

'Bring it on,' says Davy.

CHAPTER TWENTY-SEVEN

Winter solstice and the Cold Moon. In the last few days before Christmas, El hurries between the bookshop and the Pig Pen, and all the while she's thinking about Will, unnerved by the total silence, unable to contact him. Each time she thinks about texting him she loses her nerve. She still feels ashamed that he might think she was coming on to him but she wishes that she hadn't reacted so violently. She just longs to see him but doesn't know how to phrase a message that is appropriate. She believes now that Elton John is absolutely right about sorry being the hardest word, especially when she has no idea what Will is feeling. There has been no response to her call and she has no idea if Christian passed on her message. Somehow this has added to the difficulty of making a second call. Perhaps, after all, Will was simply responding to an impulse and, when she reacted so strongly, he just shrugged and went back to his own life. At last she scraped up enough courage to send him a Christmas card. It was a simple watercolour of Dartmoor in the snow and inside she wrote:

I'm really sorry about the way I reacted, Will. Just put it down to all the weird stuff I'm going through at the moment. I hate it that we've parted like this after all the good times we had and all your kindness. I think I told you about Angus's party and Midnight Mass. You're still invited and I'd love to see you.

She hesitated, wondering how to sign it, what she should put, and in the end just wrote her name. There has been no response and now, on Christmas Eve, as she moves amongst Angus's guests, she is certain that she's ruined any chance of a relationship with Will and she feels miserable and lonely, even amongst all these friends. She talks to Plum's elder daughter, Alice, and as they chat about what it's like to work at a literary agency in London, El wonders if, after all, her decision to try this life here was a good one. Perhaps she should have accepted Angus's offer to stay the night rather than return to the Pig Pen alone, but it's difficult keeping up this pretence of jollity when her heart is aching as she thinks about Will.

Even as she thinks about him, she remembers the difficulty in introducing him to her friends, the complications of his being her stepbrother. She's mentioned it to Angus, in a casual kind of way, saying that it felt odd, that she didn't know quite how to deal with it. He thought about it for a few moments.

'There's no legal tie, of course,' he said. 'And you haven't grown up together, so there's no difficulty, really, but I can see it's an odd one. I shouldn't worry about it, too much. All your friends know the situation, other people will just assume that he's a friend. Keep it simple is my motto.'

El sighs. It's been a long day in the bookshop and she's finding it hard to keep awake. It's a relief when the time comes for them to set out for church. They all go in together, Father

Steven greets her warmly, and they file into a pew near the front. She sits between Plum and Cass, and Cass smiles at her encouragingly as if she is able to imagine what this must be like for El, this first Christmas without her father.

The church is festive with holly and candles and the scent of pine needles, the choir and clergy are grouping at the back, the organ playing. El glances behind her to watch the procession forming up, and takes a little gasping breath. Will is here, standing at the end of a pew where the occupants are squeezing up to make room for him. He's in uniform, and she guesses that he must have driven straight from the airport. As she watches, he looks around, his face anxious, hopeful, and then he sees her. El is filled with relief, joy; she wants to weep and laugh all at the same time. She beams at Will and he smiles back, gives her a little nod. Then the organ plays the chords of the first hymn, the congregation stands, and she turns back, picks up her service sheet and begins to sing.

EPILOGUE

A few months later, on a sunny spring morning, Julia is walking in the gardens. Everywhere there is a wash of colour sweeping across the place, signs of new life and the sound of birdsong. She remembers how she came here after that first chance meeting with Martin, hoping to see him again, and how she found him sitting on the bench by the lake, gazing at the little dinghy, the *Nancy Fortescue*.

'I was so afraid that I would never see you again,' he said, and she sat down beside him, knowing that something momentous, wonderful, was beginning.

She goes into the tearooms for some coffee, allows herself to be tempted by some delicious chocolate cake, chats with Steve, who brings her coffee, and looks at the watercolours. Afterwards she makes her way round the side of the house to the little gift shop where she buys some Charlotte Marlow cards and a candle. Coming out again into the sunshine, hesitating just for a moment, she turns her steps towards the Arboretum. Pausing between two camellia bushes on the path above the lake, she sees that the *Nancy Fortescue* is back in the water and, at the same time, she notices the two people who are sitting on the bench beside the lake. Julia stands quite still, watching. The young man has his arm about the girl, holding her close. They are laughing together and, even as she watches them, El looks up at Will and he bends his head to kiss her.

For some reason Julia remembers Martin's first text to her:

`Crosby, Stills, Nash & Young. Woodstock.`

The words sing in her head: 'We are stardust, we are golden . . . And we've got to get ourselves back to the garden.' She longs to join them, to share in their joy, but she hesitates. She imagines El's surprise, Will attempting an introduction, being forced to explain how he approached Julia. It will be clumsy, awkward, and it's early days in their relationship. She knows in her heart that the time will come, but not now; not yet.

Julia turns back, passing between the camellias, and walks away into the bright spring sunshine.

ABOUT THE AUTHOR

Marcia Willett's early life was devoted to the ballet, but her dreams of becoming a ballerina ended when she grew out of the classical proportions required. She had always loved books, and a family crisis made her take up a new career as a novelist – a decision she has never regretted. She lives in a beautiful and wild part of Devon.

Find out more about Marcia Willett and her novels at www.marciawillett.co.uk